THE
AGED
TROUBADOUR

THE
AGED
TROUBADOUR

A NOVEL BY
KARL LODUR

SUNSTONE
PRESS

SANTA FE

ON THE COVER:
Judith Blegen and John Reardon in Debussy's
Pelléas et Melisande

Sunstone books may be purchased for educational, business, or sales promotional use. For information please write: Special Markets Department, Sunstone Press, P.O. Box 2321, Santa Fe, New Mexico 87504-2321.

Library of Congress Cataloging-in-Publication Data:

Lodur, Karl.
  The aged troubadour : a novel / by Karl Lodur.
    p. cm.
  ISBN 0-86534-404-3 (pbk.)
    1. Aged men—Fiction. 2. Philosophers—Fiction. 3. Young women—Fiction. I. Title.

PS3612.035 A37 2003
813'.6—dc22

                                        2003014880

Published in SUNSTONE PRESS
              Post Office Box 2321
              Santa Fe, NM 87504-2321 / USA
              (505) 988-4418 / *orders only* (800) 243-5644
              FAX (505) 988-1025
              WWW.SUNSTONEPRESS.COM

Acknowledgments

Much in this novel is based upon my reading of books and articles too numerous to cite. But I am indebted especially to Irving Singer's three volume *The Nature of Love* (University of Chicago Press), Emil L. Fackenheim's translation of Avicenna's "A Treatise of Love," especially Chapter V, (*Mediaeval Studies* 7 [1945]: 222, 208-228), Ronnie Apter's bilingual edition of *The Love Songs of Bernart de Ventadorn* (Edwin Mellen Press), and A. J. Denomy's article: *"Fin' Amors*: the Pure Love of the Troubadours," (*Mediaeval Studies*, 7 [1945]: 139-207). The fictional conversations reflecting the attitudes of Nietzsche and Schopenhauer toward sexual love and other matters owe something also to Walter Kaufmann's *Nietzsche* (Princeton University Press) and Alain de Botton's "The Schopenhauer Method" (*The New York Times Magazine*, February 13, 2000).

Notwithstanding any unintended superficial similarities, the events, places, and characters of this novel are meant to be wholly fictitious.

To Tälik

1

"Krr-r-a-a-ack-k-k-k! Krr-r-a-a-a-ack-k-k-k-k!"

Professor Altmann rushed to the window of his upstairs study to see what demonic creature had invaded the neighborhood. Down below, inside a big walk-in cage standing on the patio of the house belonging to his new neighbor—a divorcee who had just moved in the week before—he saw the culprit. It was a large, long-tailed macaw with brilliant red, blue and green plumage.

"I'll be goddamned!" the professor exclaimed. Several months ago he had battled with neighbors on the other side of his house about an Alaskan Husky they had tied up to a tree in their back yard and, except for throwing it a bone or two now and then, had ignored throughout most days and nights, with the result that every five minutes or so the wretched animal would fall into a fit of barking. He had tried asking them politely to either keep the dog inside, or else pay it enough attention to stop its lonely yelping, and when that hadn't worked, he had called in the police to serve them notice that if the barking didn't cease within the week, they would be fined and the dog taken into custody.

Natives of east Wyoming's wide-open ranges, they were not accustomed to any such restraints, and upon being warned by the police, immediately packed their bags and abandoned the house they had been renting, mumbling all the while—according to periodic reports Altmann later got of their departure from another neighbor up the street—that 'America wasn't any longer what it used to be!' and that he, Altmann, was nothing but 'a mean, old codger.' No sooner had they moved out, however, than another family moved in, this one with two young boys who began spending their every after-school hour bouncing a basketball on the concrete sidewalk in front of their house and periodically shooting it into a

9

barrel their father had provided them, for want of the usual backboard and goal to be found in the yards of most Midwestern homes. The dull sounds of the inflated ball thudding against the sides of the plastic container—not to mention the incessant bouncing of the ball on the sidewalk during their foreplay—would reverberate around the neighborhood, and although others seemed not to be bothered, Altmann himself had found it extremely disruptive to any line of thought he was trying to pursue.

Friendly hints to the parents—to whom, upon their arrival, he had earlier had a pizza delivered as a gesture of welcome—that their boys' behavior might be a problem, had gone completely unheeded, and he was still weighing his legal options for eliminating the nuisance. And now this! Every twenty-nine seconds—he had already timed the intervals between the macaw's outcries—the harsh squawking of a bird that even in the vast jungles of Latin America, whence it had probably been snatched by a poacher looking to make a fast buck, was enough to stop a panther in its tracks.

"How in the hell is a man supposed to think?" he muttered to himself while returning to his computer and trying to resume his scholarly writing. Some students of his had occasionally claimed that they were able to do their best work while having their radios blasting in the background, but in his more cynical moods, such claims, coming usually as he noticed they did from the weaker half of any class, only added, he thought, to the proof of Schopenhauer's assertion that one's intelligence was in direct, inverse proportion to one's ability to tolerate noise. In any event, he himself had always found it nigh impossible to get any intellectual work done without an almost total absence of noise. Even the humming of florescent bulbs could break his concentration.

It was on that account that he had moved into Brookfield's historic district in the first place some ten years ago. Located where it was, the big, two-story, white-framed house would afford him all the quiet he would ever need, his ever-so-friendly real-estate agent had assured him. And for the first eight years it had.

Having earlier published multiple articles on the Medieval-Christian-Neoplatonic roots of the Romantic conception of love as a quasi-mystical union between a man and woman transcending ordinary sexual experiences, he had, every two years or so thereafter, cranked out five scholarly books on how Blake, Coleridge, Wordsworth and other Romantic thinkers had used their idealized image of sexual love as a key for unlocking the mysterious oneness supposedly linking all humans with each other and the cosmos as a whole. For the past two years, however, he had given birth to nothing worth publishing, and although he knew, or should have known after having taught logic for so many years, that mere coincidence is no evidence of causal relationship, he was tempted to blame the recent reduction of his creativity on the increase in the neighborhood's level of noise since that time. Irritated by the repeated squawking of the macaw, he finally despaired of getting anything done, shut his computer off, and descended downstairs to dine while watching the evening news.

An hour or so later, as he lay in a lounge chair taking a catnap, a booming sound suddenly rumbled through the walls of his living room and jarred him out of his soporific state. "Now what the hell is that?" he muttered, jumping out of the chair, and racing to the back door. In the garage that stood only ten yards from his living room window, he saw the divorcee's teenage son whirling about the building to the wild rhythms of the Rock music he was trying to play on his electric guitar. So loud and shrill was the sound that all the pigeons usually perched on the roof of the Methodist Church a block away had already taken flight. Without a moment's hesitation, Altmann went across the patio to the woman's house and began beating on the back door. "Pardon me, Susie," he half-shouted when she opened the door, "but we are going to have to have a talk."

"What's the problem?" she asked, nicely enough. Twenty years earlier, she had actually taken one of Altmann's philosophy classes, and the two of them had struck up a good rapport at the time, so that even though they had hardly seen each other in the interim, there was still some mutual respect between them. On the day she had moved in behind him, the two of them had in fact had a friendly, backyard *tête à tête,* with Altmann marveling all the while at how well she had preserved the stunning beauty of her earlier, youthful years.

"Well, as you know, Susie, I spend most of my time trying to do scholarly work, and for that I have to have as much peace and quiet as possible. This afternoon I could not work because every twenty-nine seconds that damn bird of yours was squawking; now, just as I was about to try again, your son starts playing his guitar at decibels loud enough to puncture any eardrum. There's no way I'm ever going to be able to get anything done with all this noise . . ."

"Oh, I'm sorry," the woman replied with obvious sincerity. "I guess we should have been more considerate. Anyway, I'll be keeping the bird in the house from now on anytime I know that you are at home, and Sam and I will work something out until we can get the garage sound-proofed."

"I would appreciate that," Altmann stated. "I'd hate to become the neighborhood curmudgeon," he added with a sheepish grin, "but . . ."

11

"No problem!" Susie interjected, as the macaw emitted a hair-raising squawk from inside the house. "Incidentally, I just baked a cherry cobbler. Would you like a dish?"

"Well, s-sure," Altmann replied rather hesitantly, feeling all the more embarrassed by the woman's kindness after his having accosted her so roughly. During the previous week, he had ranted and raved over the telephone about being put on hold for ten minutes when he had called to clear up some confusion surrounding the billing of his Internet fees, only to discover, after declaring his own identity, that the person on the other end of the line had been another of his former students. Prior to that, a middle-aged nurse whom he had berated for being the fifth person to ask an elderly friend he had taken to the local hospital 'which funereal service he might prefer in the event of dying there,' had reminded him that he had once been her professor, and that *"back then"* he had seemed a rather "gentle fellow." On still another recent occasion, he had chewed out a clerk at U of I's library only because she was a few minutes slower than usual in processing the renewal of his borrowed books over the telephone, and almost died of humiliation upon hearing her respond: "Oh, Dr. Altmann, it's Sherri. Sherri Gray! Remember me, I was in one of your classes last year."

With Susie, his new neighbor, however, it was even worse, since there was no lack of recognition involved, and if nothing else, at least his respect for her as a former student should have inclined him to have been less confrontational. As he accepted her bowl of cherry cobbler and shuffled back to his own house, he felt foolish and not a little hypocritical. To have blamed her bird and son for his inability to work was not, he knew, altogether honest. For even after the neighborhood had been cleared of the barking dog, and before the bird and guitar had begun to screech, or the boys next door had commenced to bounce their ball around, he had been unable to make any progress on what he had been trying to write, and deep down he was aware that what was blocking his creative activity was something far more serious than the noise level in the neighborhood.

One morning shortly before his fifty-ninth birthday, he had taken a long look at himself in the mirror after shaving and came to realize, as never before, that he not only had relatively few years to live, but also, and more dreadfully, that he had let his youth slip away without ever having really drank from its fountain. Why his whitish-gray hair, liver-spotted hands, and ever-drier skin had not convinced him long ago that he had left his youth behind was something he would himself be hard-pressed to explain. Friendly colleagues from the psychology department might have accused him of being in denial. But in reality it may simply have been the result of his having spent so much of his life in the classroom. With one batch of students after another remaining every year as young as the one before, it was easy to forget or ignore the reality of his own degeneration. And so, turning forty or fifty had hardly dented the robust impression he had had of himself as a picture of virility that could, should he really want it, turn the heart of any of the post-pubescent females who, semester after semester, would congregate around his podium and scrutinize—or so, at least, he liked to imagine—his handsomely attired body as he strutted about the classroom and unloaded on them the tons of wisdom he had gleaned from his own digestion of two thousand years of philosophical speculation. Nor had the passing decades taken much of a toll on the confidence he had always had in his ability to maintain a fresh *Weltanschauung*. Although convinced throughout most of those years that Pythagoras, Plato, and their latter-day disciples had come closest to capturing the "music of the spheres," he had never lost his youthful penchant to embrace any and every new variation of thought that might conceivably put a better spin on the 'idea' with which, *à la* Walter Benjamin's metaphysics of youth, he had completely identified as a university student. Cassierer, Heidegger, Wittgenstein, Whitehead . . . he had swallowed them all, and every day in his classroom had regurgitated their various and sundry bits of wisdom with all the conviction and enthusiasm of his earliest days as a budding philosopher when he had first experienced the erotic lure of the *dialektike.*

But no more. In the growing awareness of his old age, the very mention of these Gargantuan figures of the intellectual world, like their myriad books and treatises on sale at the local bookstore for consumption by yet another gullible generation, had begun to grate on his nerves. And although he had not yet succumbed entirely to the Naturalistic dismissal of all talk of cosmic unity and things spiritual, his enthusiasm for Romanticism had certainly waned, leaving him wondering whether all his scholarly huffing and puffing in previous years to map the mysterious harmony of the whole universe had been anything more than an exercise in *hubris* to prove to himself and others that although he had had to settle for a teaching job at a lowly community college, he could hold his own with the best of them.

Full of such doubts and misgivings, Altmann had been pushing himself since the end of the school-year to revive his drooping spirit. But it wasn't working, and once again, upon returning to his house after the confrontation with the budding rock-star's mother, he found himself looking for excuses not to do the scholarly work he had earlier resolved to finish that evening after the neighborhood boys and birds had been put to rest. Instead, after gulping down the cherry cobbler, he read an article or two out of the latest *Newsweek*, flipped on the TV with his remote control, and wasted the next two hours absentmindedly watching the sophistical babble being delivered for public consumption by the Fuss News Network's latest talk-show hosts.

Then, climbing the stairs to his second floor study, he again turned on his computer to check out the day's activity on the stock market. Only a month ago, on the advice of his division dean, he had shifted almost a third of his TIAA-CREF investment funds into growth stocks, and already they had increased in value by over five thousand dollars. Once again, the report was good. In less than twenty-four hours the unit price of his shares had jumped from ninety to ninety-two dollars, affording him yet another eight-hundred dollar gain. At that rate, he surmised, he would soon be making more money per month for doing nothing than he was getting for teaching fifteen semester hours of elementary philosophy at Bridgeport's community college. Feeling a touch of shame at the greedy satisfaction he caught himself taking in such a line of thought, he flipped the computer off and crossed the hall to his bedroom, where, with luck and help from the large glass of wine he had downed with his evening meal, he hoped to get another eight hours of sleep—three more than had been his usual amount during the productive years when every night he would lie awake for at least several hours wrestling with metaphysical ruminations about the nature of love. Within minutes he was fast asleep, dreaming lustily, *pace* the Wagnerian opera he had recently seen performed in San Francisco, of water nymphs and boundless gold and power.

2

Around three o'clock on the following Saturday afternoon, Altmann backed his old Buick Regal out of the narrow garage attached to his house to begin the one and a half hour trip to Urbana. With the odometer already reading over a hundred thousand miles, he wasn't at all confident that it could get him there, but it was a chance he was willing to take to get out of Brookfield for a while to imbibe a bit of culture. Apart from a few rundown movie-houses featuring nothing but the tritest of Hollywood fare—lest in getting some of the more serious stuff, ministers of the twenty or more Protestant churches in town would be provoked into complaining again about the showing of 'pornographic' flicks, as they had done five years ago when the Moonlight had dared to run the filmed version of Eco's *The Name of the Rose*—and a Civic Theater, whose director seemed to have an insatiable taste for inane comedies about married life that Altmann had found about as appealing as the daily soap operas on TV, Brookfield offered little in the form of aesthetic consolation to anyone suffering from a bout of Schopenhauerian pessimism. When, therefore, a former student and his wife pursuing doctoral degrees at U of I had invited him to join them for dinner and a performance of Stravinsky's *The Rake's Progress,* he had jumped at the opportunity.

As he turned off of Brookfield's Main Street onto Highway 48 North, Altmann noticed a dozen or so long-haired, ragged-looking individuals standing at intervals along the road trying to hitch a ride. He assumed they were stragglers from the multitude that, according to newspaper reports, had congregated for a rock concert down on Fox Island earlier in the week. At the sight of them, many with guitars strapped to their backs, he was reminded of the twelfth century troubadours whose wandering bardic lives had been the subject of one of his scholarly papers many years ago, and for a moment he was tempted to stop and offer one or another of them a lift. But fear of being victimized by a drug addict desperate in need of money quickly got the better of him, and he drove on, oblivious to the obscene gesture the last of the hikers gave him as he breezed by.

Flipping on the radio in hopes of catching Texaco's Saturday afternoon presentation from the Metropolitan Opera, he got nothing but sporadic bursts of spiritual advice from the Religious Life Network that had recently staked out a frequency close to that of the local PBS station and was constantly drowning out the latter's programing. Not until he got some ten miles north of Stonington was he finally able to get a clear signal, and when he did, he was disappointed to hear that it was *Madame Butterfly*—his least favorite Puccini opera—that the Met was doing. Although Pinkerton's *pro tempore* marital arrangement with the beautiful Cio Cio San intrigued him, the lead male character had always struck him as being something of a stick-figure whose underdevelopment might itself, even apart from the exotic music, have been enough to incline the original La Scala audience to heap its scorn upon the composer. Switching to another PBS station, he was treated to the melancholic strains of some Mahler *Lieder*, one of which, 'The Song of a Weary Wayfarer,' especially suited his current mood, and by the time he pulled into the parking lot of the agreed-upon Italian restaurant an hour later the music had taken at least some of the bite out of the loneliness he had been feeling in recent days.

The dinner with his friends, however, did not go well. The food was good enough—far better than the cheap meals he generally fixed himself at home, but the conversation left much to be desired. Majoring as she was in Slavic Literature, the woman had little interest in the philosophical line of discussion her husband had promptly initiated with his former professor. As a result, Altmann found himself trying to keep her in the conversation by periodically raising questions of a sort that she might be interested in, while at the same time straining to listen to what her spouse was saying about the deficiencies of Kant's epistemological theory. By the end of the meal he had the impression that for all their talk they had not really communicated, and as they separately made their way to the opera house and met again to take their seats in the center of its orchestral section, he was feeling more isolated than ever, with only the most trivial of comments being exchanged between them. The seat to his right was still empty, giving him room to stretch his long legs while perusing the program notes to refresh his memory of the opera's plot. At the last minute, however, he had to retreat to his own cramped space as an exceptionally beautiful young woman rushed in to claim the seat. Except for a perfunctory, initial exchange of greetings, neither said anything to each other, until just moments before the intermission had ended and the curtain

16

was about to rise on the second act, she leaned in his direction and asked whether he was enjoying the performance. Although the answer he gave her might have sounded rather cool, so moved was he by the warm sincerity of her question that it was all he could do throughout the subsequent Act to keep his attention on the operatic performance. No sooner did the second Intermission begin than the two of them were promptly engaged in a lively conversation about their respective fields of literature and philosophy, with Altmann not letting on at all that his scholarly interests had been waning of late. By the time the opera was over, and the bedeviled Tom Rakewell had 'progressed' to the point of being purged of all passion (not to mention his reason), Altmann himself was feeling a surge of erotic desire coursing through his veins. And when, before taking her leave, Liliana– Liliana Columbra, as he had learned her name to be–suggested that they exchange email addresses for the sake of continuing their dialogue, he quickly complied, notwithstanding a suspicion that he was gambling away the last piece of his tattered soul.

3

Several days later Professor Altmann sat in his study on the second floor of his home checking his email for a message from Liliana. Finding none, and mulling despondently over the risk of making a fool of himself by expecting too much of his recent encounter with the fetching Ms. Columbra, he returned to the Netscape Navigator and typed onto its search line the title of Josef von Sternberg's 1930 classic film, 'Blue Angel.' He had read Heinrich Mann's novel upon which the film had been based, and had never suspected any semblance between himself and the petty bourgeois, tyrannical schoolteacher—Professor Unrat, as Mann had aptly named him—who, after having 'caught' his adolescent pupils ogling obscene pictures of a local cabaret dancer, had himself fallen victim to her seductive tricks, and become the laughing stock of the town. From what he remembered of the film, however, von Sternberg had not only shifted the main focus of the story from the professor's fall to the amoral woman who caused it (providing Ms. Dietrich thereby with the role of her career), but also had converted the professor himself into a prudish but loving man whose late awakening of both heart and flesh overwhelmed his better judgment and brought about his ultimate debasement. For such a vision of an essentially honorable man being destroyed by desire Altmann had always felt some sympathy, and conscious of his own increased concupiscent vulnerability of late, he had in mind to refresh his memory of the film's details.

Upon initiating the search, however, he inadvertently found himself in the midst of a porn-site filled with an array of lewd figures inviting him, like the peep-show hawkers at the county fairs of his youth, to come on in and see the naked ladies. How the word 'Blue,' with its connotation of rigid morality, or the even more religious term of 'Angel,' could have routed him into such a wanton realm was beyond his elementary grasp of computer science. And having lectured his Ethics classes in the past, *à la* MacKinnon, Dworkin, and other feminists from the sixties and seventies, on the immorality of producing, distributing and using pornographic material (without ever having viewed much of the rawer stuff himself), his first inclination was to curse the webmasters who had tricked him into this mess and to clear the screen. But every time he punched the home button on his browser to make an exit, yet another porn site would surface to grab his attention. The last of them featured an alphabetized listing of so-called 'porn stars' from around the world who promised that at the click of his mouse they would bare their most intimate secrets for his perusal and satisfaction, free of charge.

As he was about to attempt another escape, the professor's eye was drawn to the large C in the alphabetized box, and he found himself toying mischievously with the thought of whether by chance he might discover a 'Columbra' in the list's Latin-American category. For better or worse, neither a Liliana, nor any other, showed up. But as he was again about to take leave of the nasty site, another Latin-American name caught his attention. "Carmenita Consolata," he read aloud, and with a bit of a chuckle instinctively clicked the mouse to see for himself what 'consolation' the electronic gypsy-lady might have to offer.

It was far more than he had bargained for. Nothing was left to the imagination, as the screen filled with a veritable cornucopia of nude photographs of Carmenita from which he could select his desired perspective. Not a few were lurid crotch-shots that left the professor even more shocked than he had been long ago in his sophomore year of high school when one of his bolder classmates had called his attention for the first time to Gustave Courbet's infamous *L'origine du monde*. But one of them had been taken with a wider lens and showed the female body in a softer, more erotic, light. Magnifying the image with another click of his mouse, Altmann sat back, adjusted a pair of wire-rimmed glasses on the edge of his Teutonic nose, and gazed intently at the body stretched across the screen in the full-frontal, nonchalant manner of a Modigliani nude. As he felt himself becoming aroused by the erotic scene, all the old arguments about how pornography reduces women to objectified 'others' and, according to none other than the great emancipator of sex himself, D.H. Lawrence, drives the masturbating male-gawkers ever deeper into the vicious circle of self-consciousness came racing back into his mind and began gnawing at what little personal sense of integrity still lingered in his tortured soul.

Had Rousseau been right, he mused despondently, in predicting that all his years of study would only serve to exhaust his spirit, enervate his courage, and leave him incapable of resisting the slightest passion? Had he become, after forty

19

years of philosophical preachments about human dignity, just another voyeuristic, dirty-old-man? But, strong as was the shame that surged through his mind, he did not stop looking. And as he felt his excitement growing, his mind took a turn in his own defense and teased him into thinking, along with Ann Snitow and her now more fashionable feminist friends of the nineties, that perhaps pornography was not so bad after all, if, as they claimed, it could help liberate the feminine libido and will to power. The enthusiastic apology for sadomasochism by some of them, or the ironic celebration by others of a girl's discovery of sexual ecstacy through the relation with her dog, was more than he could yet stomach, but otherwise, well . . . maybe, he mused, the new feminists were closer to the truth than their moralistic predecessors had ever been. Furthermore, hadn't Ms. Steinem herself acknowledged a big difference between pornographic material that is based on the violent domination of women and erotica that is rooted in the idea of a free, passionate yearning for a particular person and leaves the viewer with a 'contagion' of pleasure? And hadn't the public reaction to Praxiteles' Knidian 'Aphrodite' proven that any nude, no matter how ideally conceived, would, as the renowned English art critic, Kenneth Clark, had written, arouse in the spectator some vestige of erotic feeling? That the photograph of Carmenita was stirring his sexual interests, therefore, was not in itself, he rationalized, any more reason to feel ashamed than he might be upon viewing, say, Francois Boucher's reclining *Miss O'Murphy* or *La Grande Odalisque* by Ingres.

His native inhibitions thus anesthetized, the professor refocused on Ms. Consolata, feasting his eyes on her naked image until, finally, his eyes closed and his body taut with pleasure, he fantasized the metamorphosis of her sensuous body to include the face of the one woman he really wanted. No sooner had his prurient appetite been sated, however, than the logic of his rationalization lost its force, and his spirit drooped under another wave of self-contempt. Disgusted at having so debased the object of his desire, and having convinced himself anew that his attraction to Liliana was something more than animal lust, he resolved never again to succumb to pornography's seductive lure. Clicking the mouse repeatedly, he finally succeeded in escaping the porn site, and returning to his email, proceeded to send a brief message to Liliana:

lcolumbra@aol.com>Tues, 10 Jun 1997 18:29
Dear Liliana,

Just a short note to see if I have your correct email address, and to make sure that the address I gave you last Saturday off the top of my head was the right one. Thanks for sharing your insights with me during the opera's intermissions. It added so much to my enjoyment of the evening. Hope we can meet again.

Sincerely,

Maurice

4

Altmann woke the following Monday morning with a sigh of relief from one of the two recurring dreams he had experienced repeatedly since the start of his professorial career. Time and again he had had to relive in his sleep the three hours of relentless grilling he had taken during his doctoral examination some thirty years ago. Inevitably, he would find himself stumped by the most elementary of questions and wake to the shameful sensation of having to inform all his family and friends that he had flunked out of the program and would have to settle for something other than a scholarly career, only to recall moments later, after shaking off his soporific state of mind, that he had in fact passed the exam *summa cum laude* and was indeed a college professor. This time, however, he had dreamed, as he had often dreamt before, of being a newly-hired professor at one or another Ivy League school like Princeton or Yale, and on the first day of the fall semester not being able to find his way to the classroom through a bewildering maze of stairwells and hallways, and later having to explain to an irate dean why he had failed to meet with his students at the appointed eight-o'clock hour.

The nightmarish, aimless racing about and the illusory panic induced by his superior's wrath had left his body in a cold sweat. Throwing back the thin white sheets under which he slept naked during the hot and humid June nights, Altmann raised himself to sit for a moment on the edge of the bed and let his body acclimate itself to the cooler temperature of the air-conditioned room before walking stiffly through the adjacent hallway toward the bathroom beyond to shower and shave. Several blackbirds that had roosted for the night on the limbs of the huge maple tree standing outside his bathroom window were just beginning to cackle, signaling Altmann that, although dawn had already broken, the hour was still very early, and that even if he had been scheduled to teach an eight o'clock class, which would never happen, given his prerogatives as chair of the philosophy department, there would be no need to rush.

So, after a leisurely half-hour of showering with the hottest of water his body could stand and trying to counter the ever-increasing dryness of his hair and skin through the application of a variety of conditioners, creams, and lotions, he strolled back to the bedroom and took another thirty minutes to execute the push-ups and other exercises his physical therapist had encouraged him to do to prevent a recurrence of the sciatica he had suffered the year before.

By the time he was finally clothed in a combination of the tan trousers, sky-blue shirt, and maroon-striped tie he almost always wore to class under a navy-blue sport jacket, it was still only seven o'clock. His summertime ethics class was not scheduled to begin until nine, so he decided to forego his usual bowl of cereal and treat himself instead to a heartier breakfast at Brookfield's House of Pancakes. There he encountered his immediate boss, BCC's Dean of Humanities, Dr. Charles Niebling.

"Well, good morning, Maurice!" the dean exclaimed upon spotting the philosophy professor. "What brings you out so early in the morning? Want to join me?"

"Yeah, sure," Altmann replied, while indicating to the waitress that he would like to order the same platter of scrambled eggs, bacon, and hashbrowns that the dean had already been served. Although they had crossed swords now and then over the many years of their tenure at BCC, he and the dean had remained good friends through it all.

"So, how's your stock portfolio holding up?" Niebling inquired, knowing full well that his earlier advice to Altmann had already reaped his friend considerable gains.

"It's doing okay," Altmann acknowledged rather nonchalantly. At last check, he had noticed that the unit price of his growth stocks had actually jumped another four bucks, and was now at something like ninety-six dollars, sixteen more than he had paid for it only a month ago. Notwithstanding his current agnostic mood, however, he remained enough of a disciple of Socrates not to want to seem more interested in getting rich than pursuing wisdom, even though the dean himself would hardly have noticed or cared, having long ago let his lust for wealth supplant the passion for scholarly work that Altmann knew had once ruled his soul.

"I told you it would, didn't I?" Niebling crowed, taking a swig from his coffee cup, and displaying the penchant for boasting that Altmann least liked about the dean. "It's really quite incredible how well the market is doing. You ought to take the plunge as I have, and shift all your money into the growth funds."

"I don't know," Altmann mumbled between sips from a glass of orange juice. "That's pretty scary. Most of the growth stocks are in the tech area, aren't they?"

"That's right, but isn't that where the future lies?," Niebling asserted. He had been one of the first at BCC to champion the computer as an academic tool, and had obviously put his money where his mouth was.

"Perhaps so," Altmann conceded. Years ago, when the dean had predicted that any faculty wanting to survive in the academic world of the future would have to become computer-literate as soon as possible, Altmann had made a bit of a fool of himself at the division meeting by declaring, only half-jokingly, that just as he had gone his whole life long without knowing how to operate a fork-lift, he fully intended to go to his grave without learning how to use a computer. It had gotten him a good laugh at the time from equally ignorant colleagues, but since then, of course, he had had to swallow his words many times over, and had, in fact, often been one of the first in line to purchase every latest version of Windows as it had come on the market.

Still, it never ceased to bother him how the computerized technology was threatening to consume so much of the money that used to go for the purchase of library books, microscopes, and other more traditional, academic tools, and on that account had recently sent BCC's head librarian an anonymous note, calling his attention to a clever mock-advertisement for the latest technological invention called the 'book.' Furthermore, he had also read enough of history to know that what goes up almost inevitably comes down. "Isn't it possible," he added, "that we're seeing a repeat of the old tulipomania? I've read where many of these tech companies have yet to make a profit and that its only wild speculation driving their shares so high at the present time."

"Oh, that's just chicken-talk by some of the more conservative brokers who missed out on the recent upswing and are trying to rationalize their lack of savvy to disgruntled clients," Niebling retorted. "Frankly, what with all the built-in checks and balances in today's market, I'd say that the chances of another collapse are next to nil. The bears may have a day now and then, but I don't think the bulls can be stopped in the long run. In any event, whatever little risk there is, is far outweighed by the odds of making tons of money for doing next to nothing."

I don't usually like to broadcast my earnings, but between us, I can tell you that in the last two years alone I've realized gains of over half a million dollars."

"On paper, you mean?"

"Yeah, of course; I haven't cashed in any of my stock; it would be stupid to do that when the future is looking so bright."

"Well, more power to you, Charles," Altmann replied, dabbing his mouth with his napkin after having downed a rather messy chunk of the scrambled eggs. "But I've worked all my life to save up the little I've got, and I'd hate to blow it all this late in the game . . ."

"That's understandable," Niebling observed, "but, as I said before, your chances of 'blowing it all' would be rather slim. Anyway, not to change the subject, but speaking of 'late in the game,' I have to tell you that the college is about to launch an early retirement plan, and your name is high on the list of targeted individuals. I was at an administrators' meeting the other day, and when the president asked for a list of names of faculty whose early retirement might be desirable, your name was the first to be mentioned . . ."

"By whom?"

"Dufus!"

"He would, the bastard!" Altmann replied, not at all afraid to share his real thoughts with a dean who had for years been his staunchest supporter in the ongoing struggle between BCC's autocratic president and its AAUP chapter, of which Altmann had long been a leader.

"From what I'm hearing, they're going to be making a fairly generous offer, something like a whole year's salary spread over three . . ."

"Well, let me tell you," Altmann declared, "Schmidt and his functionaries have got another thought coming if they think they can buy me out!"

"And I certainly wouldn't want to play into the hands of that ruthless crowd either, but . . ."

"But, what?" Altmann muttered defensively.

"Well, I've noticed that you've seemed a bit down and out lately, and wondered whether you might not want to take their money and run. With that and the benefits you'll get from TIAA-CREF you'd be making as much as you are now, wouldn't you, even though your Social Security won't kick in for another few years?"

"Probably so," Altmann admitted, a little disappointed that his dean would seem so willing to see him go out to pasture.

"Of course, I'd hate to lose you from the division," Niebling quickly added, upon detecting the slight look of hurt on his friend's countenance. "Stark, I know, has been hankering for years to get out of teaching German, and would jump at the opportunity to replace you, but I'm not sure her minor in philosophy qualifies her for the position, and finding anyone to do as good a job as you have done over the years would not be easy. I just thought it might be to your own advantage to get out from under your heavy teaching load and have more time to spend on your research and writing."

"Can't say that I've been doing much of that anyway recently," Altmann mumbled.

"Well, maybe you ought to hit the road for a while," Niebling chided. "Find a lovely soulmate, head for the mountains, and treat yourself to a bit of that terrestrial *joie de vivre* you've always been writing about!"

Altmann smiled good-naturedly. For years he had deflected similar attempts by Niebling and other colleagues to hitch him up with one or another of BCC's unattached females, and he toyed momentarily with the thought of finally offering his friend a bit of satisfaction by revealing his current infatuation with the lovely Liliana. But anticipating the ribbing he would probably have to take over the gap between his and her age, he thought the better of it, and returned instead to his earlier line of resistance to early retirement. "I appreciate your concern, Charlie, but as I've said many times before, I have every intention of staying on at BCC at least one day longer than President Schmidt!"

"That may not be very long!" the Dean chortled, after taking another gulp from his cup of coffee. "Rumors are rampant that the board has his head on the block!"

"I've heard those rumors for years, and I'll believe it when I see it," Altmann protested. "From all that I've witnessed, Schmidt has this board in his pocket, and will retire when *he* chooses to do so, not when one or another renegade trustee thinks he ought to."

"You may be right," Niebling conceded, "but all the more reason, then, for you to be on guard. He hasn't forgotten that vote of non-confidence your group stirred up against him five years ago, and if he can't get you to retire early, he'll certainly be looking for any other opportunity to run you out. So, let's not have any 'moral turpitude,' huh!" he concluded with a chuckle.

"At my age? You've got to be kidding!" Altmann joshed, albeit a bit nervously as doubts about where his fascination with Liliana might take him in the weeks and months ahead crossed his mind.

"There's no age limit on lust, you know!"

"Well, thank you, Dr. Stendhal, but I think his comment was about 'love,' not 'lust'!"

"Whichever!" Niebling quipped. "Gotta run!" he added, before scooting out of the booth and bidding Altmann a friendly farewell.

At nine-o'clock prompt Professor Altmann was in the classroom methodically calling the roll of the twenty students enrolled in the summer session of his ethics course. Satisfied that all but one of them had made it to class on time, he consumed the next fifteen minutes returning test papers and explaining what the answers to his questions should have been, and then tried picking up on where he had left off the previous day on a comparison of various theoretical approaches to morality.

"Yesterday," he began, "we took a look at two versions of the Egoistic Hedonistic Consequentialism propounded in ancient Greek times by Aristippus and Epicurus and by a host of other thinkers down through the centuries. While the one advocated the 'seeking of pleasure,' and the other the 'avoidance of pain,' both were of the view that when one is trying to decide what is the right thing to do, one should only consider how the consequences of one's action work to the benefit of oneself. In evaluating such an approach to morality, we have also already taken notice of three objections that might be raised against it. Using the example of the nobles in Boccaccio's *Decameron* abandoning their neighbors and fleeing to a country villa in order to escape the plague that had struck their city, we noted, as did also Albert Camus in his Nobel Prize-winning novel, *La Peste,* that such behavior by the nobles, or by Camus' fellow Parisian citizens during the Nazi occupation of their city, might very well be deemed 'indecent,' in view of the fact that the 'neighbors' they were leaving behind were all, as fellow human beings, in one sense or another their 'brothers and sisters.' Secondly, we noted that, contrary to the defense of capitalism by the likes of Adam Smith and Ayne Rand, any society whose members are only interested in themselves will eventually be torn asunder. And thirdly, we pointed out how both versions of egoistical hedonism can become delusory to the extent of encouraging individuals to escape the harsher dimensions of reality. There is another objection, however, that might be raised against egoism, and I'd like to discuss it with you today. As a variation of hedonistic consequentialism, egoism promises to make its followers happy. But can it deliver? Some would say that it cannot. Sean, what do you think . . . can one find happiness by going on an ego trip? Take Hugh Hefner, for example. His so-called Playboy philosophy advocates an egoistical approach to sexual relationships, and to all appearances, he is practicing what he preaches, embracing one partner after another only so long as each is young and nubile enough to satisfy his rakish fantasies. Is he a happy man? Sean, what do you think?"

"Would that I could be so happy!" the handsome student replied, to the titillation of all his classmates, except for one of the females, whose feminist wrath Altmann had earlier experienced in a discussion on abortion when he had observed that a woman's right to privacy may not be as absolute as Roe v. Wade seemed to imply.

"You think living in a mansion like that, surrounded by all those . . ." Altmann hesitated for a moment before using the term that initially came to mind, ". . . *chicks*, would be paradise, huh?"

"Could be worse!" Sean mumbled with a wry grin.

"Well, Hefner does look rather happy, what with that silly grin and suave, constant puffing of his pipe, and were we to ask him, I'm sure he would claim to be in a state of bliss. But can we say that he is happy just because he looks happy and thinks that he is happy? What did Aristotle say in this regard? The miser thought that happiness consisted only in hoarding all his wealth, but was he a happy man according to Aristotle? Sarah."

"Not really," Sarah answered hesitantly.

"Why not?" Altmann asked, not without a small pang of conscience over his own ever-increasing preoccupation with daily fluctuations in the stock market.

"He didn't know what he was missing?" Sarah guessed.

"Like what?"

"Knowledge, friends?"

"Yeah," Altmann elaborated, "remember how according to Aristotle wealth is only one of the goods we humans need to find happiness; friendship is another, and if we think we are happy without friends, that just shows how stupid we sometimes are, not that we really are happy. So, if going on an ego-trip deprives us of the chance to make friends, then no matter what we think, we can't really be happy according to Aristotle. What do you think, Sean, does Hefner have any friends?"

"I guess it depends on how you define friendship," Sean replied.

"True," Altmann conceded, "and would you say that your friends are those who care at least as much about you as they care about themselves? Someone probably wouldn't be your friend for long, would he, were he to think only about himself and never show any consideration for *your* interests?"

"Not really," Sean agreed.

"So, what do you think about all those chicks and other folks hanging around the Playboy mansion? Do you think they really care about Uncle Hugh, and does he really give a damn about any of them, or are they all only looking out for themselves? Are they friends in any real sense of the word?"

"Some of them might be," Sean contended.

"Let's hope you're right, and you probably are. But I daresay that *if* you are, it's only because Hefner and his crowd are not always living up to their own egoistical philosophy, for egoism by its very nature precludes the kind of consideration of others that we expect of friends. So, if you agree with Aristotle that friendship is in fact essential to the pursuit of happiness, and you think that egoists cannot really make friends, then you would have to conclude, wouldn't you, that egoism cannot deliver what it promises? Sean? You don't look entirely convinced."

"Isn't the concern friends have about each other also motivated by self-interest? In the final analysis, aren't we all basically looking out for number one, even when we befriend or fall in love with others?"

"That's what Freud, Sartre, and other so-called psychological egoists claim; they think that as a matter of fact everybody—parents, teachers, lawyers, doctors, students—are all in it for themselves. But are they right? Jessica, what do you think? If your boyfriend tells you he loves *you,* or even walks up the aisle eventually and tells the world that he will take *you* for better or worse, will you believe him, or will you, like Sartre, suspect that he is only using such sweet talk to disguise his intention of exploiting you to his own advantage?"

"Sartre's right; men are all wolves!" Jessica asserted, evoking general laughter from her female classmates, but to judge from the bitter tone of her voice, meaning exactly what she said.

"And women aren't?" a male student grumbled from the back row.

Altmann thought of playing the devil's advocate for a moment by taking Jessica's side and sharing with the class the words of a country hit that was popular back when he was growing up: *"Now come ye young maidens, and listen to me . . . Never place your affection on a green willow tree; for the leaves they will wither, the leaves they will die, and you'll all be forsaken and never know why . . . They'll hug you and kiss you, and tell you more lies, than the crossties on a railroad or stars in the sky!"* But upon pausing to recall all the words, he glanced at the clock on the wall and noticed that the class-time was about to run out. With a promise to continue the discussion the following day, he dismissed the class and returned to his office where for the next half-hour he sat staring at the wall and wondering whether he was a fool to think that a man as old as himself still had any chance of finding a bit of happiness with a woman only half his age, and one so beautiful as Liliana.

5

A light breeze gently rustled the sheer curtains of his open, upstairs-study window, as Altmann rested the down-loaded message in his lap and listened to the melancholic sound of doves cooing to each other across the neighborhood rooftops. A moment later, he picked it up again, and perused its gentle words a second time:

> <maltmann@netscape.net>; Fri, 13 Jun 1997 11:27 (EDT)
> *Recordado Mauritio,*
>
> *Como estas?* I received your message and was so glad you were able to contact me. I will always remember the musical event we shared last Saturday evening. 'There' I had the courage to speak to the person sitting next to me! 'There' I felt the vibration of great voices and the waver of musical instruments! 'There' we spoke about philosophy, literature and paintings! 'There' are numerous reasons why 'There' will always remain such a magical place! I hope you will continue coming to Urbana for these musical events. Please let me know your opera schedule and I will help you get tickets.
>
> P.S. Have you ever read any of Gabriel Marquez?
> *Hasta pronto!*
>
> *Liliana*

Reaching behind him, Altmann pulled a small, Spanish pocket-dictionary off a bookshelf to check the meaning of the word *Recordado*. He assumed it was the equivalent of the English, epistolatory salutation Dear, but Spanish never having been among the modern languages mandated by his own doctoral work years ago, he wasn't sure of its exact connotation. All he could find, with the help of the magnifying glass he had begun keeping close at hand since the onset of old age, was an entry for *recordar,* which Langenscheidt informed him was a transitive verb meaning To remind; to remember. *"Also . . ."* he mused aloud in the Austrian dialect he had picked up from a year of graduate study in Vienna, ". . . *Recordado Mauritio!* She must be implying that there is something about me that is unforgettable! " "How nice!," he murmured with a smile.

But on second thought, he admitted to himself that if the word had any special connotation at all, it might be nothing more than that she thought of him as being worth remembering. Still, to be deemed at his age worthy of embrace by the memory of so young and vibrant a woman was not, he recognized, anything to be scoffed at. For a day or two, after having received no immediate reply to his own email, he had begun to suspect that Liliana Columbra was but an operatic phantom of his own delusory making, and that he would probably never hear from her again. All the greater his thrill now, then, to realize that he had been wrong, and that she had not forgotten him after all. And how sweet of her, he thought, to try enshrining poetically their relatively fleeting encounter within the sacred space of 'There'—infinitely beyond the average Main Street, USA, where, in an Existentialist nightmare of subjective isolation, he and other Giacometti-stick figures so often drifted past each other like ships in the night. If anywhere, it was 'There,' in the intimacy of their instant rapport, and not in the swamp of witless voyeurism, that his best chance of still finding some *praemortem* bit of earthly happiness might lay, and it was 'There,' he told himself, that he would be wise to stay. No sooner had his noble resolve been made, however, than his imagination quickly went to work again and began filling his mind, facet by facet, like the screen of a computer, with the digitalized, naked figure of 'Carmenita.' He tried flushing his brain of the obscene imagery by returning his attention to the email from Liliana, but his graphic recollection of her own sensuality only fired his passion the more, and despite his best intentions, he soon found himself exiting the email, methodically typing "Blue Angel" once more onto the search line of his Netscape Navigator, and with a few more clicks of his mouse, retrieving 'Ms. Consolata' from the alphabetized soup of stars still being served up on the porn site.

A bit shocked at the ease with which his will had succumbed to temptation, he fretted for a moment over the possibility of his becoming one of the two hundred thousand or more Internet users, who, according to a recent article he had read in *The New York Times*, were hooked on porn sites, X-rated chat rooms or other sexual materials online. From his undergraduate reading of Rousseau's 'scientific' analysis of civilization's 'dangerous supplement to reproductive coitus,' he had learned that it was the imagination, with its constant recollection of beautiful women who had been visually devoured at an earlier time and who could be called into lascivious service at any moment without needing their consent, which was the real culprit behind the epidemic of onanism that had swept the nineteenth century and supposedly sapped its dreamier chaps, like Rousseau himself, of their creative juices.

Nor had he forgotten Aristotle's sage advice to the effect that habits of virtue and vice are formed one step at a time through the repetition of right or wrong choices. He did not doubt, therefore, that some people could, if not by force, at least through a steady sequence of bad choices, become addicted not only to drugs and alcohol, but also, as recent issues of *The Chronicle of Higher Education* were reporting, to gambling and other forms of behavior, including sex. But recalling also how much control he had kept over his own libido during the first sixty years of his life, he reassured himself that, notwithstanding a periodic lapse or two, he was still the master of his own will, and could, if he wished, forego the pleasures of the moment in the interest of achieving the kind of long-term goal that Aristotle had associated with the pursuit of genuine happiness.

It then dawned on him though that having lost much of his hope of life beyond the grave, and with only a decade or two left to his earthly existence, it didn't make a lot of sense to be thinking of any end beyond immediate gratification . . . Unless, perhaps—the thought crossed his mind—Liliana's 'There' was all the room he might ever need to bring the shattered pieces of his identity back together and make the whole of his life good again. Illusory though it might have been, the thought was enough to incline his will to erase the image of Carmenita, and with multiple clicks of his mouse, he waded through the pornographic swamp back to the email site to begin another note to Liliana:

<lcolumbra@aol.com>; Sat, 14 Jun 1997 8:45 (EDT)

Greetings, Liliana,

I received your email, and was very touched by your poetic rendition of our rather serendipitous encounter. 'There' is such a common word, and usually connotes a certain spatial-temporal distance that limits one's access to whatever reality it locates. By impregnating it with such depth of meaning, however, you would seem to have converted it into what Walter Benjamin or Karl Rahner would call an *Urwort*—one of those words, that is, which, precisely because of their uselessness as technical jargon, are pregnant with the totality of being, capturing as they do the mysterious unity of the part in the whole, and the whole in the part. But lest my own plethora of words kill the magic of the moment you wanted to save, let me check this penchant of mine for philosophical rumination and simply say how much I too will treasure forever the excitement of our first encounter. Rahner and Benjamin used to say—here I go again—that the *Urwörte* constitute an *Ursprung*, a primordial pool of meaning from which all linguistic expression must repeatedly drink if it is to stay alive. So, let's hope that the 'There' of which you sang so beautifully will always remain for the both of us something like a Fountain of Youth to which we can return time and again to refresh our . . .

Our *what?* Altmann asked himself. By inviting him to keep in touch, Liliana, he suspected, had probably been looking for nothing more than a friend with whom to converse about something other than the latest graduate-school gossip of faculty-student sexual liaisons. And, given the dearth of intellectual life on his own community college campus, he would himself gladly welcome the friendship of so bright and articulate a female as she had shown herself to be. But the feelings she had instantly stirred in him, he knew, were something more or less than friendship alone. But what? Considering how quickly his aged imagination had recently converted her beautiful body into just another piece of porn, he could hardly deny that whatever else he was after—friendship or maybe even love—it was the prospect of a *'nuit de plaisir'* that most attracted him. Should he write then ". . . to refresh our passion," or perhaps, to tone it down a bit, ". . . to refresh our passionate friendship"? In both Schopenhauer and Nietzsche he had recently read about the outside chance of a man and woman becoming sexually passionate even while enjoying each other's company as friends. And perhaps, he mused, his relation with Liliana could prove to be one of those rare cases. Not daring to hint at such a possibility, however, he proceeded to type in the word that had initially come to mind:

34

. . . friendship.

And speaking of youth and friendship, were you aware that Tchaikovsky's *Eugene Onegin* is being performed next month? I already have two good tickets, and would be very pleased to have you join me. Let me know by email if you would be free and interested. Perhaps we could also have dinner together before the opera. What do you think?

P.S. I am sorry to say that while I have heard much about Gabriel Marquez, I have never read any of his works. But I intend to go to the bookstore tomorrow to buy some of them, and hopefully will have a chance to read one or another before we meet again.

Cordially,

Maurice

6

"Why did Schopenhauer think that way? Tess, did you get a chance to read his essay?" Altmann asked in an attempt to get a class discussion going on the meaning of life.

"Think what way?" the long-haired girl in the front row queried, as she quickly leafed through her textbook to find the essay in question, having obviously failed to do the assigned reading.

"That human existence is a joke," Altmann prompted, but to no avail, as Tess only looked the more bewildered. "Joe, help her out. Why was Schopenhauer so pessimistic?"

"Probably because he had messed up his own life so badly," Joe Jackson half-sneered. A handsome business major with total confidence in his own ability to succeed, he had little sympathy for losers in any society.

"So you think he was just projecting his own misery out onto the rest of mankind?"

"Yeah. I read somewhere that after losing his father early-on in his life, he came to hate his mother and women in general, had no friends or lovers, and after quitting his job as a professor because no one showed up for the lectures he had scheduled at the same time as Hegel's, he spent the rest of his years wandering around the Alps whining about the mess he had made of his own life. Frankly, I think the guy was sick!"

"Perhaps he was," Altmann conceded, mindful of his own recent bouts with depression, "but probably no more so than other philosophers of his time. Rousseau, for example, claimed in his *Confessions* that it was a 'sensitive heart' that had caused all the 'misfortunes' in his life, but there is no question that his lifelong inability to relate to others was to some extent also the result of his periodic depression and delusory thinking. Both Kierkegaard and Tolstoy suffered from melancholia, a neurotic condition which some claim is often accompanied by a pathological fear of sexual involvement. And even before he went stark raving mad, Nietzsche, whose own father had died from a softening of the brain, had suffered terribly from migraine headaches and mental anxiety. Nietzsche, in fact, was of the view that man is by nature 'the sick animal,' to the extent of constantly being torn psychologically between different ways of trying to satisfy the will to power. And in this latter broad sense of the word, Nietzsche would have agreed with you, Joe, that Schopenhauer, with his life-denying asceticism, was indeed 'sick'. But we can't assume, can we, that just because one or another thinker like Schopenhauer experienced a little pain in his life that his philosophy is nothing more than the projection of his own personal misery? I don't deny that Schopenhauer's outlook may have been colored by the mess he had made of his own life, but he did provide some rational arguments for the conclusions he drew, and our acceptance or rejection of the latter ought to be based on a consideration of the reasons he gave. So, again, Joe, what reasons did Schopenhauer give for concluding that human existence is a joke?"

"Well, okay . . ." the student reluctantly answered, ". . . for one thing, he argued that our lives are temporally and spatially insignificant."

"Was he right, Patty?"

"I don't know," the girl mumbled, rather defiantly.

"How old are you?"

"Nineteen."

"You've been around nineteen years! Wow! How does that make you feel? Like you're fairly important, huh? Well, all of us sometimes get to thinking that we're pretty hot stuff, because we subconsciously assume that the world did not begin until we came along. But, let's see . . . what year is this? Nineteen ninety-seven? Were our universe no older than that, Patty here might still have some reason to feel significant to the extent of having been around at least one-hundreth of the time. But how old is our universe, Steve? Only two or four thousand years, as biblical mythology would have us believe?"

"More like ten billion . . ." Steve, a science major, promptly declared.

"So, how does that make you feel, Patty? Like a drop in the bucket of time?" Altmann queried, after writing the mega-number out on the blackboard and juxtaposing Patty's age under it. "A bit insignificant, temporally speaking? And what about our place in space? Measured over against the limits of the city, state, or planet-earth in or on which we live, our own backyards might seem rather impressive, but what does it add up to in the context of outer space, with all its billions upon billions of galaxies? Not much more than an inconspicuous speck of dust, according to Schopenhauer. Religious people, of course, would say that even if time and space are of such infinitude, God, in his omniscience can still keep us in mind and endow our lives with lasting meaning. But Schopenhauer was an atheist, and was thus left with the conclusion that humans are fools to think that the little bit of time and space they take up amounts to anything significant. What other reason did he give for concluding that our lives are jokes? Joe, can you help us out again?"

"Frustration," Joe replied in his usual prosaic manner.

"That's right," Altmann proclaimed. "Schopenhauer thought that none of the desires generated in us by the will to life are ever satisfied . . ."

"Not even love?" Tess inquired.

"Not even love!" Altmann asserted. "In his view, love of any sort, including the passionate kind, is merely a disguise for the sexual impulse toward reproduction contrived by the will to keep the species afloat. Nature dupes individuals into thinking that sexual intercourse will afford them their best chance of happiness, but no sooner has the seed of the next generation been planted than they experience profound disillusionment, lose their passion, get bored, and often end up hating each other."

Several male students in the back row looked at each other and smirked knowingly, and before continuing with his summary of Schopenhauer's pessimistic appraisal, Altmann paused to give them time to vent their bitterness. "The only possible exception to this rule he says, is the rare case of a man and woman conjoining their sexual passion with real friendship, but even then it is likely that the harmony of their relationship will only surface after their sexual passion has dissipated. The main question, then, is not so much whether human existence is or is not in and of itself wretched, but how we humans can best cope with the reality that we know is, if not absurd, at least very tragic. Joe, you seem to be our resident expert on Schopenhauer this morning. How does he answer this latter question?"

"Doesn't he say that we should just throw in the towel?"

"Well, not to the extent of encouraging suicide, but certainly in the sense of advocating a cessation of desire through distinterested aesthetic appreciation and the practice of asceticism. In this way he thought we could exorcise the demon of sexual desire altogether and already here and now experience a little bit of the self-annihilating bliss the Buddhists call Nirvana. So, what do you think, Joe? Was Schopenhauer right?"

"I think he sucks!" Joe replied.

"Well, you may be right. But what alternatives do we have? Steve, if we don't take the route pointed out by Schopenhauer, how else can we cope with the misery of human existence? Did you read the Tolstoy piece?"

"Yeah-h," Steve half-lied, having assumed, like most of the students in the class, that he could get by just reading the text's introductory summary of Tolstoy's *Confession*.

"What was *his* answer to the question?"

"What question?"

"About the meaning of life. Did he agree with Schopenhauer that this life in and of itself is worthless?"

"Yeah," Steve guessed.

"His whole life long?"

Seeing the defensive, quizzical smile on Steve's face, Altmann decided to spare the lad any further embarrassment and answered the question himself: "Well, you're right, Steve, Tolstoy did eventually come to agree with Schopenhauer, but only after—according to his own testimony—he had experienced a very joyful childhood and a rather exciting twenty years of early manhood during which he was entirely devoted to ambition, vanity and, above all, lust. At first he thought this profligate lifestyle was the height of human bliss, but at about the age of thirty-five or forty, he came to the conclusion that the life he and his high-society companions were living was altogether hollow."

"Including his sex-life?," a student queried with a snicker from the back of the room.

"*Especially* his sex-life!" Altmann solemnly declared.

"Why was that? Was he too old to enjoy it any longer?" the student persisted in asking, obviously in hopes of getting another cheap laugh from his classmates.

With his own libido still raging at sixty like the Platonic wild beast, Altmann was in no mood to humor the typical assumption of youth that after thirty, one could not possibly have any sexual drive left, and toyed with the thought of humiliating the smart-ass in the back row with an insult or two about how any female could possibly enjoy sex with witless young bucks like himself, but thought the better of it, and explained instead that at least according to Tolstoy's own account, his sexual appetite remained as strong as ever up to the day he died at the age of eighty-two, and that though he thought at first that his youthful promiscuity was satisfying, he later came to the conclusion that it was only serving to exacerbate his feelings of emptiness and loneliness.

"But wasn't he just talking about his experience of premarital sex when he made comments of that sort?" a female student named Donna Jo inquired, "And didn't his attitude change after he fell in love and got married?"

"Quite the contrary!," Altmann explained. "Already in *War and Peace* and *Anna Karenina* which were published in the decade following his marriage, his fictional married couples, shamed by their erotic behavior during their honeymoons, are depicted as spurning sexual allurements in favor of the demands of domestic life, concluding finally that their only chance of happiness lay in purging themselves of passionate desire and devoting themselves instead to charitable work in and outside the family home. He may occasionally have expressed some tolerance for marital sex as a cure for concupiscence or as a means of reproduction, but he was bitterly opposed to any humanistic attempt—Christian or otherwise—to glorify it under the aegis of connubial bliss. Sexual intercourse, in or out of marriage, was in his view a mere contrivance of civilization, and as such totally 'unnatural.' Far from being elevated by marriage, marital sex actually reduces the latter to the wretched state of cohabitation that he describes it as being in his later writing, *The Kreutzer Sonata*. Marriage, he claimed, is simply the price that couples have to pay for buying into the false allurements of sex."

"And what he says about sex, he also says about life in general?" one of the more middle-aged students inquired.

"Right. In and of itself, life holds no promise, he thought. The only way to find meaning in this life is to see it as a preparation for the next through the practice of charity as dictated by the teaching of Jesus. Sexual abstinence is only one step toward supplanting disgusting 'animal man' with a race of superior loving creatures."

"Did he practice what he preached?," Marian asked.

"As a matter of fact, he did, eventually giving away much of the tremendous wealth he had earned from the sale of his very popular novels, and emulating the simple faith of the Russian peasant, whose unsophisticated lifestyle struck him as being most consistent with his love of Nature."

"What caused him to change his approach to life so dramatically?" the senior student inquired further.

"Mainly a fear of dying. The sudden death of one of the companions of his wild youthful years set him to wondering whether anything on this earth is of any lasting value, and led him finally to the conclusion that only the next life holds any real promise."

"So, in his view religion alone could afford any meaning to our human life?"

"Correct. But I would caution you not to think that Tolstoy's interpretation of the teachings of Jesus is the only way to conceive of a religious, or even a Christian, response to the question about the meaning of life. Not a few religious people, including many, if not most, Christians, would argue that while self-denial is one way of trying to find meaning through union with God, it is not the only, or even the best, way to do so. Others would say that it is precisely their religious faith that inclines them to embrace this world and bury themselves in it through a love of one's fellow human beings that includes an erotic dimension."

"But what if one doesn't believe in God?" Marian persisted in asking.

"Well, Schopenhauer was atheistic, and we've already seen his response. But is his the only non-religious alternative?" Altmann asked. "Can one deny the existence of God, human immortality, and everything else traditionally propounded by various religions, and draw any other conclusion than that human existence is a joke? Take Bertrand Russell, for example. He was as atheistic as they come, but did he agree with Schopenhauer about the meaningless of human life? I asked you to read his essay, 'A Free Man's Worship.' Did anyone get a chance to do that yet? You did, Steve? Great! So what did Russell say in this regard?"

"He argues that we can in fact make our lives meaningful if we stop worshiping false gods and devote ourselves instead to human ideals of truth, goodness, and beauty through the pursuit of projects bigger than ourselves."

"So the trick, he thinks, is to get out of ourselves?"

"Exactly. It's only when we get off the ego-trip that we have any chance of finding happiness."

"And if we succeed at that, then even though our universe is not going anywhere in the long run, and is instead heading for doomsday, we can still find some meaning here and now."

"That's what I interpreted him to mean."

"And I think your interpretation is accurate and well put, Steve. But how is what Russell is saying any different from what Tolstoy and other religious folks are suggesting. Both are saying, aren't they, that to find happiness or meaning in life one must get out of oneself through service to the human community. So wherein lies the difference?"

"Well, I guess it's in the fact that religious folks, like Mother Teresa, who claims that it's seeing the face of Jesus in all the poor and dying people she serves that keeps her going, think they need a relationship with God to get out of themselves, while Russell and his kind claim to find the relation with their fellow human beings exciting enough in and of itself to sustain their interest."

"So who's right?" another of the students called out.

"Well, I'd say the proof is in the pudding," Altmann replied. "But you can decide for yourself who has made the greater contribution. So give it some thought, as I'll probably be assigning you an essay on the subject in the near future. Have a nice weekend."

Back in his office, Altmann collapsed into his armchair, threw his long legs over the edge of his desk, and sighed deeply. Trying to sustain his interest in the elementary issues he was expected to cover in his ethics class had become increasingly difficult with the passage of years, and all the more so now when, given his agnostic mood and bouts of depression, he had to fake his own enthusiasm for the material he was delivering. Exhausted, but satisfied that he had once again pulled off the trick, he let his mind wander onto more pleasant turf, and spent the next ten minutes fantasizing about the possibility of a man as old as himself ever finding a bit of erotic bliss with so young and lovely a woman as Liliana had seemed to be.

Altmann knew enough about the lives of famous philosophers to know that he would not be the first in his field to have ever entertained such thoughts. Rousseau, Novalis, Goethe, Stendhal, Schopenhauer, Nietzsche, Heidegger were only a few who came to mind. But no sooner did he think of them than he also recalled how almost all of them had failed to capture the youthful objects of their amorous desires. Would his chances be any better? Probably not, he mused dejectedly, before picking himself up and heading for the parking lot. While driving home and having to wait five minutes for a train to cross the road he was on, however, he remembered reading Rousseau's fictional account of an older man's passion for an idealized younger woman, named Julie d'Etange. *La Nouvelle Héloïse* it was entitled, and may very well have been nothing more than an attempt on the part of its author to purge himself of the desire to love which he had never been able to satisfy, or more specifically, of the hopeless passion he was still feeling, even while writing, for the beautiful Countess d'Houdetot, his junior by at least twenty years. But like Stendhal's later work on the nature of love, *De l'Amour,* it may also, Altmann suspected, have been intended by Rousseau as a thinly disguised picture that he could send to his beloved in hopes of sharing with her the innermost feelings of affection that he dared not express directly, and by the time he had arrived home, he had convinced himself that a similar ploy might well work to his own advantage.

7

Altmann fell into a fit of creative labor, agonizing throughout the next several days about how best to arrange the raw material of his erotic feelings into a story that might appeal to Liliana's aesthetic taste, while at the same time giving her some subtle hint of his own affection towards her. Finally, while paging through a recently published biography of Goethe late Friday night, it dawned on him what should probably have been obvious from the start, that being the aging, disillusioned philosopher that he was, his infatuation with a beautiful young woman was not without a Faustian undertone. Arising the next morning at the crack of dawn, eager to begin processing the words that would put some flesh on the bones of a plot that had come into his head the night before, he quickly showered and shaved, gulped down his breakfast, and by seven o'clock was at his computer typing in a variation on the name of Faust as a provisional title:

PROFESSOR KLAUER
A Novel
by
Maurice Altmann

Knowing only too well that he had gone his whole life churning out nothing but drab scholarly pieces that had next to no literary value, Altmann cringed momentarily as he reflected upon the pretentiousness of identifying himself as a 'novelist.' But the thought of engaging Liliana thereby in a romantic dialectic of sorts overrode any doubts he had, and he proceeded on with his writing.

CHAPTER ONE

One Saturday afternoon in early summer, Professor Klauer set out for Urbana, deftly steering his '97 Monte Carlo off the main highway onto a narrow country-road that would cut at least ten minutes off the time it would otherwise take to get there. Over the years he had made the drive hundreds of times to take advantage of U of I's "Big Ten" library or the copious productions of its School of Music. But it had become increasingly tiresome to travel the hundred and fifty miles to and fro, and recently he had checked out the possibility of buying a house close to the Krannert Center in the heart of the university town, hoping that when he retired four or five years down the road, he could actually walk to the performances of his favorite operas. Shocked, however, by the exorbitant prices set on the few houses within walking distance of the Center, he had dropped the idea, and resigned himself to negotiating central Illinois's much neglected back-roads anytime, as now when he was off to attend a performance of Gounod's Faust, *he felt in need of some cultural enrichment.*

In the late afternoon sun much of the farmland through which he was passing was aglow with golden brown hues of the stubble left behind by the recent harvest of winter wheat. The first of the season's dull-orange, black-bespotted tiger-lilies were already beginning to sprout amidst the lush, green undergrowth of the ditches alongside the road, and at the edge of one pool of standing water an elegant blue heron waited with total concentration to strike at its next victim. Here and there a farmer could be seen dutifully racing his tractor across a plowed field in a last-minute attempt to finish the annual planting of corn that had been delayed by seemingly incessant rains during the month of May, while a bunch of black birds, their erratic flight creating a scriptic arabesque against the soft blue sky, followed him around and periodically dove to steal one or another of the precious kernels from the chthonian bed into which they had just been dropped.

As recently as two or three years ago such pastoral scenes would likely have stirred the professor's imagination along lines of philosophical speculation about Nature's mysterious beauty and left him in something approximate to the 'rapt mood of transcendent ecstacy' Wordsworth and his Romantic kin were said to have experienced. But now the early-summer rituals being reenacted in the surrounding fields only served to exacerbate his feelings of despair, and more than once along the way he contemplated plunging his Monte Carlo into the raging waters of the river over which the serpentine road would periodically take him.

Lacking, however, the courage to drown himself, he cursed the signs of early summer that everywhere mocked his senescence, and drove on. He had made plans to attend the opera and dine with some friends—a married couple, the McIntires, one of whom, Josh, the husband, had been among the brightest of the six thousand or so philosophy students he had taught down through the years—and pulled into the parking lot of the agreed-upon Italian restaurant just as they too were arriving. After exchanging handshakes and friendly hugs, they hurried into Mazzoli's only a minute ahead of their reserved time. Not long into their meal together, his former student began unloading some material from his ongoing doctoral dissertation about Kantian epistemology, while Olga, his wife, a lovely woman of Russian origin, whose limited fluency in the English language made it difficult for her to appreciate any such esoteric discourse, was delicately slicing the calamari she had ordered over a dish of linquini. Like Sartre, Professor Klauer had always detested the eating of any food that had not been wholly fried, baked, broiled or otherwise worked over by human hands, and notwithstanding the woman's exquisite manners, her genteel consumption of the half-cooked squid left him feeling slightly nauseated and all the more agitated by the convoluted twists and turns of her husband's monologue. Ten years ago he would have plunged right into the conversation, and the two of them, oblivious to the passage of time and the undisguised boredom of whichever female Josh might have been currently dating, would have chewed the philosophical cud until their carafe of cheap Chianti table-wine had been emptied of its last drop. But his sexagenarian despondency had soured whatever taste he had ever had for such dialectical verbiage, and nipped in the bud a slight temptation to re-engage himself. Pushing aside his own plate of canneloni, he sipped pensively at his half-filled glass of Merlot, and instead debated within himself whether simply to humor the younger man's graduate-school fervor, or to chance spoiling the whole evening by dousing it with a bitter shot of the Rortyian skepticism he had himself been imbibing of late. But recalling that it was he himself who had first set the younger man on fire intellectually, and how, over the years, the budding philosopher had traveled with him half around the world with no less devotion than an Antonius for his emperor, he could not bring himself now to try blowing the flame out, and preoccupied himself instead with nonchalantly sharing a piece of Tira Misu with the charming Olga, while her husband further expounded on the intricacies of Kant's transcendental critique of traditional metaphysics.

An hour later the three of them settled into the prime orchestral seats which Professor Klauer had reserved at a bargain price (compared to the going rate at the Met) of twenty-two dollars each. With Olga and Josh seated at his left, the seat to his right remained unoccupied at first, and the professor hoped that it would stay that way so that his six-foot-four-inch body would find some extra room to stretch during the impending three and a half hour performance. At the last minute, however, before the lights were dimmed and the orchestra had struck up the fortissimo chords of the adagio to introduce Faust's melancholic brooding, Klauer glanced to his right and noticed the attractive figure of a dark-haired, amber-skinned female of moderate height in a plain black dress hurriedly wending her way down row G past already-seated, slightly disgruntled opera-goers toward the vacant seat next to himself. Pulling his lanky legs back in front of him, and drawing his right arm closer to his own body, he gave the young lady a nervous, perfunctory nod and dutifully surrendered the empty space to her duly-proportioned body. She, in turn, instantly flashed him a friendly smile that even in the dimmed lights revealed a pair of dazzling dark eyes and a set of immaculately white teeth behind out-stretched lips of the most sensuous sort. As though an arrow had been shot direct into his heart, the old professor felt such a surge of excitement pulsing through his veins that when, midway through the second scene of the first act, Faust aired his melodic plea for the pleasures of youth, it was all he could do to refrain from singing along. But not daring to show any sign of his internal commotion, he became all the more cautious about having an arm or leg of his accidentally brush against one of hers within the charged confines of their juxtaposed seats, and when—the theatrical transmogrification of the aged Faust into a dashing young suitor of lovely Marguerite completed—a fifteen-minute intermission came at the end of act one, he immediately rushed off to the men's room, and then, upon returning, promptly initiated an exaggeratedly-intense conversation with Olga and Josh in a feigned attempt at gentlemanly propriety toward the comely incarnation on his right. But just as the curtain was about to rise again, and he had returned his attention to the stage in front of him, he felt a gentle nudge on his right arm, and upon discretely leaning in that direction, heard the young lady ask him in whispered English, accented by an obviously Latin American inflection: "Are you enjoying the performance?" "Oh, yes!" he replied with a boyish exuberance that belied his old age and earlier depression. "Good!" she cooed softly into his ear, as drunken revelry broke out on the stage, and the two of them settled back to watch half-inebriated students and soldiers vying before their slightly jealous seniors for the attention of the town's sprightly maidens. As further scenes of diabolical intrigue and machination finally gave way to the consummation of erotic yearnings, and he was listening to the rejuvenated Faust's singing of his ecstatic night of love with Marguerite, the professor happened to glance to his right and out the corner of his eye caught a glimpse of the young lady next to him poised, like a hummingbird hovering before a floral pool of nectar, on the edge of her seat, joyously absorbed with every ounce of her being in the amorous action unfolding before her. Whether from aesthetic appreciation of the theatrical performance or vicarious identification with the opera's angelic heroine, she was a picture of total abandonment to the pleasure of the moment. Long accustomed to the lanquid inattention of so many of his students in the classroom, the professor was momentarily stunned by the young woman's enraptured countenance, and because of his fixation almost missed the concluding brief scene of act two (three in the original Barbier and Carre libretto) when Marguerite pours her heart out to the night in expectation of her lover's return in the morn. No sooner had the curtain fallen, however, and the second intermission begun, than she immediately turned her attention to him, introduced herself as a graduate student in the field of Spanish literature by the name of Teresa Bellezo, and after learning his own name and profession, told him how her recent reading of Sophie's World *had whetted her appetite for a deeper study of the history of philosophy, and especially of some of the more modern thinkers like Schopenhauer and Nietzsche.*

"Schopenhauer?" the professor murmured with a skeptical smile. Although he himself had come to share the nineteenth century, German philosopher's pessimistic assessment of human existence on grounds of its temporal insignificance and frequent frustrations, he was not yet ready to embrace asceticism as the best way to cope with all that energy supposedly coursing through his veins in the form of Will. Even if his life

were not going anywhere in the long run, and he periodically was tempted to throw in the towel, he still liked to think that it would be better to go out on a 'bang' of immediate gratification than to follow the example of some whimpering monk, like the Buddha, and stop desiring altogether. "I like Nietzsche too," he added in a friendly tone, "but why Schopenhauer?"

"Well, from what little I've read of him," Teresa replied without any hint of being intimidated by Klauer's professorial air, "he seems to have had a keen appreciation of all the fine arts, and not least of all for the kind of tragic literature to which I've devoted much of my scholarly life."

"That's true," Professor Klauer replied. "Although he thought of music as the highest of all the arts because of its ability to exhibit the Will in all its subjective passion, he did consider tragedy the supreme poetical art."

"What about painting?" Teresa asked. "I do a little of it myself on occasion and have often sensed a special affinity between that and my literary interests."

"You paint!" Klauer exclaimed in a hushed voice. "I do too . . . or, I should say, I did in my younger days before I buried myself in the library and let my rationalistic proclivities chew away the better part of my soul. Anyway, Schopenhauer would probably have agreed that painting and tragedy are closely allied, since in his view, painting, unlike sculpture, which he thought of as being primarily concerned with beauty and grace, is chiefly an expression of character and passion."

"So why shouldn't I like the man?" Teresa queried, picking up on the professor's earlier hint of disapproval.

"Well, far be from me to try dictating your philosophical taste, but I just don't care for the way he tries to subject everything to the third of Buddha's so-called Four Noble Truths."

"And what would that be?"

"The cessation of desire," Klauer replied. "The only real value Schopenhauer saw in aesthetic contemplation was the temporary escape it could afford one from the slavery of the Will by encouraging disinterest on the part of the observer in the beautiful object of desire. To get lasting relief and to finally cage 'the beast that resides in the human heart,' the Will to Live, he said, must be renounced entirely through the practice of asceticism."

"Didn't Nietzsche also encourage a form of asceticism?"

"Only as a disciplinary means to artistic sublimation, and never as an end in itself. He despised any and every attempt to emasculate the human spirit of its natural instincts to live."

"So what do you think of Faust's erotic desire?" Teresa interjected. "I recall Charles Lamb posing the question in one of his essays: 'What has Marguerite to do with Faust?' Apparently he didn't think the episode with Marguerite really belonged to the Faust legend. Was he right?"

"Well-l-ll," Klauer muttered, a bit taken aback by the sudden shift away from his own field of expertise, "it's been a while since I've last perused medieval literature, so perhaps I ought to throw the question back to you. Was Lamb on target?"

"I don't think so," the budding literary scholar promptly replied with the inimitably musical cadence of her native tongue. "The earliest popularizations of the legend, bent as they were on condemning the sixteenth century necromancer's preference for science over divine revelation, may only have hinted at Faust's hedonism, but Marlowe's 1588 Tragical History of the Life and Death of Doctor Faustus *certainly does have a scene wherein, after having surrendered up his soul to the devil in exchange for twenty-four years of intellectual and voluptuous living, the Doctor pleads for a wife or paramour, and finally has his soul sucked out by a kiss from none other than the imaginary, sweet Helen of Troy."*

"Ah, that's interesting!" the professor purred, while pensively surveying the face that could itself have launched a thousand ships. "But was the romantic element so dominant in Marlowe's drama?"

"Not really," Teresa answered rather hesitantly. "You can blame Goethe for that. In Marlowe's account, the erotic experience is little more than a crumb thrown to Faustus as compensation for the devil's inability to deliver on the universal knowledge he had promised. It was Goethe who first fully developed the love story. But even in Goethe, or at least in the drama's second part, the romantic relationship plays second fiddle to the larger theme of Faust's yearning for something more than earthly meat and drink, and Gounod's French librettists were certainly digressing from the German original in making Marguerite so central a figure in their operatic rendition."

"Were Barbier and Carre justified then in placing the woman at the heart of the Doctor's tragic struggle?" Klauer asked with a touch of

Socratic irony over the din of instruments again being tuned in the orchestra pit.

"I would rather know what you think," Teresa replied with a mischievous grin.

"Well, it probably brings the legend a bit more down to earth and renders it somewhat truer to life, don't you think?" Klauer muttered hesitantly, reluctant to confess openly his current distaste for the kind of transcendentalism oozing from Goethe's text, but convinced by his own libidinous disposition and the recollection of late-life ruminations by the likes of Rousseau or Emerson, that the promise of sensual delight more than anything else would likely have lured the aging philosopher into selling his soul.

"It certainly captivated nineteenth-century Parisian audiences, didn't it?," Teresa added with an appreciative smile and a tender pat on his right arm, before shifting her attention back to the stage.

His heart skipping a beat at the gentle touch, Klauer returned the smile, and after exchanging a perfunctory whispered word or two with his slighted friends on his left, tried focusing on the tragic scene of the abandoned, pregnant Marguerite that was beginning to unfold before him. But neither Valentine's valiant efforts to chastise her seducer, nor Faust's own desperate attempt to rescue her from Mephistopheles and the prison into which she had been thrown for having killed her illegitimate child, were exciting enough to keep his mind from toying, all throughout the final two Acts, with the slim chance of his ever striking up an amorous liaison with so young and beautiful a woman as the one next to him.

It was not the first time Professor Klauer had felt his orectic proclivities being pricked. There had been Clare, a voluptuous classmate from his undergraduate days; Barbara, Lisa, Ruth, and many another nubile creature who had crossed his path in the hallowed halls of wisdom where he had plied his trade in subsequent years; and last, but far from least, Sarah, the lonely and hungry wife of a fellow dialectician, whose ever-so-delicate formal features had once struck his middle-aged, Platonically-attenuated heart as the quintessence of feminine pulchritude. But his pretense of philosophical bemusement, with its supposedly all-consuming dedication to the pursuit of wisdom, and an ongoing frenzy of scholarly activity—not to mention mere professorial absentmindedness and procrastination of the sort that had kept Immanuel Kant from ever landing

51

a bride or even once experiencing sexual intercourse —had always retarded or altogether stifled the growth of such erotic impulses in the past, so that notwithstanding all his talk about sexual ecstacy along romantic lines, he had himself never experienced the climax of any amorous relationship. Now, however, given the new-found lucidity of his older age, his disillusionment, that is, with idealistic or any other claim to certitude, there was nothing to keep him from letting his imagination run wild with the thought of consummating his aroused passion, except perhaps, he feared, old age itself. While conversing with Teresa he had tried calculating what her age might be, and guessed that she was probably not much older than thirty. As the shocking realization sank anew into his besotted brain that this was only about half his own advanced age, and as he passively watched Marguerite being snatched at the last minute from the arms of Mephistopheles, he felt a wave of despair washing away the châteaux en Espagne *his mind had begun to construct out of the sandy-hued pile of beauty that Fate had deposited within his reach. His recollection of Rousseau's passionate love for Sophie d'Houtetot or of Goethe himself for his young bed rabbit—women their juniors by twenty and sixteen years—or of a host of other philosophers who had fallen madly in love with women half their own age, provided a moment of consolation, until he also recalled how the beautiful, seventeen year old Flora Weiss had almost kicked the middle-aged Schopenhauer out of the boat where he was romancing her with the offer of a bunch of white grapes. An image of Marlene Dietrich smashing rotten eggs on the skull of the clown-like figure of Professor Unrat also flashed across his mind. But then, just as he was about to bid the amber angel farewell and go his own way—despondent, but with his dignity still intact—she gave him another of her disarming smiles, thanked him for his friendly* tête-à-tête, *and asked whether he might not like to have her email address so that they could continue their intellectual dialogue.*

"Well, sure!" he replied with the same boyish exuberance he had answered her initial question.

Exhausted from his non-stop writing, Altmann ran off a copy of what he had written, and went downstairs to his kitchen and living room just in time for the evening news on TV. Sipping at the wine he had fetched along with some cheese and crackers, he listened passively as the Fuss Channel once again focused its newscast on the month-old story about the disappearance of a young female intern who allegedly had been having an affair with one of Washington's senior congressmen. Speculation was running in every direction, with one pundit conjecturing that the poor woman had probably been dumped into the Potomac by the jilted politician, another hinting that she may have been targeted by a betrayed spouse, and a third guessing wildly that the missing woman herself might be playing a vicious game of hide and seek to embarrass the man for having dropped her. Disgusted by the circus some in the media were making of the tragic event, Altmann switched to CBS, but not without his mind having already been pricked into fretting, however slightly, that he could himself be getting into a dangerous liaison. Stories of older, wealthy men being preyed upon by ravenous young females from south of the border, were not at all uncommon in the news these days, and although Liliana had impressed him as being as kind and gentle as a lamb, he would have to admit that in reality he knew very little about her background other than what she herself had told him. Ashamed, however, that such thoughts could surface on his mind, Altmann cursed the boob tube for its pernicious influence, and turning it off altogether, ate the rest of his meager meal in silence, and then went out for a leisurely walk around the neighborhood, reflecting all the while on how the little hope Liliana had given him had been enough to get him writing again, albeit in a less than scholarly manner.

8

Upon awaking Sunday morning and realizing that he still had a full day to go before having to be back in the classroom, Altmann jumped from his bed with no less excitement than he had once felt as a youth when, dabbling in the fine art of painting, he had discovered the seductive lure of an empty canvas. By six o'clock he was already at his computer, rereading what he had written the previous day. He was somewhat taken aback at how full it was of erotic innuendo. It hadn't necessarily been his intention to make it so. In fact, he hadn't really had a clue where he was going with the material when he had started writing that morning. But like the action painter whose first line on the canvas evokes another and then another, one sentence had lead to a second and a third until before long he had felt that he was no longer in control, but was instead being directed to write what he did by the lines he had composed before. And it had all happened so fast, as if, like a Handel, whose *Messiah* was said to have been born in a rush of creative frenzy, he were a wind tunnel of sorts through which some muse was blowing her poetic stuff with divine rapidity.

He hardly dared, of course, to think that his inchoate writing was in any way inspired, but he did like what he read, and all the more when he got to thinking about how it might stir Liliana's own imagination. But when he set out to write the second chapter, words of the sort that had come so easily the day before were nowhere to be found. For hour after hour he sat there, staring at the blank computer screen, sweating blood—as he recalled the American novelist, James Baldwin, having once said about the occasionally futile effort to unlock the writer's imagination. Part of the problem was trying to settle on the form in which to cast the second chapter. But even after he had finally decided to follow the example of

Rousseau and structure it in the form of an exchange of electronic letters between Klauer and Teresa, he was still at a loss over what to have them say to each other. It all depended, of course, upon where the imaginary relationship between them was going to go. But being at least remotely based as he had intended the novel to be upon his own relationship with Liliana, he had no idea what direction to set them on, since he was so unsure about where he himself would be going, or would even want to go, with Liliana. All kind of possibilities drifted across his mind: a one-night stand of sexual bliss, climaxed perhaps by a dramatic *Liebestod* when their initial friendship is soured by lust; an unrequited love affair that never gets beyond the stage of epistolary wooing; a purely friendly relationship; or perhaps a friendship with a sprinkling of erotic affection.

Unable to make up his mind about where to take Klauer and Teresa, he finally gave up, and abandoned the novelistic project, if not for good, at least until such time as he could get a better feel for where he stood with Liliana. Getting her response to the first chapter, he thought, might help get him out of the mental bottleneck he was in. So, taking out a card he had purchased from Boston's Museum of Fine Arts depicting Prendergast's *Eight Bathers,* he scribbled a note to Liliana asking her indulgence for his lack of talent on grounds that he was still trying to learn how to write by actually putting pen to paper, invited her to provide him with some feedback—should she still have the time and will—and then slipped it, along with the completed chapter, into a brown envelop that would carry it all safely to her Urbana address.

9

"In the Platonic dialogue entitled the *Phaedo*," Professor Altmann began, "we are told that as Socrates lay in prison awaiting his execution, he had another of the many recurring dreams in which he hears himself being admonished to cultivate and make music."

He had been asked by Dr. Norma Smead, the chair of the English department, to make a presentation at the monthly forum it sponsored for the sake of encouraging dialogue between faculty and students of BCC and any interested individuals from the local community. She had suggested that he might like to share with them something about the scholarly research project on Schleiermacher's epistemology that she had heard he was working on of late. Without confessing that no such undertaking was any longer in the works, he had demurred on grounds that having heard him give several scholarly lectures before, his likely audience would probably have wearied of such heavy stuff and might prefer a reading from a novel he was currently trying to write.

"A novel! You, the Prince of Footnotes, are writing a novel?" Dr. Smead exclaimed, tweaking Altmann's ego a bit over the notorious reputation he had gotten for loading all his earlier works down with an excess of scholarly apparatus.

Altmann took no umbrage at her friendly joshing, motivated at it was, he suspected, by legitimate surprise at his having had the *chutzpah* to announce with a straight face to the chair of the English department that he, a philosopher by trade, was not only writing a novel, but would like to do a public reading of it. "I'm a new man!" he crooned.

"I'll believe that when I see it!" Dr. Smead retorted, "but I must confess that you do seem to have lightened up a bit these past few weeks. What's going on? You're not hitting the bottle again, are you?!"

"Again?" Altmann chortled, accepting the fallacy of the woman's complex question for the joke that it was meant to be.

"What then? You're not getting married, are you?"

"Ha! You think that would lighten me up?"

"A *few* folks now and then do find connubial bliss."

"How many? One out of three these days? Sorry, but I'll need better odds than that," Altmann protested.

"Well, whatever it is that's lifting your spirit, I'm glad to see it. Frankly, some of your colleagues, including myself, were getting a little worried about your despondent moods this past year. So, I'll be more than happy to schedule you for the June meeting. How should we bill your presentation?"

"Let's call it 'Making Music Philosophically'," Altmann had suggested.

Before actually reading from his novel on the day of the meeting, however, Altmann had thought it wise to provide some exegesis of the Platonic text from which he had gleaned the nebulous title of his presentation.

"Socrates tells Phaedo," he continued, "that upon being admonished to make music he had first imagined that this was only intended to exhort and encourage him in the study of philosophy, which had been the pursuit of his whole life, and the noblest and best of music. But being as he was under the sentence of death, he began to develop the scruple, he says, that the dream might perhaps have meant music in the popular sense, and so, to satisfy the scruple, he thought it safer to compose a few verses before he departed. He thereupon sat down and wrote a lyrical ode to Apollo. But considering, he said, that a poet, if he is really to be a poet, should not only put together words, but should invent stories, he also felt compelled to try his hand at a little fiction. Well, notwithstanding my advanced age and a growing awareness of human mortality, I can't say that I have many scruples," Altmann declared, pausing to acknowledge with a wry smile a few snickers from the audience. "Still," he continued, "the thought has repeatedly occurred to me as I have grown older, that perhaps it's time to put my reason out to pasture and, like Socrates, to try making a little music philosophically along more imaginative lines. What I will be reading to you is an excerpt from my first attempt to do just that. Its chapter one of a novel I have begun about an aging, disillusioned philosophy professor who becomes enamored of a beautiful young woman while attending a performance of the opera, *Faust*."

"Is this autobiographical?" a colleague in the front row half-whispered to a friend next to her, just loud enough for Altmann to hear.

Altmann laughed. "Before I start reading," he observed, "let me remind you of Tom Wolfe's famous comment to the effect that while all serious creative work must be at bottom autobiographical, and that a man must use the material and experience of his own life if he is to create anything that has substantial value, it cannot merely be a literal transcription of his own experience. So-o-o, *Lou*-ise!" Altmann chided the woman in the front row who had been whispering to her friend, "don't think that this is all about me! As Wolfe asserted in regard to his own first novel, *Look Homeward, Angel,* 'I do not believe that there is a single page of it that is true to fact.'"

Louise smiled back, and Altmann began reading in the deep bass, but mellifluous voice that had become his trademark during twenty years of professorial lecturing. Even without his use of the battery-charged, snake-like microphone Dr. Smead had provided him, it carried easily across the small, public library room where the audience of about fifty people had congregated, and gave the story he was delivering an extra bit of profundity, or enough at least to keep even the few students in the back row, whose slouching posture and defiant stares betrayed the duress Altmann assumed they were under to meet a class assignment, awake.

No one, in fact, fell asleep on him, and for all that he could tell, his audience seemed enraptured by the story he was reading to them. But when, after some thirty minutes, he had read the last line, the only reaction he got was dead silence. This had happened to him before, when several years ago, in a rather foul mood, he had used Kundera's scatological analysis of *Kitsch* to challenge a local church group of social workers, who had invited him to address the banquet they were holding to celebrate another year of their good works, to wipe the self-congratulatory angelic smile from their sanctimonious faces, and had been left standing on the podium at the end of his talk without receiving even the most perfunctory applause or word of thanks.

But he wasn't aware of anything in what he had delivered this time that might have personally offended anyone in the crowd, unless perhaps they had somehow detected his ulterior motive in writing all this stuff, or, like Dr. Smead when he had first proposed to do the novelistic reading, were a bit taken aback by the effrontery of his intruding upon their literary turf, and weren't quite sure how to respond to the feebleness of his creative effort. Rushing to head off the latter possibility, Altmann quickly called their attention back to the conversation between Socrates and Phaedo with which he had introduced his reading.

"The conversation between Socrates and Phaedo" he reminded them, "had been prompted by a jealous concern on the part of a local Athenian poet named Evenus who wanted to know why Socrates, who had never before written a line of poetry, was now versifying the fables of Aesop. Tell Evenus, Socrates had declared, that I had no idea of rivaling him or his poems, for to do so, I knew, would be no easy task. Well," Altmann concluded in a self-effacing comment that he hoped would deflate any resentment or embarrassment his audience might be feeling, "it should be obvious that our own local poets need fear no competition from this quarter. And so, as Socrates saluted Evenus and his kind, let me bid all of you budding and blooming bards to be of good cheer and invite you to sing along as I leave my reason behind and whistle my way to the grave."

It was enough to break the ice. And although they later gave Altmann few compliments or even comments about the chapter of fiction he had read to them, preferring instead to gossip witlessly between nibbles and sips at the cookies and punch provided them, most in the audience seemed to get a chuckle out of his last remark, and prompted by Dr. Smead, gave him finally a round of light applause.

Reflecting while driving home on the cool reception his novelistic reading had received from the local high brows, Altmann convinced himself that it hadn't mattered all that much anyway, since the only reaction to his work that he really cared about was Liliana's. And upon entering his house, he promptly went to check for mail in hopes that within the several weeks since he had sent her a copy of the first chapter, she had found the time to read it and give him some feedback.

He was not disappointed. A large brown envelop with her return address on it was awaiting him. Tearing it open, he found a lengthy letter and a copy of Max Frisch's *Montauk*. He was not familiar with the novel, and took a moment before turning to the letter, to read the blurb on the book's back cover. It told him that the story was about an erotic weekend affair out on the northern point of Long Island between a young woman and a much older, visiting Swiss writer. Had he gotten into the text itself, he would have heard the novel's heroine warning the writer at one point against turning their affair into grist for his literary mill, and Altmann might have taken the gift of the book as a hint from Liliana not to use her for any further development of his novelistic project. But going by the summary of *Montauk's* plot alone, he interpreted the gift instead in exactly the opposite direction, and turned to the letter fully expecting Liliana to be resonating to the erotic tones of the material he had sent her. But the letter contained nothing of the kind. What he got instead was an extremely sophisticated literary critique of the way he was structuring and writing the novel. It was 'Bakhtin this' and 'Bakhtin that,' as she went on for two full pages repeatedly citing the famous Russian theorist about the importance of embedding any text with polyphonic voices and balancing out mimetic and diegetic elements. Much of it, along with all the rest of her talk about hermeneutics, sailed right over Altmann's head. Many years ago he had wrestled with Heidegger's metaphysics in an attempt to gain a better appreciation of the pre-Socratic sense of wonder, but he had not kept up with the many theories of textual criticism that Heideggerian disciples like Gadamer, Ricoeur, and Derrida had been spinning in recent years out of a combination of their mentor's linguistic philosophy, Freudian psychology, and Sausurian semiotics. Still, he wasn't so far behind that had Liliana given some tiny hint of having 'deconstructed' his own purposeful 'phallocentric' presuppositions in writing the piece, he would not have picked up on it. But he searched in vain to find between the lines of all her scholarly discourse any clear indication of how she was reacting to his erotic innuendoes. She did, to be sure, drop in a comment toward the end of her letter about Faust's fixation on Margurite being so typical of the traditional idealization of feminine beauty, but if she had intended thereby to reveal something of her own sentiments about what was going on between them, Altmann failed to get it.

Tossing the letter aside, he went to bed not knowing anything more about where he stood with Liliana than he had known before. His only consolation was that in the letter's postscript she had indicated a willingness to accompany him to U of I's presentation of *Eugene Onegin* on June 31, and to have dinner with him earlier in the same evening.

10

Searching through a chest of drawers in his bedroom, Professor Altmann finally retrieved from the bottom of one of them a navy-blue, polyester swimsuit he had not worn for twenty years. Its 1970s skin-tight, bikini style was not something he would any longer want to be seen in on the public beach, but it would be perfect for sunbathing and affording his body maximum exposure in the relative privacy of his backyard where a row of four-foot high Roses of Sharon along his property line blocked at least the downstairs view of his next-door neighbors. His waist having expanded no more than an inch or two during the interim years, it took only a minimum wriggling of his lower torso to pull the suit, with its thirty-four inch waistband, onto his naked body. Stepping before the floor-length mirror that hung on a closet door across the room, the aging professor paused to survey the damage that forty years of scholarly work and the lack of physical exercise after he had given up the playing of tennis and golf ten years ago, had done to his bodily appearance. Except for the minor bulge around his midriff, however, and the slightest wrinkling of lateral skin when he bent this way or that, he could find no cause for excessive concern. Compared to his youthful friend Josh, whose disrobed Doryphorian figure had often, during the nights of their travels together, left him embarrassed at the Cassian, 'lean and hungry' shape of his own 'thinking man's' relatively ectomorphic physique, he had never been, he knew, all that much to look at, and certainly not the kind of 'hunk' being stalked by the *Playgirl* photographers roaming Cape Cod's seaside strip and the other beaches he and Josh would periodically visit for an hour or two of afternoon basking in the sun to break the monotony of their long-distance trips.

Still, judging from the many female advances he had had to ward off in the interest of his hot pursuit of wisdom down through the years, his slender body was not either, he had come to believe, without its own appeal. And despite its having been hunched over books and manuscripts for all too long, it could, with a little effort by its brainy master, still strike a rather impressive pose, if for no other reason than its magisterial height. Taking a deep breath to expand his chest and suck in the loosened muscles of his stomach, Altmann turned slightly to his left to get a better view of his body's profile in the mirror. "Got to work on those hams!," he mumbled to himself, before grabbing a towel and a copy of *Love in the Time of Cholera,* and heading for the backyard.

With the late-June sun at its zenith, Professor Altmann winced as he stretched his body onto the hot, multicolored plastic ribbons of the cheap recliner he had recently purchased from Walmart. The heat reminded him of the chance he was taking, basking in the sun at this time of the day without any protective screens. But getting a good tan before his next encounter with Liliana seemed more important at the moment than worrying about the long-term consequences of overexposure to the sun. Bare-backed labor in the hayfields or hours of seminude play on the tennis court during his teenage and subsequent years had often resulted in his skin being baked to a golden bronze, and if ever his amber angel might deign to cast her gaze upon his naked body, as he fantasized she might in his wildest dreams, he wanted her seeing it in as much of its former glory as possible. At the very least, he had figured, a good tan might help to neutralize the telltale marks of old age that had suddenly begun to blotch the back side of both his hands—blemishes, which his dermatologist had recently informed him were irremovable, because, contrary to popular belief, they had nothing to do with any defect of the liver, but were merely the result of the body's photoaging after years of constant bombardment by ultraviolet rays. Within half an hour, several rivulets of sweat were trickling down the professor's chest, sensuously tickling its soft, brownish hairs along the way, before running finally into the umbilical pit of his belly and forming a minuscule, salty pool. But he refused to surrender to the god of light, and in fact rather savored the scent of his own sensuality wafting past his nostrils on the faint summer breeze. Instead of seeking shelter, he rolled over onto his stomach to let the solar radiation stimulate the production of melanin on his back side too. An hour of this each day for the next few weeks, he reckoned, and he could be ready to strip down at a moment's notice without too much fear of being humiliated by the pallor of old age.

Adequately roasted for the day, he finally pulled the recliner over into the shade of the huge, hundred-year-old oak tree that stood on the northwest corner of his lot, adjusted the chair's angle to accommodate the comfort of his lanky frame, and positioned himself to begin reading his first Gabriel Marquez novel. *"It was inevitable:"* the story began, *"the scent of bitter almonds always reminded him of the fate of unrequited love . . ."* He had not yet finished reading the opening line, when all of a sudden, seemingly out of nowhere, a ruby-throated hummingbird flitted into sight and hovered momentarily not more than a foot from the book he was holding, obviously mistaking its bright orange jacket for one of the similarly colored zinnias now beginning to bloom in several of the neighborhood gardens. Birder that he had been for many years, Altmann immediately recognized the tiny creature as the female of the species, lacking as it did the sexy, carmine pigmentation of the typical male's throat-feathers. The subtle, silvery-gray plumage of its underside, however, highlighted all the more the iridescent blues and greens of its head and back, and in the professor's view at least, made it even more attractive than its flashy mate. "What brings you here, *Archilochus colubris?*" he half-hummed, knowing that Colombia was the species' primeval motherland, and playing humorously with the thought that, instead of just looking for another nectareous handout, the bird might actually have sensed an evolutionary kinship with the book's Colombian author. "Was it *moi?*" he chuckled in response to her weak, unmelodic chippering. And as she darted off in a blur of wing-beats to search elsewhere for the real nectar, he mused for a moment more, before returning to his book, on what possible concatenation of biological and historical events might have brought that other product of the Andean north-land across his path. "Was it *moi*, Liliana?"

11

"You say his name is Adam?" Professor Altmann asked somewhat prosaically, trying to disguise the hurt he had felt upon being informed by Liliana of the long-standing romantic relationship she had with a fellow graduate student.

"Yes," she replied softly, "and I hope you don't mind, but I took the liberty of inviting him to stop by the restaurant when he goes to work this evening. I told him all about you the other night, and that I wanted him to meet you."

"I'll bet he was excited about that!" Altmann responded rather grumpily, while spearing a piece of asparagus and biting off its phallic head with more than his usual vigor. There was no reason on earth, he knew, why he should be surprised to learn that a young and beautiful woman like Liliana would have a lover, or why he, a sixty year old man, should begrudge her the chance to find a lifetime of connubial bliss. She had been kind enough to initiate a conversation with someone whom she had probably perceived to be a lonely widower, and even kinder to try putting on it a more profoundly personal spin. But that had hardly been an invitation to love. And judging from her cool reception of the personal references he had injected into his novel in hopes of stirring her romantic interests, little had changed in that regard. The plight of Klauer and Teresa had not even arisen during their dinner conversation. Clearly, he was making a fool of himself to think that she shared his amorous feelings. Still, crazy as it was, his heart ached, and though he immediately resolved to cultivate, as honestly as possible, the soulful camaraderie she certainly did seem to offer and want, he lacked the strength and will to tear from his heart all the desires and feelings their chance encounter had planted there, or to rule out once and forever the possibility of a Faustian *'nuit d'amour'.*

"Why do you think Fermina married Dr. Urbino?" he finally asked, trying to shift their conversation away from himself and back to the Marquez novel they had been discussing earlier. "Was it just for his money?"

"Well, that, of course, is what one of Florentino's disgruntled lovers claimed after she lost the Golden Orchid award in a poetry contest presided over by Fermina, accusing her of being the lowest kind of whore for having married for money a man she did not love."

"But doesn't Marquez have Fermina herself admit at one point in the novel that all her husband had had to offer was security, order and worldly goods, and that at the time of their marriage she had felt a greater need for such things than for love?" Altmann queried earnestly, recalling with a bit of shame how he had himself toyed with the idea of trying to lure Liliana into his amorous embrace by dangling before her some of the half million dollars he had stashed away over the years.

"I think you're partly right," Liliana concurred with a sip of her iced tea. "Although the two of them seemed to have found some romance along the way, she certainly had not married the man out of love. But you'll recall from another passage that she states explicitly that she gave very little importance to Mr. Urbino's 'legendary wealth,' his 'youthful glory,' his 'handsomeness,' or 'any of his numerous virtues.'"

"So if it wasn't love, or money, or sex appeal, what was it?" Altmann asked. He thought he knew the answer, but wanted to see if Liliana had also caught the author's clue.

"Well," she started to say, before politely stopping to chew and swallow the thin slice of salmon she had just taken into her mouth, "wasn't it that she had reached the age of twenty-one, 'her private time-limit,' as she says, 'for surrendering to fate,' and was afraid of letting 'an opportunity slip away?'"

"Exactly," the professor declared, with a touch of bitter masculine pride, "and in the process erases Florentino from her memory as though their earlier love affair had been nothing but an illusion, leaving him feeling for fifty-one years by her 'indifference' that he was 'ugly, inferior, and unworthy not only of her but of any other woman on the face of the earth!'"

"The 'Poor Man,'" Liliana replied, mimicking the 'final sigh' the novel's guilt-ridden heroine had permitted herself before dismissing Florentino with a wave of her hand and telling him to 'Forget it!' "Oh, here comes Adam!" she added with a smile, while rising to give her boyfriend—short, but as handsome and debonair as Altmann had fully expected any lover of Liliana to be—an affectionate hug, and introducing him to the professor as 'Adam Schwartzkopf'.

"Why don't you join us for a cup of coffee?" Altmann volunteered with less than heartfelt enthusiasm.

"Yes, do!" Liliana chimed in. "You don't have to be at work till seven, do you? Dr. Altmann here was just expressing his concern about Florentino getting jilted by Fermina in Marquez's *Love in the Time of Cholera*"

"Well, he gets her in the end anyway, doesn't he?" Adam interjected, while taking the seat offered him, and adding with a bit of a smirk that "but by then, I guess, the both of them were too old to enjoy their geriatric love-making."

The smart-ass! Altmann thought to himself, as he motioned for the waitress to bring more coffee, and Liliana rushed to remind her beau of the eternal dimension Marquez had ascribed in the novel's last chapter to the final, mutually erotic feelings of his ill-fated, fictional pair of love-birds.

"Yeah, I know," Adam stated, "but wasn't that just a bit of youthful idiocy on the part of Florentino—and, I might add, Marquez—to think that there was something immortal about young love? I personally prefer Schopenhauer's view."

Careful, you arrogant bastard!, Altmann mused, I'll have your balls on a platter!

"The professor is an expert on Schopenhauer," Liliana warned, sensing from Altmann's silent stare how turned off he was by her lover's impertinence.

"Oh, you are!" the young man exclaimed with feigned deference, while ignoring the red flag being waved by Liliana, and continuing with his venture onto Professor Altmann's philosophical turf. "Schopenhauer, as I was saying, would simply have dismissed Florentino's rejection by Fermina as a result of Nature's conclusion that their potential offspring could contribute nothing to the equilibrium of the human species."

"Is that right?" Altmann mumbled sarcastically. He had read the same *New York Times Magazine* article from which Liliana's boyfriend was obviously quoting.

"Yeah," Adam gushed, "and on that account would have offered the brokenhearted fool the consolation of knowing that his rejection was no cause for hating himself. Just because he found himself unfit to produce a balanced child with one particular person was no reason to think that he was ugly or inherently unlovable."

"So what was our lovesick, rejected hero supposed to have done?" Altmann asked. "Lavished his affection for the rest of his life on a succession of poodles, as did Schopenhauer himself after being scorned by his Lolita?"

"I thought her name was Flora, but anyway, as Liliana here can tell you, there is something to be said for the pleasure a dog can give one in the dark of the night. Right, Lil?"

She ignored the not-so-subtle slap at her insistence upon sleeping with her own dog, Jeremiah, even and especially on those nights when Adam would make love to her, and continued pensively sipping her coffee without saying a word.

"Well, in summary, then," Altmann began, while rather ruthlessly slicing in half the piece of chocolate-moose he and Liliana had earlier decided to share, "your interpretation of Schopenhauer's pre-Darwinian theory would have us believe that the Will to Life is driven toward the neutralization of all the variegated noses, chins, or body sizes that Nature, in its blindness, has concocted, lest by the persistence of such imbalances, the human race would quickly founder in oddity. Right?"

"That seems to be the drift of his thought," Adam concurred.

"And with your taste for the old German curmudgeon, you would also think, therefore, that not only Florentino, but all of us erotically-minded chaps, should humbly submit to Nature's balancing act, and stop whining when some female—or bitch, as you might say—kicks a little dirt in our face?"

"Well-ll-l, first of all, let me say that I've never thought of any woman as a bitch," Adam protested, with a defensive look toward Liliana, "but, yeah-h, I don't think we have any choice but to go along with Nature."

"So, if, to strike a balance, Nature dictates that shorter women should fall for taller men, you would have no objection! Well, I'll drink to that!" Altmann exulted, before excusing himself, and lifting his six-foot, four-inch frame from his chair and heading for the men's room. Upon returning he found Liliana's boyfriend ready to leave, insisting against the professor's effusively polite protestations that he had only ten minutes to get to work.

"Well, you sure chopped him down to size!" Liliana said, after Adam exited the restaurant and could be seen riding off on his bicycle.

"I'm sorry," Altmann uttered, "I guess I should have been more respectful of any friend of yours. But the guy really bugged me."

"Don't worry. He got what he deserved!" Liliana replied, as she reached across the table and patted the aging professor on the hand he extended to her.

"So, have you had any other such dogs in your house in years past?" Altmann asked.

"Too many to talk about now," Liliana confessed. "I'll tell you about them someday if you really want to know, but we'd better be moving on. The opera will be starting in forty-five minutes, and parking, you'll recall, is at a premium."

"And we certainly don't want to miss Tatyana's song of unrequited love for the adorable Mr. Onegin!"

"Not on your life!" Liliana chirped merrily, as Altmann dropped a fifty on the table with a nod to the waitress, and the two of them exited the restaurant arm in arm.

12

"Why don't we have a cup of coffee back at my motel room?" Professor Altmann suggested, as he and Liliana sat in his car after the opera and debated where to go next. "It's already eleven-thirty, and I doubt that Sully's will still be open." Rather than trying to drive the seventy-five miles back to Brookfield in the dead of the night, he had reserved a room at the local Day's Inn, and the thought of having Liliana accompany him there had set his adrenalin flowing. "We can continue our discussion about whether Tchaikovsky's music is faithful to Pushkin's poetic masterpiece," he quickly added, in an attempt to allay any suspicions she might have about his intentions.

Much to his surprise, she agreed to go along, and as they drove to the motel and made their way across its parking lot to his ground-level room, he marveled at how indifferent she seemed to the possibility of their being spotted by someone—not to mention, her beau Adam—who might know them. In the jaundiced view of strangers, the sight of an older man escorting so shapely a young woman to his motel room in the middle of the night would no doubt leave but one impression. And even the best of friends, he knew, would find their kind credulity tested by such brazen behavior. As for Adam—well, like Lensky, he suspected, the young buck would probably fall into a jealous rage and challenge him to a deadly duel. But the recollection of Onegin's triumph in the operatic shoot-out gave the professor himself, despite its tragic implications, a moment of perverse pleasure, and dismissing the image of his haughty competitor from his mind, he actually thought of taking Liliana into his arms and, for all the world to see, carrying her across the threshold of his room, confident that she, at least, would appreciate the comedic aspect of such a gesture. Fearful, however, of exacerbating a bulging disc, or worse yet, the inguinal hernia he had left unattended for several years, he settled instead for simply opening the door and inviting her, with an exaggerated display of etiquette, to enter the humble abode he had reserved for the night.

"Looks rather regal to me!" Liliana joked, as she walked into the room and surveyed its contents. Judging from what Professor Altmann had seen earlier in the evening of the sparse furnishings of her own room in the two-story house she shared with another female grad student, she might well have meant what she said. For apart from a small writing-desk and chair, one rather dilapidated dresser, a bookcase constructed out of a few boards and concrete blocks, several paintings of her own hanging on the walls, and a mattress placed directly on the floor, her room had struck him as being, albeit nicely kept, pathetically spartan, reminding him of the days long ago when, like any other doctoral candidate out of whom the university had already sucked every available dollar and reduced to the indentured servitude of the typical 'TA,' he too had lived on the edge of poverty.

"You won't mind if I strip down a bit, will you?" Altmann asked, while discarding the coat and tie he had worn to the opera, and loosening the top two buttons of his chalk-white, Geoffrey Beene shirt, not without the thought of revealing thereby a bit more of the skin he had worked so hard over the past month to bronze.

"Not at all! Where are the filters? I'll help you get the coffee brewed."

"Oh, yeah! The coffee! That's why we came here, wasn't it?" Altmann joshed. In the room's soft light, he was finding the young woman's sensual beauty all the more appealing, and he struggled not to let his imagination run wild. "So-o-o," he sighed, launching into a line of conversation that he hoped might take his mind off its less noble sentiments, "What did you think of Tchaikovsky's treatment of Onegin's cool rejection of Tatyana's confession of love? You know, at the end of act one, where he tells her that he loves her only like a brother, and admonishes her to practice more self-control?"

"Well, as I mentioned before, some critics think that Tchaikovsky misunderstood the role of music in opera, but frankly, I thought his treatment of the whole letter-scene was very effective. The calm, collected rhythms of Onegin's aria clearly support what the composer—himself wrestling with his conscience at the time over ill-fated, amatory advances from a female student of his—wanted the audience to think of a man who would so cavalierly reject an admirer's sincere avowal of love."

"He does come across as a rather cold and heartless coxcomb, doesn't he?" Altmann observed, while pouring a half-filled carafe of water into the GE coffee-maker provided by the motel management.

"And all the sweeter, therefore, Tchaikovsky's ironic touch toward the end of act three when he accents Tatyana's final, *andante molto mosso* rejection of the repentant dandy with fleeting references to the music he had used to underscore Onegin's initial rejection of her."

"His heart was certainly with Tatyana, wasn't it?"

"No doubt," Liliana concurred. "Pushkin notwithstanding, Tchaikovsky clearly turned it into her story."

"Like the rest of human history, huh?" Altmann teased.

"Oh, really?" Liliana retorted, jumping up from her chair and playfully tickling the right side of the professor's rib-cage as he was leaning down to fetch some cups from the cabinet below. "Try selling that to Luce Irigaray someday!"

"To whom?" Altmann asked with a quizzical smile, while throwing an arm around Liliana's waist and drawing her body toward his own for a friendly hug.

"Luce Irigaray!" Liliana repeated, as she gently disengaged herself and again took her seat. "You know, one of those post-structural, deconstructionists *fathered* by Jacques Lacan! She wrote *Speculum of the Other Woman* and many other pieces that challenged the traditional phallocentric interpretation of reality."

"Ah, yes, now I remember: 'The view from the womb!'"

"Well, I guess one could put it that way," Lillian replied with a laugh. "And it certainly makes more sense than Freud's silly notion of a young girl's penis envy. If female sexuality is indeed an aspect of the radical lack of being which, according to Lacan, underlies all human desire, it is, as Irigaray claims, an ineffable nothingness that, willy nilly, determines the male gaze in the same way that the gynecologist's *speculum* is shaped by the vaginal passage."

"In her view, then, the 'Other' of whom, according to Lacan, 'desire is the desire,' is not just the negative reflection of the male, Cartesian self, but a mysterious being in her own right."

"Exactly!"

"So, like I said, 'his-tory' in the final analysis is really 'her-story,' right?!"

"That's the way it *should* be, she says, but that's not the way it's always been, and to turn things around she calls for a new, truly feminine form of creative language, writing and thought."

"Well, here's to Luce, then!" Altmann proclaimed, as he lifted the cup of coffee he had just poured himself and invited Liliana to join in the toast. "Now let's forget her, and talk about you!" he added, after setting the cup down on the lamp stand, and seating himself in the chair next to hers. "You've told me earlier that you were born in Colombia, but tell me more. How did you ever end up here in the boondocks of Illinois?"

"It's a long story, but basically I can thank my mother for that. As a sixteen year old girl she had an affair with a married man, and I was the child of their love. But when he found out that she was pregnant, he abandoned both her and me. Once, some five or six years later, when I saw my mother conversing with him at the butcher-shop he operated, I ran up to him and naively asked: Are you my father? No, I am not! he answered coldly, crushing my childish heart that longed for a virile hand to hold. It was the last I ever saw of him until he was killed by someone robbing his shop nine years later, and my mother thought that I ought to accompany her to his funeral. On the day he was killed my mother had just returned from the States, where she had gone five years earlier, at the prompting of her sister and with the help of an uncle already there, to start a new life for me and the two other children she had borne since my own birth. To my great good fortune, I had been left during those five years in the care of my aunt, who, God rest her soul, was as kind to me as any mother could ever be, and ignited in me whatever spark of the Colombian fire it is that still burns within my heart. But with all the drug wars going on down there, and the societal havoc they wreaked, my mother knew, and her sister readily agreed, that the only chance I and my brothers would have at finding a better life, or at least avoiding a violent, premature death, would be to accompany her back to the States, where she still had the promise of a job. And so, with concern for nothing but the well-being of her children, she severed the last heartstrings tying her to her native land, packed us up, and hauled us off to a small town in New Jersey called Manville."

"*Man*ville, huh! Luce would love that!"

"Wouldn't she, though!" Liliana snickered, with a quick toss of her head to throw back several strands of the dark-brown hair that had fallen across her left eye. "Anyway, being the precocious brat that my mother tells me I've always been, I excelled in my high school studies, and upon graduation was granted a scholarship to Princeton, where I majored in world literature."

"Humm-m," Altmann mused aloud, "So Liliana was a Princeton Tiger! A tiger-lily!"

"Ti*gress*!" Liliana insisted, mimicking the feline's reputed fierceness, and then, just as quickly, taming it with one of her more kittenish smiles.

"I can imagine!" Altmann purred, while feasting his eyes on the graceful lines of her facial features, which, except for the fuller lips and dark, deep-set, bigger-cat eyes, were actually more like those of a cheetah. Two amber earrings and a matching cameo around her neck accented her smooth skin, like the jewelry bedecking a consort of Shiva, with the sensuous hues of the cat's native land. Notwithstanding its decent neckline, the short and tight, ruby-red, sleeveless dress she had worn to the opera created by its tautness an exciting play of lines between her moderately curvaceous breasts, and barely covered half the thighs of the relatively long legs she had honed to the muscular perfection of Cranach's *Venus* by daily runs along U of I's miles of forested paths. As Altmann let his eyes wander down the length of her body, and allowed his imagination *à la* Rousseau to devour visually the woman's impressive beauty, he was reminded again of the art critic's conclusion that even the most idealistic conception of the woman's body cannot but arouse some vestige of erotic feeling. "No doubt you have had many a ti*ger* on your trail, right?" he observed, only half in jest.

"Oh, now and then a tom or two would stray in my direction, but I was a real nerd during my undergraduate days, which landed me another scholarship at Princeton for further study, but not many dates. And it was not until I finished my Master's degree and had a job teaching Spanish at a high school in Trenton that I loosened up and ran a little wild. That was at about the time I met Steve."

"Steve?"

"Yes, Steve Bolero! Poor fellow! I didn't know it when I first started dating him, but I soon discovered thereafter that he was hooked on porn. Four, five hours everyday, after he would get home from his computer-programing job at *Interspace,* he would lie around his apartment viewing one piece of porn after another and working himself up into a masturbatory frenzy."

"So, why didn't you dump him?" Altmann asked, rather sanctimoniously for a man who knew his own vulnerability in this regard.

"Well, he was one handsome fellow and I, at the ripe old age of twenty-six, was one hungry woman. Furthermore, on weekends, when he seemed to get a little more control over himself, he could be quite witty and charming. We had many a good time together, going to the movies or dances, and usually ending up in bed, where, I must admit, he could be quite the Valentino! I kept thinking that as our love would grow, he might overcome his dependency on pornography, and settle into a normal relationship with me. But, sad to say, emotional invalid that he was, matters only got worse. Within the next year he got involved in all kind of voyeuristic escapades with some homosexual friends of his. On one occasion, they invited him to engage in sexual intercourse with a female friend of theirs while they stood around and watched. Before agreeing to do it, he asked me if I would have any objection."

"The sleaze-bag!"

"I found the thought of it rather disgusting too, but told him that it was his decision to make."

"And he decided to do it?!"

"Yes, he did, after telling me exactly when and where—in his apartment only three doors down from my own—the event would occur, and trying to convince me that being nothing but an erotic game they were playing, it would take nothing away from his love for me."

"I remember the wife of Gay Talese trying to make an argument like that several years ago when her husband claimed to be doing research for his book on the sexual behavior of the American male by sleeping all around town. To many an incredulous ear of *Esquire* readers, she wrote that Gay's sexual infidelity would take nothing away from the love they had developed for each other. I trust that an intelligent woman like you would never have fallen for such a line."

"I didn't really, although at first I tried to be as understanding as possible. As I sat alone in my apartment, however, thinking about what was going on between Steve and his wild friends only half-a-block away, I became increasingly distressed. It was really quite painful. I had had some strong feelings for Steve, and to realize that he didn't care enough for me or have sufficient character to forego the exotic pleasure of a voyeuristic moment and spare me the humiliation I was feeling, was the closest thing to psychological torture I have ever experienced. So, when he came crawling back to me, I told him to get lost, and that I was finished with him forever, whereupon he promptly went to pieces emotionally, tried to commit suicide by overdosing, and eventually, after recovering somewhat at the rehab center where I dumped him, disappeared for good."

"And then you started dating Adam?"

"No, there were half-a-dozen others before him, but none very serious. I didn't meet Adam until I came to Urbana two years ago to start my doctoral program."

"How serious are you with Adam, if you don't mind my asking?"

"I'm not sure. You may find it hard to believe after your encounter with him earlier this evening, but he *can* be a very pleasant fellow. I think you may have intimidated him and brought out a side of his character that I hadn't much noticed before."

"You may be right," Altmann conceded. "And I guess I baited him unfairly, but his opening crack about older peoples' lovemaking really ticked me off."

"It wasn't a very nice thing for him to say," Liliana agreed, "and he was rather haughty in flaunting what little he knew of Schopenhauer."

"So now that you know what a snob he can be, are you going to stay with him?"

"Well, even before this evening I had had some doubts about whether I really loved him. Sometimes I suspect the only reason I'm still dating him is a reluctance on my part to add to all the pain he's already experienced."

"What do you mean?"

"For one thing, his father died when he was only thirteen, and he's had a hard time coping with the loss ever since, especially after his mother, only a year following his father's death, up and married another, much older man with whom Adam doesn't get along. Then he had a rather traumatic experience about five years ago when a girl whom he had apparently loved very much walked out on him the very night before their planned wedding. Invitations had already been sent out, the wedding reception planned, gowns and tuxedos all rented, and so forth, but as the prospective bride was about to practice her walk up the aisle during the rehearsal the night before she suddenly announced to the stunned wedding party and her pastor that she could not go through with it, walked out of the church, and, can you believe it, within several months married someone else! You can imagine how embarrassing and painful that must have been for Adam."

"Yeah, of course, but he's not the first man to lose a father or to be stood up at the last minute by a fiancé, and I sure hope the sympathy you feel for him is not your main reason for staying with him. Nietzsche, you may recall, once wrote— I think it was in one of his letters to the Overbecks, in which he was trying to justify severing once and for all his relation with Lou Salome—that the feeling of pity can turn one's life into a hell by constantly interfering with the pursuit of one's own ideals."

"I remember reading the passage too," Liliana observed, "and I basically agree with him, but it's going to take me a while to sort out all my feelings."

"What's Adam majoring in?"

"Journalism. After getting his Master's, he wants to exploit his language skills to become an international reporter."

"That could be a very dangerous profession. I heard just the other day that last year alone some thirty-five journalists were killed in the line of duty. Wouldn't it bother you to be married to someone like that, not knowing from one year to the next whether he would still be alive?"

"Not if I really loved him. The possibility of losing him after only a few years together would not in and of itself keep me from pursuing the relationship further, *if* I were certain that I really loved him. But that, as I said, is what I'm still trying to decide."

Not wishing to seem overly solicitous about the possibility of her break-up with Adam, Altmann dropped the subject and asked if she cared for another cup of coffee.

"What time is it?" she asked.

"Only twelve-thirty," he replied. "The night is yet young."

"Well, perhaps half-a-cup, but then I will have to be going. I've got a paper due on Monday, and will still have to do a lot of work on it tomorrow."

"Ah, yes! Papers, and more papers! The bane of the doctoral student's life! What's it on?"

"I'm trying to do an analysis of Nietzsche's critical appraisal of Cervantes."

"Didn't Nietzsche like to identify himself with Don Quixote?"

"He did. He loved Don Quixote, but hated Cervantes."

"Why?"

"Well, in the first place, for fear, perhaps, of having the chimerical nature of his own philological profession ridiculed, he despised the way Cervantes disparaged his hero's quixotic character. Secondly, he faulted Cervantes for mocking the victims—the heretics and idealists—of the Spanish Inquisition, rather than holding the feet of its perpetrators to the fire. Finally, he was most upset about Cervantes' attack on the romance of chivalry. By having its fictional knight-errant come to such a horrible end, climaxed by a dreadful illumination of his illusory state of being, Cervantes' *Don Quixote,* Nietzsche said, threatened to level all of mankind's higher aspirations, and to expose its noblest specimens, like himself presumably, to an ignominious denial of oneself at the end of one's striving. For all these reasons, he concluded, the book should be considered a national misfortune and a symptom of the decadence of Spanish culture."

"Wow, that's pretty strong stuff," Altmann uttered, "and spoken, no doubt, as a true son of Luther!"

"What d'you mean?"

"Well, Luther, in my view, was his own worst enemy by virtue of his constantly overstating whatever point he had in mind to make, and Nietzsche, I suspect, may have picked up the same bad habit, if not from the Lutheran minister who was his father, probably from all his reading of the Reformer's works. In any event, his criticism of Cervantes seems no less exaggerated than Luther's of Leo X."

"I agree, and that, in fact, is what my paper is all about. I try to show, in other words, that Nietzsche's criticism of *Don Quixote* is not really consistent with what he wrote elsewhere about the 'birth of tragedy' out of the ancient Greek capacity for the tenderest and deepest suffering. But we'd better leave that for another time, don't you think?"

"As you please," Altmann replied, with a touch of resignation. "Let me get my coat back on, and we can be on our way."

"Better pull the plug!" Liliana cautioned, before taking the professor's arm and leading him out the room and across the motel's parking lot to where his Buick Regal had been left an hour or so ago.

13

Although he had gotten an affectionate hug and even a labial peck on the cheek from Liliana when he took her home and walked her to the door of her house on Orchard Road, Professor Altmann felt tired and rather defeated as he drove back to the motel, and trudged alone across its asphalt parking lot into the barren room that was all his for the night. After a quick shower and a perfunctory brushing of his teeth, he flipped off the overhead light, pulled back the covers of the king-sized bed he had requested upon making the reservation, and climbed in, kicking the heavier, topmost comforter off to the side, and stretching his naked body on its back, spread-eagle, under the remaining white sheets.

"Professor of Desire, indeed!" he mumbled disgustedly to himself as he reflected on his failure to have made even the most elementary of romantic moves toward the object of his desire, and calculated how his own performance paled by comparison with the sexual prowess of the hero in the Roth novel he had been reading earlier in the week. Not that Kepesh's animal aggressiveness was something that after forty to fifty years of gentlemanly propriety he would ever be able, or even want, to approximate. But should he not at least have grasped the moment of opportunity she had afforded him when, dressed as seductively as a Madonna, and looking no less delectable, she had come back to the room with him, and at one point at least seemed inclined to a bit of erotic play herself? Even in his latter years, Kepesh no doubt would have had her disrobed in no time flat and making love this way or that, in or out of bed, on the floor, in the shower, or had there been one, hanging from a chandelier. And although Roth's hero might be dismissed as a nymphomaniac—at least prior to his saner final years when the illusory nature of his earlier quixotic quest for sexual bliss came home to haunt him—could one not still ask whether any other, more normal representative of the male gender would ever have let such a chance for erotic pleasure slip by untaken, or even untested? Had his years of wandering in the ethereal realm of philosophical speculation rendered him totally inept at something so practical as the making of love? Or was it, he wondered, simply cowardice that had caused him to blow this chance? Doubts had indeed crossed his mind on several occasions about whether at his age he could any longer find the courage to open himself to the demands of a serious sexual relationship, not to mention the challenge of having to walk up the aisle should the object of his desire actually ever want something more than an overnight romp in the hay. It was not, of course, entirely inconceivable, he reminded himself, that notwithstanding the fact of his having thrown overboard most of his earlier philosophical convictions, he was still, to some extent, a man of principle, and that it may, in fact, have been his basic sense of decency that had kept him from taking advantage of Liliana's overly-trusting disposition. For whatever else he no longer believed in, freedom of choice was still something precious in his eyes, and he would not ever, he reassured himself, have thought of actually forcing himself upon any woman, least of all Liliana.

'Altmann's Law of Delicacy' he had labeled his position in this regard when, in years past, he had lectured his ethics students on how to avoid what had come to be known as date rape: "Never give more than the other wants to receive, and never ask more than the other wants to give!" Such delicacy is required, he had always explained, if sex between humans is to remain anything more than the mere mating of jungle cats.

But, as he lay there taking some drowsy consolation in the thought of having perhaps retained at least a modicum of delicacy through the respect he had supposedly shown for Liliana's freedom, he remembered also having told his students that the feminine No need not always be taken as final rejection, nor the man's, for that matter, as a female member of the class had been quick to remind him over the laughter of several feminists in the room who apparently found it hard to imagine that any man would ever turn down an invitation to sex. Far from precluding the Art of Wooing, he had theorized, Altmann's Law of Delicacy actually makes it all the more requisite, since otherwise, given the native fears we all have, none of us would ever freely come out of ourselves far enough to make love. The trick, he had further expounded with such cocksureness, as though he actually knew what he was talking about, was to delicately break down the other's irrational defenses by making oneself irresistibly attractive. Not only do you have to develop an eye and an ear for the more subtle, often whispered sounds and nuances of love coming from your mate, you must yourself also learn to speak and act beautifully, lest your rough language and behavior only serve to exacerbate the fears, distaste, boredom or whatever else might turn her—or him, he had been quick to add—off!

Mulling further over the events of the day, he chastised himself anew for failing to practice in his own life what he had always preached to others. Like Stendhal, he had obviously not been delicate enough. Liliana had hardly found him any more irresistible than had Metilde the great analyst *De l'Amour!* And perhaps he was a fool to think that at his age, without the advantage any longer of the disarming charm of a young, hard body, he could ever break down her resistance and woo her into his loving embrace. But then again, he mused, maybe he had failed this day only because, after learning of Liliana's ongoing affair with Adam, he had stopped trying very hard to win her love, and had settled instead for an evening of good music and intelligent conversation. And now that he had more time to think about it, he would have to admit, he conceded, that even without any erotic moments, the evening had been quite enjoyable. All the talk with Liliana had even seduced him into dropping somewhat his own, recently acquired, skeptical guard. And reflecting dreamily on how, if only for a moment or two, he had once again felt the joy of his youthful studies, he toyed with the thought of shelving altogether his romantic interest in the woman, and settling for the friendly camaraderie that had developed between them. But what if she actually ended up marrying Adam? What chance would he have then of continuing even their conversation? More than once he had experienced in past years how the marriage of one or another of his friends had reduced them to babbling idiots in the presence of their jealous spouses, and wrecked altogether the rapport he had once enjoyed with them.

So why not go for it all, now while he still had a chance with Liliana, and add a bit of erotic spice to what, admittedly, was the dialectical substance of their relationship. Had it been so unreasonable of the agonizingly-lonely Nietzsche to have asked something similar of Lou Salome, his intellectual soulmate for years, before she ran off to marry Fred Andreas and flirt thereafter with Rilke and Freud to assuage her marital pain? So what, if because of his advanced years, he could offer Liliana only a decade or two of companionship? Had she herself not said in regard to her relation with Adam that where there is love, time is of little significance? And wasn't that what Marquez was also saying about old age, that love, in other words, transcends the law of gravity? And even if, therefore, Liliana were half-committed to someone else, it would not have hurt, he berated himself again before falling asleep, to have let her know that he too would like a chance to woo her affection while she weighed her love, or lack thereof, for more youthful suitors.

Toward six o'clock in the morning he was awakened by the slamming of a door down the corridor from his own room. Rolling over, and pulling the comforter back over his body, now chilled by his having run the air-conditioner on high the whole night through, he promptly fell back to sleep, and as often happened to him on such early morning, soporific occasions, he began to dream. In a scene very much like a painting by Marc Chagall entitled Morning Mystery, he saw himself and Liliana, locked in a passionate embrace, floating weightless through a fiery space that was otherwise filled with the strange, coital-like conjunction of a Cyclopean Blue Hen and the spiky foliage of a bouquet of red, yellow, and white roses. When he awoke an hour later, wet with the sweat of his imagination, the scene came back to him in vivid detail, and for the rest of the day, as he checked out of the motel, drove back to Brookfield, and resumed his now daily summer routine, when not teaching, of reading novels, walking, and sunbathing, it would periodically resurface in his mind and leave on his otherwise saddened countenance the slightest, quixotic look of delectation.

14

"So, what you're saying," Altmann asked during a faculty senate debate about a new policy being drafted on the use of BCC's computers, "is that reading another user's files is the same as breaking and entering?"

"That's right," Bob Wissen, the long-time director of the school's information center, replied. "It would be just like reading papers on someone's desk, a violation of privacy."

"Why, then, on page four of the draft is it stated that BCC reserves the right to examine files and other computing material without notice? Wouldn't such an investigation require a search warrant?"

"Not really," Wissen contended. "Privacy is mitigated by Illinois and federal law that affords any institution the right to have its administrators control the use of its own computers."

"But that doesn't mean that they or technical staff people can casually or routinely monitor traffic content or search files, does it?"

"Not at all," Wissen acknowledged. "The content of files should only be examined when there is a reasonable suspicion of computer misconduct."

"You say 'should,' but 'could' they not just go on a fishing trip?" Altmann queried, looking around the room at his fellow senators and wondering why more of them were not as concerned as was he about the looseness of the document under discussion.

"Legally speaking, they probably could, but as noted, the draft indicates that it should be done only when there is 'reasonable suspicion' of abuse."

"As determined by whom?" another senator—Paul Mason, from the Psychology department—finally chimed in.

"By me, the chief information officer, and appropriate college authorities," Wissen declared rather defensively, knowing how little trust faculty had left in him and other college officials after years of confrontation over salary and governance issues, during which many of them, Altmann included, had long suspected their phones had occasionally been tapped.

"I think it would be better," Altmann interjected, "to have some third party, like a committee of peers, review the evidence before administrators and staff are given such license. And on that account, I would move that we not approve the policy statement at this time, but instead send it back to the *ad hoc* committee for further revision."

"Second!" Mason half-shouted.

The motion carried by a nearly unanimous majority, and it being already five-o'clock—a whole hour having earlier been consumed by the dean of faculty's lengthy report about the possible implementation of an early-retirement plan in the spring semester of the following year—the meeting was quickly adjourned.

"So, what have you got to hide?" Altmann was asked in a muffled voice as he brushed past Sam Deety on his way out of the small auditorium. Deety, the only senator to vote against Altmann's motion, was a professor from the business department with whom Altmann had repeatedly done battle on every issue facing the Senate in recent years. "Still into all that porn?" Deety added with a sneer.

Altmann knew that the business prof had to be bluffing. For even if Deety or anyone else at the college had somehow gained access to Altmann's college-owned, home computer, they would not have been able to discover the few hits he had so far made on the porn sites, since early on he had learned how to clear the computer of any of the so-called cookies or other electronic codes that might tell a snooping administrator or technician where he had been. But among the flaws in his character, one of the worst, by his own estimate, had always been his inability to slough off an insult or stupid comment from an opponent, and so, once again, instead of ignoring Deety's complex question as the cheap sophistical trick that it was obviously meant to be, Altmann chose to return the insult.

"Very funny, Sam," he muttered right into the business professor's face, "but if I'm not mistaken, it's you and your capitalistic swine who have cornered that market."

"Forget it, Maurice!" Professor Mason whispered upon overhearing the nasty exchange of comments. Taking Altmann by the elbow, he steered his friend past the hostile business professor and out the door onto the campus parking lot next to the library.

"One of these days I'm going to stomp on that rodent!" Altmann fumed. And well he could have, given his aging, but still well-honed, wiry frame as compared to the puny physique of his much younger opponent.

"Oh, that would make great news!" Mason chided. "I can see the headlines now: BUSINESS PROF MURDERED BY MAD PHILOSOPHER! President Schmidt would love it. He'd lose one of his favorite sycophants, of course, but seeing you hang would surely be reckoned a net gain."

Altmann laughed at the reminder of how for years the autocratic president of BCC had been looking for an excuse to fire his rebellious, but tenured, philosophy professor. After bidding Dr. Mason farewell, however, and climbing into his car to drive back home, it crossed his mind, as he was pulling out of the parking lot, how vulnerable he had recently become to the president's wrath. The threat to exterminate a fool like Deety was, of course, mere bluster, and notwithstanding the natural proclivity he always felt coursing through his veins to fight back—nurtured by the competitive spirit of the big family and rough neighborhood he had grown up in—he was confident of being able to keep his anger enough in check to refrain from use of physical force. But his recent dabbling in electronic erotica—a fact he had not yet shared with his friend, the psychology professor—pointed to a temptation of another, much stronger, sort, and he was not at all sure of being able to withstand it. He would need to be cautious, he knew, and upon arriving home, he promptly went to his computer and checked to be sure that any indication of his previous activity had been erased. Seeing that it had, he took an extra moment, before dining on the Fettucini Alfredo he had picked up on the way home, to see also how his stock had performed during the day, and was pleased to note that the unit price had soared beyond the hundred-dollar mark, increasing his one-month gain on his relatively small investment in the growth stocks to well-nigh ten grand.

15

Early on the next morning, Professor Altmann took the time to compose the email message he had been wanting to send to Liliana for several days.

<lcolumbra@aol.com>; Wed, 23 July 1997 7:30 (EDT)

Hello again, Liliana.

> I can't tell you how much I enjoyed our time together last Saturday. The opera was great, and I'm reading Pushkin again to appreciate better some of the points you made about the comparison of his original text to the libretto of Tschaikovsky's composition. How did anyone so young as yourself ever find the time to read so much, and become so astute! No kidding, you amaze me! I'm almost ninety-nine and haven't yet read half as much as you . . .

Altmann knew, of course, that what he was writing was not altogether accurate, since from the earliest days of his undergraduate studies, he had read voraciously every morsel of philosophical material he could get his hands on. But neither was it mere flattery, for although the *quantity* of his reading had been such that Liliana would have to live to be a hundred before she could catch up with him on the actual number of books he had read, the *quality* of her reading—embracing as it had, despite her major focus on the *Siglo de Oro* of Spanish literature and a personal taste for the likes of Lorca, Coelho or Marquez, almost all of the world's great literary classics—struck him as being far higher than that of his own.

True, the history of philosophy had its great classics too, and despite his current skeptical mood, he had no real regret for the time he had devoted to reading works of the calibre of Plato's *Dialogues* or Nietzsche's *Thus Spake Zarathustra*. Nor did he feel any inclination to try discouraging Liliana from pursuing her own new-found interest in 'Sophie's World.' Still, much of what he had read, he was now convinced, had indeed been worthless, speculative gibberish mouthed by dabbling dilettantes who had never really lived themselves and who, from their ivory-tower perspectives, had not a clue of what life was really all about. How much better might it not have been for him to have been reading, in depth, and not just the superficial skimming of texts that had gone on in his undergraduate World Lit courses, Homer, Aeschylus, Sophocles, Ovid, Virgil, Dante, Chaucer, Boccaccio, Ariosto, Cervantes, Shakespeare, Dostoevski—maybe even Zorilla, whose profligate hero, Don Juan, is finally saved, he recalls, from eternal hellfire by the love and devotion of the pure and virtuous Dona Ines —Melville, Ibsen, Joyce, Faulkner, Wilde, Updike and so many more of the outstanding literary figures with whom Liliana seemed so conversant, rather than having wasted so much of his time trying to unravel the Idealistic abstractions of a Hegel or the equally abstruse, Naturalistic ruminations of a Wittgenstein. Could the knowledge he had supposedly gained from having read the 'nonsense' of the former—as the Naturalists liked to ridicule Idealistic speculation–or from having played the 'language games' of the latter—as the Idealists were inclined to dismiss the Linguistic Analysis of the modern Naturalists—have ever compared to the concrete, practical wisdom he might have imbibed from the literary pool at which Liliana had long been drinking? Once, not so many years ago, a female colleague whom he had been dating off and on, had told him, out of the blue, that she had yet to meet a truly wise man. "What about *moi?!*" he had joked in reply, knowing all the while that the woman had hit the nail on the head, so far at least as her comment might have been meant to apply to himself. For, despite all the so-called knowledge that he had stuffed into his brain during myriad hours of heavy, philosophical reading, he had grown, he knew, only in age, and not in wisdom, even if by wisdom was meant something less than the 'divine perspective' his very Presbyterian girlfriend had probably had in mind with her humiliating remark, and connoted nothing more than what the French like to call *savoir vivre* or *savoir faire*. In the classroom, to be sure, he could talk for hours on end about the diachronic and synchronic stuff of selfhood or the intricacies of I-Thou relationships, and make his students believe that he was speaking from personal experience, but put him out on the streets where life was really going on, and he knew that for the most part he would be lost, lacking even half the savvy of his dumbest students.

... But I *am* working on it. You'll be happy to know, for example, that I'm reading another Marquez novel, namely, *The General In His Labyrinth*. Wow! Bolivar certainly did 'plow the sea,' didn't he, and not only on the revolutionary battlefield, but in bed as well! Besides Manuelita Saenz, his favorite mistress, there were apparently—not counting the one-night birds—thirty-four other women whom he 'conquered' without ever committing the least part of his life to them. And all because of the early death of Maria Teresa Rodriquez del Toro y Alayza!? Am I reading him right? Is Marquez really suggesting that all of the Great Liberator's successes and failures, in and out of bed, can be ascribed to the untimely loss of the woman who was his wife? He does have Bolivar say at one point that he'll 'never fall in love again . . . because it's like having two souls at the same time.' I guess that would imply that with the premature death of his wife, he had felt as though half his own soul had been lost. Certainly, as we follow him on his seven month voyage down the Magdalena River, the old general does seem in his senescent disillusionment to have lost a good part of his soul. But was that because after the death of his wife, he had never again really put his soul into anything else, and had pursued all his revolutionary and sexual exploits only as a distraction from the pain he had never gotten over? Can the love of a woman be so powerful in the life of a man that the loss of it can so reshape the rest of his days, and have such an impact on those around him, for good or—as happened in Bolivar's own life (so honestly portrayed by Marquez), and even more so in the case of ancient Rome's worst emperor, the butcher Caligula, whose tyranny you'll recall was also triggered by the loss of his young wife—for ill? Having never been married or even deeply in love in the past, I find it intriguing to think that the loss of erotic love can be so overwhelming. I guess it's really no different from what we see when a man like Don Jose in Bizet's *Carmen* is willing to sever all ties to the past and ride off into the mountains to capture such love in the first place—a phenomenon which our simple-minded, modern psychiatrists would probably want to write off as nothing more than the work of the 'noonday devil' luring supposedly neurotic, middle-aged fools into blind pursuit of some 'wild thing,' but one which I prefer to take far more seriously. Dudley

Moore's panicky chase after Bo Derek, the 'Perfect Ten,' may have been fun for the college jocks, sitting around in their semen-bestrewn animal-houses, to watch, but I, for one, would rank it, like so much of the other trash produced by Hollywood in recent years, on a par with TV soap opera. When presented in its original *opera-comique* version (as I saw it done at U of I many years ago), or even in the older, silent movies where Don Jose is being played by Charlie Chaplin as a clownish 'Don Hosirey,' there is a certain element of sadness to the phenomenon that the psychiatrists, and Hollywood's humorists, seem incapable of grasping.

Well, I'm sorry. I didn't really mean to ramble on like this. But it's nice to have someone with whom one can talk about something other than the latest baseball scores. I enjoyed our long conversations last Saturday immensely, even more than the opera! It was Mephistopheles, I know, who dropped the lovely Marguerite into the lap of the aged Faust, but meeting you has almost made me believe again in a provident God! No devil could ever be so kind . . .

'or dumb!' he thought of adding upon recalling how, far from robbing him of his soul, his encounter with Liliana had come closer than anything in recent months to putting him back in touch with the real world from which his pursuit of speculative wisdom had cut him off. And wasn't that what the Greeks of old had meant by 'soul' in the first place, namely, that part of ourselves that connects us with everything else? But for fear of overplaying his hand so early in their relationship, he shelved the thought and completed his email on a more mundane note:

Since you expressed an interest in them, I am sending you some photographs of a few of my paintings, most of which were done years ago before I sold my soul to Reason. But I can still feel a bit of the excitement of having worked on them, and who knows, perhaps someday the Muses will strike again, and give me some relief from the rigors of analysis!

I don't recall if I told you or not, but I have agreed to take my fifteen-year-old, great-nephew on a trip to the Rockies. He's got the legs and lungs of a potential Olympic runner, and the brains to be a nuclear scientist, but at this point in his life apparently thinks there could be nothing more exciting than being a forest ranger. So, the task jokingly assigned me by his mother, who has already checked out how little such guardians of our woods make, is to clue him in on just how wild it is out West and, hopefully, turn his sophomoric mind around to thinking of some more lucrative alternative to a lifetime vocation. We'll be leaving August the sixth and be gone for about a week. I'll give you a call when we get back. The new opera season, you know, will be starting up in September, so perhaps we can take in another performance or two, maybe Mozart's *Don Giovanni*, which I think they're doing sometime in October, or perhaps the December production of Verdi's *La Traviata*, one of my favorites!

P.S. *Hasta luego!* (I'm trying, but have my doubts whether a dog as old as I can learn another language, or for that matter, any other new tricks! Ha, ha!)

Altmann debated whether to erase the double entendre of his final parenthetical remark, but let it stand, and signed off.

16

Patience, Professor Altmann had learned from his earlier reading of Augustine and Thomas Aquinas, was the virtue by which humans could best protect themselves against what the *Book of Ecclesiasticus* described as the 'useless, destructive force of sadness.' But he had little of it. It was, in fact, an inability to endure the daily vicissitudes of life brought on by what he considered to be the slovenly ineptitude of so many of the administrators under whom he had had to work these many years that had gotten him into so much trouble at BCC. Unlike his parents, who had raised a brood of seven children with Job-like patience, he had always found it hard to adjust to the pace of others slower than himself, and the older he got, the harder it had become to brook any dilly-dallying on the part of the people around him. He still had as much 'sensibility,' or 'fellow-feeling' as Hume liked to call it, as any of his Romantic heroes had ever displayed in the works of Fielding, Richardson, Prevost or Marivaux, and was always ready to support any benevolent cause, but only so long as it was being pursued as expeditiously as possible. Even if he had lost the motivation that had inspired his earlier scholarly work and had little inclination left to undertake any new studies of his own, he was in no mood to let others waste what little time he had left by luring him into projects to which their own commitment was only half-hearted. Developing a friendly or loving relationship was not, he knew, the same as getting a job done or seeing a project through, but his impatience toward the latter nonetheless often carried over also into his personal life, so that when a week had passed, and he still had had no response from Liliana to the email he had sent her, what little joy in living he had recently begun to feel was quickly evaporating. Every day, after checking the status of his TIAA-CREF account, he had clicked on to his email to see if there was any word from her, and not even the remarkable daily gains on his stock investments were enough to offset the disappointment he had felt upon repeatedly having had to read on the screen that he had no new messages. Several times he had gone back to scrutinize his own email, thinking that perhaps she had somehow been offended by what he had written. But finding nothing that to his way of thinking could reasonably have given her cause to be angry with him, he was left with the impression that her silence could only mean that her feelings for him had a long way to go before catching up with his own toward her. And even though commitment to his own 'law of delicacy' deterred him from trying to rush her into some sort of reciprocal expression of love, passion, desire, or whatever it was that he himself was feeling toward her, there was no denying his lack of patience. He was, in fact, fit to be tied, and finally, after waiting a full seven days, had gone to his email site with the intention of firing off to her a rather terse inquiry as to why it was taking her so long to answer, only to discover that she had that very morning sent him an email, and a very lengthy one at that. Ashamed that he had ever thought of criticizing her, and embarrassed by his senile impetuosity, he emitted a deep sigh, before downloading the message and treating himself to its friendly, sagacious content.

<maltmann@netscape.net>; Tues, 29 July 1997 10:03 (EDT)

Hola Mauritio,

Please forgive my slowness in responding to your email. Over the weekend I made a quick trip out to New Jersey to visit my mother, and with what other little time that left me during the past week I have been busy trying to finish an 'incomplete' left over from the spring semester. I finally turned it in today, and so can return to a bit of normal life again, if studying the 'dead' language of Latin at least seven hours per day can be considered anything like 'living'! The two chapters of grammar and vocabulary that we are supposed to cover every day can really exhaust one, as you have no doubt rediscovered through your recent plunge into *Espanol. Verdad?* But I must say, reading the original of Virgil's *Aeneid,* as we are—we're right at the part now where Aeneas, hell-bent upon fulfilling his mission to found a new city for his defeated fellow Trojans, pushes again out to sea from the port of Carthage, leaving his beloved Dido behind in a suicidal rage—certainly beats watching the soaps.

I received the photographs of your paintings, and loved them! The 'Women of Jerusalem' and the 'Job on the Dung-heap' pieces were very moving too, but I liked best the one depicting the humiliated, half-stripped Jesus being exposed to the indifferent stare of the public while all of Nature is blushing in the background. I hadn't suspected that you had ever been of such a tender religious bent, but then, as you say, most of your painting was done before you reached the Age of Reason! Next time we get together, we'll have to talk more about some of your other paintings. (Incidentally, when is the best time to call you? I tried several times to reach you in the afternoon, but without success. I teach an intensive Spanish grammar course every morning, and during the early hours of the evening try to help out at the local center for the children of Mexican migrant workers. When do you retire? Would it be too late to call you after nine?).

"After nine!" Professor Altmann mumbled, "How old does she think I am! I haven't gone to bed before, well . . ." Thinking about it, he realized that as a matter of fact he had been hitting the sack much earlier of late. As recently as ten years ago, the light in his study could be seen burning into the wee hours of the morning as he would be tracking down yet another piece of historical or philosophical trivia to stuff into the plethora of footnotes his Germanic disposition had inclined him to think indispensable to any genuine piece of scholarly work. But after the publication of his last book several years ago, his fifth in ten years, he had decided to grant himself a temporary reprieve and had started retiring, not, to be sure, nearly so early as his ninety-two year old father, who liked to brag about beating the chickens to roost, but . . . yes, he would have to confess, around nine every night, joking to himself all the while that he could thereby test the truth of old Ben Franklin's aphoristic claims that those who are 'early to bed' will be 'early to rise!' and that it will be the 'early bird' that 'gets the worm!' Well, in good Aristotelian fashion, one act of going to bed early had led to another and another, until he had actually gotten into the habit of being the earliest in the neighborhood to retire, as well as the first to rise. Still, for a call from Liliana, he mused, he would be willing to stay up the whole night and miss forever whatever 'worm' it is that the early bird is supposed to get.

In regard to your comments about the force of a woman's love in the life of a man, let me say, first of all, that I think you are you stretching the story a bit to compare Don Jose's pursuit of that 'wild bird,' Carmen, to

Dudley Moore chasing Bo Derek. For, notwithstanding the movie version of the opera in which Carmen's suitor is played by a less than youthful Placido Domingo, Bizet's Don Jose is hardly a middle-aged man. Be that as it may, however, I think your remark about Hollywood and the modern psychiatrists, with all their flippant talk about middle-aged crises, missing the element of sadness behind the sexual exploits of men like Don Jose or General Bolivar is right on target. What has generally impressed me most about the works of Gabriel Marquez, or for that matter, of any truly great writer (eg., my beloved Cervantes) is the deep melancholy that touches all their stories and forms the background against which any *joie de vivre* of their characters is always played out. I think it derives from the appreciation that all such writers seem to have for the 'Androgynous Myth' mouthed, as you'll recall, by Aristophanes in Plato's *Symposium*. When Bolivar, for example, implies, as you noted, that upon losing his beloved wife to an early death he had lost half his soul, and spends the rest of his life futilely 'plowing the sea,' was he not in a sense giving expression to the maddening grief that all mankind, male and female alike, have felt since having been split asunder in the beginning of time by a Zeus resentful of having been assaulted by the primeval, roly-poly *hermaphroditoi?* Aristophanes, I know, was a comedian, but should his final conclusion that love is but the desire and pursuit of the whole be dismissed as a mere joke? I think not, for in my view it is precisely the dreadfully sad division between the sexes that constitutes more than anything that 'lack of being' or nothingness which Lacan and Irigaray see lying at the root of all human desire.

I hope you and your nephew have a wonderful trip out West, and that you won't try too hard to talk him out of becoming a forest ranger. After all, as Voltaire's Pangloss would say, 'man was placed in the Garden of Eden, not for 'idle theorizing,' but '*ut operaretur eum*–to dress and keep it!' I have myself often been tempted to throw out all my books and head for the woods, or at least the garden.

P.S. I will be more than happy to accompany you to *Don Giovanni* or *La Traviata*. Adam hates opera and will be glad that he doesn't have to take me. And no, I don't think you are too old to learn Spanish! But a new body language, well . . . that might be another story! Ha, Ha! Just kidding!

Ciao!
Liliana

17

"Are you *ready?!*" Professor Altmann asked his nephew as he steered their rented Grand Marquis onto the highway running out of Idaho Springs toward Mt. Evans. He had saved the drive up the fourteen thousand two hundred sixty-four foot mountain as a final climax to their week in the wild West.

"Boy Scouts are always prepared!" Gregory bragged with a sheepish grin, undaunted by the skeptical tone of his uncle's voice. Only a step or two away from being awarded his Eagle badge, he prided himself upon his survival skills.

"Not many scouts ever been up Mt. Evans!" Altmann retorted. "In fact, they just opened the road several years ago, and most tourists are still unaware of it."

"So much the better!" Gregory muttered, still chewing on the disappointment he had felt earlier upon finding the Estes Park region where they had spent their first night in the Rockies overrun by motor homes and recreational vehicles.

To get to Route 5 that would eventually snake up the mountain and take them within one hundred and thirty-four feet of its summit, they had to travel through the remote back country of Chicago Creek Canyon, which already at ten in the morning was cooking close to ninety degrees Fahrenheit. "A breakdown out here," Altmann observed, "and a man will be buzzard-meat in no time flat!"

"Or cougar-chow!" his nephew added facetiously. Several days earlier, before starting a short hike along the Tonahulu Trail at the southern tip of Rocky Mountain National Park, they had been warned by a ranger to be on the lookout for one of the wild cats that had recently killed a young boy in the area. The youngster had apparently put some food out for squirrels the night before, and upon checking to see if they had taken it the next morning, had been grabbed by the puma and carried off before the very eyes of his parents who had let him run a bit ahead of them on their early morning stroll. Gregory had seemed unconcerned about the danger of their being attacked, cooly informing his great-uncle as they walked along that it was only the cats that were too old to catch other prey that would attack human beings, and that they could easily defend themselves against any such senior feline with the two-inch-thick walking sticks they both had in hand. Circling back through the forested, rocky terrain to the trail-head and emerging onto the lot where they had left their car, Altmann had tried discerning whether Gregory, for all his bravado, was not as relieved as he was himself at being out of harm's way, but detected no sign of fear on his nephew's part.

"Says here," Gregory noted, reading from the Mt. Evans brochure he had picked up at their motel back in Idaho Springs, "that there are more cougars in this canyon than anywhere else in eastern Colorado."

"Well, a cougar's not a cheetah, you know, and with your speed, you could probably outrun one!" Altmann joked.

"Yeah, but what about you?!"

"At my age, I'm too old to be chased! These cats like meat that's young and not so tough!"

"I suspect though that if they're really hungry and can't catch me, they might settle for a senior citizen!"

Altmann laughed. He was glad to see that after their week on the road together his nephew felt comfortable enough to display his native wit, having relaxed the initial formality that his mother, intent upon having her son properly respect the authority of an elder, had no doubt dictated. "Well, I'd better get out of here fast, then!" Altmann declared, while depressing the gas pedal and briefly accelerating the Grand Marquis up to eighty miles per hour. Upon emerging from the canyon onto the sagebrush steppes beyond, however, his playful mood quickly dissipated as he felt the car suddenly being buffeted by a strong wind. Stopping for a cup of coffee at Echo Lake Lodge, where, according to their map, the ascent up the mountain was supposed to begin in earnest, they were warned by the matronly woman behind the counter that the wind was blowing sixty to seventy miles per hour and that this was no day to be driving up the mountain.

"No sweat!" Gregory mumbled under his breath, fearful that his uncle might lose his nerve and decide against going up.

"Well, let's see what the ranger has to say," Altmann stated cautiously, as they got back into their car and approached the toll-booth at the entrance of the scenic byway. "Anybody driving up there today?" he asked the neatly-groomed, well-tanned brunette manning the station.

"You're the first!" she chirped.

"Any chance of the wind abating?"

"Probably not until late afternoon."

"So, what do you think, are we fools to want to drive up there this morning?'

"Stay away from the edges, and you shouldn't have any trouble," the pretty ranger predicted.

Knowing that no road could run behind the talus slopes, and that its cliff-hanging precipices could not, therefore, be by-passed, Altmann worried for a moment about whether the young woman knew what she was talking about, but finally threw all caution to the wind, and decided to make a run at it anyway. Within half an hour he was having some second thoughts. Already at the lower elevations, not a few of the lodgepole pines had seemed on the point of snapping as they were being whipped to and fro by the blustery winds. As the road ascended still higher, however, through the broad expanses of Englemann spruce, subalpine fir, and finally, at about twelve thousand feet, a stand of Colorado's oldest trees—sixteen hundred year old bristlecone pines, according to Gregory's brochure—and then began a slight descent toward still half-frozen Summit Lake across a four-mile-long escarpment, so ferocious had the blowing of the wind become that there were moments when Altmann doubted his ability to keep the car any longer from being swept off the side of the cliff. That field of danger having been traversed, another immediately appeared on the horizon, as the road took a sudden dramatic turn upward, past massive rocky outcroppings and several clusters of twisted, arboreal dwarfs clinging tenaciously to the eastward side of the mountain.

"*Es ist das Krummholz,*" Gregory calmly reported, after checking his brochure, and reading from it in his best high-school-German accent.

"They have more sense than do we!" Altmann responded, as he nervously glanced at the diminutive trees and took notice of how nature had endowed them with the perspicacity to hug the ground and, with their twisted branches growing only to leeward, shielding each other against the brutal winds.

"*Hoch, hoch, und immer höher!*" Gregory observed, without a hint of acrophobia or any other fear, as the road ahead of them seemed to soar right off the side of the mountain into the sky beyond, and his uncle steered the wind-buffeted car at the last minute around another hair-pin curve.

Shifting into the lowest of the car's gears, Altmann guided the Grand Marquis through the alpine tundra up the road's last steep incline, past several marmots basking in the sun, and finally into the summit parking lot at fourteen thousand, one hundred and thirty feet, as indicated by a sign warning people about altitude sickness. Except for a female mountain goat and her pair of kids, the lot stood empty.

"Going up?" Gregory asked.

"We are up!" Altmann retorted.

"Not quite. According to my brochure, we've still got another one hundred and thirty-four feet to get to the summit."

"Be my guest! But be careful! I don't want to have to tell your mother that you're gone with the wind!"

Clinging to one rock after another to avoid being blown over the side of the mountain, Gregory raced up and down its pinnacle in less than thirty minutes, as his uncle stayed all the while inside the car, munching on peanut-butter crackers, and worrying about the trip back down, which, he knew, could be even more precarious than had been their coming up, what with having to be in the outside lane on all the curves, and the danger of brakes giving out at any moment.

"Wow! I thought I was a goner there a couple of times!" Gregory exclaimed excitedly, as he jumped back into the car, and pulled the hood of his parka away from his boyish face.

Altmann grunted his relief at seeing his nephew safely back, and immediately started up the car to begin their descent. Driving no faster than the Bighorn sheep they encountered along the way were walking, it took them almost an hour to reach the valley below. "Whew! That was something else!" Altmann uttered, while shifting back to Drive and letting the Grand Marquis return to normal speed on the flatter pavement of Highway 103. "So, do you still want to be a forest ranger?" he asked a half-hour later, as he turned onto Interstate 70 outside Idaho Springs to begin the trip back home to Illinois.

"Forest ranger?" Gregory queried, as if the thought had never crossed his mind.

"Yeah, your mother tells me that that's all you ever talk about."

"Well, I do like the outdoors, and there was a time not long ago when I thought being a ranger would be rather cool, but . . . I haven't told Mom or Dad yet . . . but I've been thinking lately about maybe going to the seminary after I graduate from high school."

"You want to be a *priest!*" Altmann interjected. "Whoever put *such* an idea into your head?" Recalling how he had himself been lured into the seminary some fifty years ago, before he'd had a chance to make an informed decision of his own, he knew only too well how vulnerable a young boy can be to the clever promptings of an idolized priest.

"Earlier this summer I went with Father Mike and some of my classmates to a retreat at our diocesan Youth Camp, and after hearing Father talk about the shortage of priests these days, I got to thinking that perhaps I could help out."

"You like Father Mike, do you?"

"Yeah, he's cool."

"And you think you'd like to be like him?"

"I'd like to do *some* of the things he does."

"Like what?"

"Working with youths, helping them cope with all the problems they have at home, in school, and with each other . . . that sort of thing."

"Well, young people certainly need all the help they can get, and I'm sure you would be very good at it, but you know, don't you, that priests can't marry?"

"Yea-h-h."

"And that wouldn't bother you?"

"Not really," Gregory replied rather bashfully.

Glancing sideways and raising one of his eyebrows, Altmann gave his nephew a kind, but skeptical look, debating within himself whether to try disillusioning the handsome lad in the way that he had often wished someone would have done for him those many years ago—before he had ever come alive sexually and looked at girls as anything other than tomboys with whom he could play softball or kick-the-can—when, at the tender age of fourteen, he had packed his bags and gone off to the seminary with nary a thought of the sensual pleasures he might be leaving behind. Once, to be sure, after breaking a leg during a freshman football game and being taken to the small seminary-town's medical clinic, a doctor had come into the operating room where he had been stripped almost naked to have his leg set, and upon striking up a conversation and discovering that he was a seminarian, had commented, only half in jest, on what a waste it would be for such a fine specimen of a body never to be loved. Though surprised and secretly pleased at the time to hear someone say that his tall, thin body was not as ungainly as he had always thought it to be, he had dismissed the cynical implications of the physician's remark as just another of the many anti-Catholic slurs he had heard so often while growing up in his Protestant-dominated hometown. And after that, noone to his recollection had ever sat him down to talk seriously about how good could be the sexual love that he was so casually sacrificing. Suddenly, during the summer following his sophomore year, while playing in a church-sponsored volleyball game on the beach, he had discovered for himself how excitingly beautiful a female body can be. But far from encouraging him to leave open the possibility of exploring a relationship with Mary Lou or any other of the lovely creatures who had caught his eye that day on the beach, his pastor and spiritual mentors at the seminary had only increased the penances they laid upon him whenever he would confess to them the supposedly dirty thoughts his awakened libido had generated. Never once did they, or, for that matter, his parents or any older aunt or uncle, ever think to suggest to him that the bouts of moodiness to which he had thereafter fallen prey might have been the result of his having cut himself off from the normal play of teenage life, and that he might on that account want to reconsider whether he was really suited for the celibate life of the priesthood. Having themselves been sold on the theological line that their own marriages were of only secondary value compared to the excellence of the celibate life, they seemed blinded to all but the honor supposedly accruing to the family as a result of having one of their own dedicated to the service of the Lord. And although he had ultimately disappointed them, leaving the seminary after eight years to pursue full-time the lust for knowledge that had taken hold of him after a year of philosophical study, he had still found it difficult to shed the expectations of self-denial they had willy-nilly helped to instill in him over the years, and so, instead of accepting himself for the very sexual being that he had come to know himself to be, he had simply transferred the sacrifice of his sexuality from one altar to another. No longer a eunuch 'for the sake of the kingdom,' he had let himself become, with no less high-mindedness than a Kierkegaard dumping his Regina, a philosophical *castrato,* singing shrill sounds of abstraction without ever indulging in any serious way his heartfelt need for concrete love. He knew, of course, that in the final analysis, he had no one to blame but himself. For although others had not stepped forward to help bring him back to his senses, neither had they purposely or consciously ever forced him to sacrifice himself for the church, for the academy, or for anything else. Still, there was no denying either that had they offered him occasionally a better word of advice, he might well have more readily found within himself the sense and strength to have made a saner decision. "Have you ever dated?" he finally asked his nephew.

"Nope."

"Why not? Because your parents wouldn't let you?"

"That's part of it, but I haven't really wanted to either."

"You'd rather play soccer, huh?"

"Yeah, and I can't really imagine any girl wanting to go out with me anyway," Gregory replied with a self-effacing snicker.

"Well! Don't be too sure of that. You're a pretty handsome fellow, you know!" Altmann stated, aware of the embarrassment it might cause his nephew, but thinking again of how a similar assertion might have helped build up his own self-confidence years ago and possibly nudged him down a different path. "How old did you say you are, sixteen?"

"Fifteen and a half."

"Fifteen!" Altmann exclaimed, and then added with a sigh, "Oh, to be young again!"

"Really?" Gregory exclaimed, rather incredulously.

"Yeah, I wouldn't mind starting over again."

"Would you do anything different?"

"Well, for one thing, I would do what I am telling you to do now, and that is, to give yourself more time to explore relationships with the opposite sex before running off to the seminary. It's all fine and good to be thinking about helping young people as a priest, but you have to ask yourself also whether you are really suited for the kind of life priests are made to live. Most young men probably are not." Altmann was thinking of the many former classmates of his who, according to reports, had baled out of the priesthood in recent years, or, more tragically, had stuck with it, some only to become victims of alcoholism, drug addiction, or worse yet, pedophilia. Most had been wonderful human beings when he had known them in the seminary, and it pained him to think that his nephew's life might be similarly ruined by the institutional myopia of bishops intent upon preserving the law of celibacy, and the monastic lifestyle it reflected, for no other reason apparently than to defend the *status quo* and prop up their own princely authority.

"*You* were in the seminary?"

"Yes, for eight years in fact."

"Why did you leave?"

"I got hooked on philosophy."

"So, why didn't you get married then? Philosophers can marry, can't they?"

"Yes, they can, and in the past a lot of them did. But many others did not."

"Why?"

"Well, for a variety of reasons," Altmann replied, while recalling how various philosophers as different from each other as Kant, Schopenhauer, Thoreau, or Nietzsche had each, in their own unique way, bungled their chances of ever finding a suitable mate. "Some were probably just too bashful, inept, ugly, egoistical or stubborn to attract a partner. Others got so involved in their work that they never found the time to go looking for a mate. And a few, like Kierkegaard, whom you've probably never heard of, got to thinking that just as the poet is doomed to be different from other people, so the philosopher, because of his whole-hearted dedication to the pursuit of truth, has to forego the joys of marriage."

"Did you agree with K-Kuerr . . . what's his name?"

"Kierkegaard."

"Did you agree with him?"

"There was a time when I did."

"So, you never got married?"

"That's right."

"And did you find the truth?"

"Well-l-l, that's a whole other story," Altmann replied, hesitant to impose upon his bright nephew all the weight of his own recently acquired agnosticism. "As your mother has probably warned you, I am not all that religious anymore, and . . . well, I can't honestly say that I'm any longer very sure of anything."

"How old are you?" Gregory asked.

"I am sixty, going on a hundred!" Altmann joked. "Think you'll ever live that long?"

"Sure hope so. Anyway, sixty's not that old when you measure it over against the age of our universe," Gregory replied with a wry smile and a tinge of sympathy in his voice. "In a world that's ten billion years old, as we learned in biology class last semester, sixty years is just a drop in the bucket!"

"Tell that to Liliana!" Altmann muttered half-aloud.

"To whom?" Gregory asked.

"Oh, just a friend of mine," Altmann replied, as he pulled off the interstate to gas up again for the long trek across the plains of Kansas.

18

"Speaking of mountains," Professor Altmann added, as he finished sharing with Liliana the details of the experience he and his nephew had had ascending Mt. Evans, "I was reading Kierkegaard's comments in *Either/Or* the other day about tonight's opera, and came across a passage where he states that 'Don Juan was the first-born on the Mountain of Venus' . . ."

"Mons Veneris!" Liliana echoed playfully in her recently acquired Latin tongue, while slowly twining a slippery piece of angel-hair pasta around her silver fork.

Altmann smiled knowingly. It had been more than forty years since he had taken a course in physiology, and back then any reference to the female anatomy would have been made in only the vaguest terms, and certainly without the benefit of the kind of explicit graphics used to illustrate modern-day textbooks on the subject. But having used the latter over the years to fill in the gaps left by his seminary education and lack of experience, the aging professor was not altogether ignorant of that piliferous mound of adipose tissue overlying a woman's pubic symphysis and surrounding the vaginal orifice with no less mysterious an air than did the hilly dark wood around the entrance to Dante's eternal world. He could readily appreciate, therefore, the more imaginative references to it, and all the more when coming so unabashedly from the mouth of Liliana. He liked the way she and so many of her generation, in sharp contrast to the puritanical inhibitions of his own, could talk so easily about their sexuality. Still, he suspected that the *mons pubis* was not exactly what Kierkegaard himself had had in mind by his comment. Pausing to sip from his glass of Pinot Noir, and giving the ruby-red wine a moment or two to work its magic upon his taste buds, he said as much to Liliana.

"Don't bet on it!" she replied. "From what little I have read of his life, I suspect he had mapped the body of more than one female, and could not have talked the way he did without some recollection of the lay of the land!"

"That may be, but in the passage I was referring to he explicitly mentions the medieval mythology surrounding the Mountain of Venus, and that's what I wanted to ask you about. Are you familiar with any such mythology from the Middle Ages?"

"Vaguely. The Germanic tribes, I know, had some legends about a certain mountain of delight and love that they called the *Horselberg*, because Holda, the Goddess of Spring and Love, supposedly dwelt there and used her seductive charms to lure passing knights into her erotic embrace. Wagner, you may recall, based his opera *Tannhäuser* on some such legend."

"You're right! I can't believe I didn't remember that myself!" For some reason, the abhorrence, perhaps, of some of the School's Jewish Board members for Wagner's music after Hitler's evil misuse of it, or the difficulty, experienced from the very start by Wagner himself, of finding anyone, much less students, capable of playing the demanding roles, U of I had not presented any performances of Wagner's operas in recent years, and it had been at least fifteen years ago that Altmann had heard them do the *Tannhäuser*. Still, it bothered him to be reminded again of not remembering something that in his earlier years would immediately have popped into his mind. Although he knew that the jokes about the memory being one of the first things to go in old age had no real foundation in fact—at least not so far as it applied in any general way to the majority of older people like his father, who at ninety-two still had the memory of an elephant—he was also aware that instances of forgetfulness could be the first sign of Altzheimer's disease. Taking another sip of the Pinot Noir, he let the worrisome thought furrow his brow for a moment before picking up again on Liliana's reference to Wagner. "Now that you mention it, I recall reading somewhere that Wagner, in fact, originally entitled his opera *Der Venusberg*, and only changed it to *Tannhäuser* after his publisher warned him that professors and students in the Dresden Medical School would probably turn the original title into an obscene joke!"

"And no doubt he was right! I've never met a medical student yet who could talk any way other than dirty."

"Why do you think that is?"

"I guess it's got something to do with their constant preoccupation with body parts . . . Familiarity, you know, breeds contempt!"

"But medical students aren't really any worse in that regard than other students, are they? In Wagner's opera, you'll recall, Tannhäuser was not a medical student, but a budding *poet* who gets in trouble for talking dirty, when during a Contest of Songs, he derides what the other minnesingers have sung about the beauty of *virtuous* love, and to the horror of everyone around and especially his beloved Elizabeth, bursts out into a reckless ode to lust."

"Not unlike Rod Stewart, huh?"

"Rod Stewart?"

"Yeah, the rock star who a couple of years ago had this hit entitled 'Passion.'"

"Can't say that I ever heard of him or it," Altmann confessed with a bit of chagrin at having to acknowledge yet another foot or two in the gap separating his generation from that of Liliana. "And you say his song was also an ode to lust?"

"Yeah, with its pounding rhythm and prurient insinuations it was obviously intended to celebrate the wildest of sexual yearnings."

"And was his girlfriend as embarrassed by the dirty lyrics as was Elizabeth by those of Tannhäuser?"

"Are you kidding? She was as wild as they come, and no doubt inspired every word Stewart sang."

"Well, that sort of illustrates the point I'm trying to make. It was not any clinical familiarity with human anatomy, but the recollection of the year he had spent in the company of Venus and her orgiastic court of nymphs and sirens that inclined Tannhäuser to talk dirty. After becoming bored and descending from the Mountain of Venus, he thought that with an act or two of repentance he could quickly get back to a genuinely loving *tête-à-tête* with his Elizabeth, only to discover that his whole being had become so thoroughly imbued with lust that, despite his best intentions, whatever he said came out dirty. And come to think of it, that's probably what Kierkegaard was hinting at when he described Don Juan as 'the first-born of the Mountain of Venus.'"

"What do you mean?"

"Well, that Tannhäuser and his kind are reincarnations, so to speak, of Don Juan. In Kierkegaard's view, Don Juan is the supreme seducer and ultimate womanizer precisely to the extent that his sensuality is so buoyant and immediate. Because of his reflective, verbose and penitent disposition, a character like

104

Tannhäuser, therefore, would no doubt have struck Kierkegaard as being in some ways more like Goethe's Faust than Don Juan. Still, what drives Tannhäuser to think and talk so dirty is his recollection of having once lived like Don Juan on Mt. Venus."

"So, what you're saying is that Kierkegaard would have interpreted Tannhäuser's dirty talk as simply a linguistically muted version of the demonic music played originally by Don Juan."

"Exactly, and I might add that that is why Kierkegaard was so enthusiastic about Mozart's *Don Giovanni;* he thought that only music could express the raw force of Don Juan's elemental sensuality, and that no composer could ever blend such an idea more perfectly with musical form than had Mozart in the overture to *Don Giovanni.*"

"Wow! I can hardly wait to hear it! But first, I just have to have a taste of that *crème brûlée* the waitress was raving about! How about you?"

"Yeah, let's split one. You don't think Adam would object to our sharing a bowl of custard, do you?" Altmann joshed, while signaling to the waitress to bring one serving of the caramelized dessert.

"What he doesn't know won't hurt him!" Liliana declared.

"Hum-m-m . . ." Altmann purred, ". . . so, it wouldn't hurt if you and I were to steal away to the mountains some weekend?"

"What mountain did you have in mind?" Liliana asked with a mischievous smile.

"Oh! Mt. Evans, of course!"

"Yeah, I wouldn't mind doing that."

"You wouldn't!? What about Adam? He would surely know if we were on the road together for a whole weekend, and things can get rather intimate, you know, when two people travel together."

"Well, I'm not married to Adam, and frankly our relationship has cooled considerably in the last month, to the point where I'm not sure we'll be able to hold it together much longer."

"I'm sorry to hear that," Altmann mumbled, grateful for the possibility of not having to compete any longer with Adam for Liliana's attention, and mildly ecstatic at the prospect of having her accompany him into his beloved mountains, but still caring about the pain she might experience in the breakup of any relationship. "Ah, here come's *la crème brûlée!*" he exclaimed, as their portly waitress set the dish in front of Liliana, and offered them each a clean spoon.

Sliding the dish a bit closer toward Altmann, Liliana delicately broke the dessert's sugary crust, dipped out a tiny portion of the creamy substance for herself, and playfully invited Altmann to take his turn. As he did so once and then—after pausing each time to give Liliana a chance to make her next move—again and again until the dance of spoons had emptied the bowl, a *joie de vivre,* as light and fanciful as the erotic chattering of violins they would soon be hearing in Mozart's overture, warmed his heart.

"About that trip into the mountains . . ." he half-whispered an hour later, as he and Liliana sat waiting for the opera to begin, ". . . we'll probably have to wait until next summer, since this late in the season the higher roads will all be snowed in." He was also thinking that perhaps by then he could have Liliana all to himself. For even if they could slip away without anyone knowing of it, it would not be the same were she still dating Adam or anyone else. As unrealistic as he knew it was to entertain any thought of holding her in a long-term romantic relationship with himself, it was still his fondest hope that the two of them could find some time when they could be together—talking, laughing, playing—to the exclusion of everyone else. Just as the orchestra was striking up the deathly D-minor chord of the opening *andante,* Liliana leaned in his direction, whispered 'Alaska!' into his ear, and then, upon seeing the look of incredulity upon his face, smiled ever so kindly and nodded slightly in confirmation of what she had said.

19

Upon returning from Urbana the next day, Altmann immediately set to work researching via the Internet how best to travel to Alaska, and what such travel might hold in store for him and Liliana should the idea she had planted in his imagination ever come to anything more than a mind-trip. It being mid-October, traveling to the North country any longer in the current year was out of the question. But all the initial electronic advice he was getting warned him that it was never too early to start planning for a trip in the summer ahead. So, with no less zeal than a prospective bride planning her June wedding day, Altmann set off in hot pursuit of all the information he could get, and within weeks his mailbox was crammed full every day with literature he had found advertized on the Internet. From *Amazon.com* came two guidebooks that told him what to expect, mile by mile, should he and Liliana decide to drive the six thousand miles to and from Alaska along the world famous Alcan Highway. Stacks of material from the Alaska Marine Highway, Alaskan Airways, Alaskan Railways, Holland/America, Princess, Carnival and other cruise lines arrived daily, inviting him to consider alternative routes. The state's Tourism Marketing Council checked in with the 'Official Alaska State Vacation Planner,' while Anchorage, Kodiak Island, Fairbanks, Denali National Park and almost every other Alaskan city and park came through with visitor guides of their own. Lists of hotel, motel, and B & B accommodations poured in from every corner of the state, even such remote places as Nome and Prudhoe Bay. Amidst the daily heap of material could usually be found also a couple of slick brochures advertising small commercial outfits that for exceptionally low rates would take the visitor white-water rafting, wildlife-viewing, whale-watching, halibut, salmon, or trout fishing, back-country hiking, biking, helicoptoring, kayaking, or on a host of other wilderness experiences of a lifetime. Altmann devoured it all as voraciously as a grizzly on an autumnal feeding frenzy, and before long his every level of consciousness was saturated with Alaskan scenarios of one sort or another involving Liliana and himself. By day, when not in the classroom or sitting in front of his word processor mulling in vain over where next to go with his fictional characters, he would walk the neighborhood streets for hours on end, imagining himself and Liliana treking, if not to the top of Mt. McKinley—which he read only the most foolish of Japanese tourists would ever think of attempting—at least into the wild country around its base or along some of the other hiking trails through the Kluane and Wrangle mountain ranges, and trying to build up the heart and leg muscles he would need to keep up with his young, cheetah-like friend in such strenuous activity.

It was during the night, however, that his imagination would run especially wild. Worn out by all his daytime walking, he would retire early to bed, and within minutes fall into a deep sleep that would almost always end up with him dreaming about Liliana and himself engaged in one or another, often dangerous, Alaskan adventure. In one such dream, he and she were hiking late one afternoon along the banks of the Dezadeash River outside Haines Junction, where they were spending their last night in the Yukon before crossing the Alaskan border, when suddenly, out of the huckleberry bushes less than fifty yards ahead of them, a grizzly bear rose up on its hind legs, and from the height of its full nine-foot stature asserted its territorial imperative with a look and growl as mean as any rational intruder might ever need to be convinced not to take another step forward.

"Don't move!" Altmann whispered, recalling what he had read about how best to survive such an encounter, and freezing in his tracks. But Liliana paid him no heed. Stepping gracefully out into an opening, she began dancing in slow motion the elegant moves of the tango, as though her sensuous beauty would be enough to tame the wild beast. Altmann kept wanting to warn her that it takes two to tango, but paralyzed by his fear, he could not get the words to come out, and awoke in a cold sweat without ever learning how the bizarre event might have ended—with the bear dancing, or with Liliana being mauled.

On another night he had dreamt of letting Liliana talk him into going with her on a white-water rafting trip down the Nenana River. After signing papers not to hold the rafting company responsible should either of them be killed along the way, and having donned the thermal suits and life-jackets that might help to save them should they be tossed overboard into the river's raging, icy cold waters, the two of them joined a family of four that had been assigned to the same raft, and listened nervously—Altmann at least—as their muscular oarsman, before pushing out into the current, gave them last minute instructions on how best to sit on the rubber tubing while at the same time holding on to the rope running around its periphery. The ride started out calmly enough, and the first two rapids, rated by the oarsman as a 'two' and 'three' respectively, gave Altmann little concern. But rounding a bend in the river half an hour later, they saw themselves approaching another rapid which the oarsman promptly warned would be close to a 'four'. Altmann braced himself for the worst, but glancing side-wise, noticed on Liliana's face that same wide-eyed look of gleeful absorption that he had observed when sitting next to her during the performance of Mozart's *Don Giovanni* or any of the other operas they had attended together, and glimpsed her exuberant response to every nuance of dramatic action. A teenage boy about to go on his first date could not have looked more blithesome. And when, after riding out the rapid's relatively tame foreplay, the raft was lifted up on the foremost swell of the aquatic currents, she could be heard screaming delightfully, like a woman in ecstasy: "Yes! Yes! This is Life! This is Life!" A moment later, as the back end of the raft slammed down against the river's surface, Altmann's legs were suddenly thrust up over his head, projecting his whole body backward into the turbulent water. Clinging desperately with one hand to the peripheral rope, he felt himself being sucked under the raft and for a split second had the impression that this was death. And well it could have been, what with the possibility of having had his unhelmeted head smashed against a boulder, or of having lost his grip and being swept down the wild river and drowning before a helping hand could be given him. But when finally he was able to pull himself back to the side of the raft and popped up out of the water, the mighty oarsman was there—having been alerted by the shrieks of alarm emitted by Liliana when she had looked around and noticed her companion gone—to grab Altmann by the shoulder straps of his life-jacket and drag his limp body back on board. The danger past, Liliana fell into a fit of convulsive laughter, stopping only long enough now and then to try explaining to Altmann that what she found so funny was the fact that of all the people it could have happened to, it had to be him—he, who of all the individuals on the ride, had been the one most reluctant to go, and who would never have gone except for her persistent prompting! The family of four, as well as the oarsman, were also getting a good chuckle out of the incident. And trying to be a good sport, Altmann laughed right along with them, satisfied that though he had had to sacrifice a bit of dignity and a treasured set of prescription sunglasses to the river gods, he was still alive, with yet another adventurous story to share with his ethics students when next discussing Aristotle's theory of the good life.

Not all the dreams he was having played on the fears generated by his reading about the dangers that would be facing them in the Alaskan wilderness. His libido hardly ever went to rest, and not infrequently during the night would churn the stuff he had been reading into positively hedonistic dreams of erotic pleasure. One—triggered no doubt by his having read the day before of Japanese couples, intent upon conceiving superior children, paying huge sums of money to stay at a glass-roofed, Nome hotel on nights when southern winds were blowing and the Aurora Borealis was most active—had him and Liliana playing erotically with each other on the top deck of the M/V Matanuska as it sailed through the Inside Passage under a clear nocturnal sky draped with curtains and hooks of green, blue, white and red light, and resonating with the whistling and cracking sounds of departed Inuit souls trampling about on the celestial snows. In another wet dream, he and Liliana, after a long day on the Alaskan Highway, have pitched their tent in an isolated spot near the Laird Hot Springs, and under a full moon are gleefully skinny-dipping in its soothing, sensuously warm waters, altogether oblivious to the threat of grizzlies Watson Lake's 'Bear Lady' had warned them about.

But none of these earlier dreams could compare for erotic verve to the one he was having on this particular night. Before retiring he had fetched himself a glass of Pinot Noir and gone to his computer to check out on the Internet what Santa Fe's world-renowned opera house might be offering in the summer ahead. Much to his delight, he had discovered that on the night of August 1 there would be a performance of Claude Debussy's *Pelléas et Melisande*. "*Perfecto!,*" he had exclaimed, as his imagination immediately set him to thinking about how a night at the opera in Santa Fe could be a perfect climax to the Alaskan trip that had begun taking shape in his mind during the preceding month. After driving in his new Monte Carlo to and from the major attractions of Interior and Southcentral Alaska, they could take the ferry from Haines through the Inside Passage to Bellingham, and then, with a week still to burn before either he or Liliana would have to be back to work, drive down the Oregon and California coasts, visit some friends in San Francisco, cut across the Mohave Desert for one night at Las Vegas, another at the Grand Canyon, and then, who knows, a post-operatic '*Nuit d'amour,*' perhaps, in one of the most romantic cities in all America! Just the thought of it had sent waves of desire pulsating through his veins, and when finally he had made it to bed, his brain was still racing so fast that notwithstanding the dose of soporific wine he had downed, it took him two full hours to turn it off and get to sleep. Even then the sleep was so light that every half hour or so he would be awakened by a household noise, and have to suppress anew the tendency of his mind to replay the fanciful itinerary his imagination had earlier concocted. Not until the neighborhood birds were already beginning to chirp did his slumber run deeper. But this had always been his best time for dreaming, and once again it was happening.

His sun-tanned body resting against a pillow and clad only in the bottom half of the olive-hued, Turkish sleep-wear he had bought in anticipation of this night, he is lying on a king-sized bed in Santa Fe's Hacienda Hermana, watching Liliana's every move as she loosens the rose-colored, satin evening gown she had worn to the opera, lets it drop to the floor at her feet, and steps out of it—as gracefully as the first Aphrodite from the sundered head of Zeus—into the soft light of the bedside lamp. For thirty-one nights the two of them had shared the same room and sometimes, ignoring Othello's sage warning against tempting heaven, even the same bed, but never in all that time had she allowed him a glimpse of the more intimate dimensions of her physical beauty. And even now, as she reached with both arms behind her back to unsnap a snow-white, silken bra, and then let her hands slide slowly down over her hips to remove the last piece of clothing, a delicate bit of lace no bigger than a fig leaf, covering her secret parts, there was nothing immodest about her moves, nor anything prudish either—just that same fetching, unabashed directness that he had come to expect of all she did.

"O beautiful, adorable vision!" Altmann murmured, mouthing the words of his operatic, Faustian counterpart, as Liliana stretched her naked, lithesome body to its full height, and turning her head slightly to one side, ran her uplifted hands around the nape of her neck to let fall across finely-honed, shoulder muscles several strands of long, dark-brown hair. "*Pas le ciel! Que de grace!*" he added in a low, awestruck voice. Charmed by her irresistible beauty, his body lifted itself slowly from the bed, and like one of Chagall's weightless lovers, flew to her side. Falling to his knees, he wrapped his arms around her lower back and pressed the side of his face against her soft belly, muttering "*Chere ame!*" and other such amorous ejaculations all the while. The adulation left Liliana feeling no less admired than a Galatea by her Cyprian king, and brought her statuesque figure all the more to life. Running her delicate fingers through his hair and down over his shoulders to the underside of his extended arms, she gently drew him back up to his feet, and with the playfulness of a Scheherazade, teased loose the string-knot holding up the bottom half of his Turkish pajamas, and saw his member, like a sword unsheathed, yearning for action. As he moved to embrace her, she took his hands into her own, stepped back a foot or so to feast her eyes for a moment on his handsome nakedness, and then invited him with a delicate tug to follow her back to the bed. Throwing themselves amidst the oversized pillows that lay around the sea of sheets like seals on a bed of ice, they let their unbridled, entangled bodies ride the waves of unrequited passion for better than half an hour, while outside the hacienda's window the storm that had earlier threatened to drown out Melisande's doleful singing in the city's open-air opera house, was again drenching Santa Fe and rocking its adobe homes with ear-shattering thunderbolts. The Diamond Sutra flashed through both their minds and brought a whimsical smile to Liliana's face, as Altmann continued, without the slightest Tantric intention, his erotic foreplay of kissing and fondling her breasts, running his fingers up and down the inside of her downy thighs that by now she had spread like the sepals of O'Keeffe's Black Iris, and periodically caressing the calycine folds of her fleshy *mons.* Her excitement close to peaking, Liliana slid her one free hand around Altmann's buttocks, and as the fragrance of patio primrose wafted through the open window, and the storm played itself out with a final pitter-patter of raindrops against the saturated earth outside, she guided him gently into herself, and surrendered whole-heartedly to the passionate thrusts of his *mort d'amour.* "Ah! *Qu'il est doux de vivre!,*" she moaned ecstatically, just before the neighbor-hood garbage truck performed its usual early morning ritual and roused Altmann from his erotic slumber.

20

"So why not go wild?" Professor Altmann asked his ethics class by way of introducing it to the subject of sexual morality. "You've probably heard it said that 'In love and war, anything goes!' Well, we'll see later that even in war the line must be drawn somewhere, but what about love? Can you come up with any reasons why we shouldn't go wild sexually?" Leaning back in the wheeled armchair which he had taken to using since the onset of his lower back problems, he waited for one or another of his brighter students to venture an answer. "Meredith, what do you think?"

"To avoid becoming a victim of AIDs," the tall, black-haired girl responded from her seat in the front row.

"Yeah, engaging in promiscuous sex these days would be like playing Russian roulette, wouldn't it?" Altmann readily concurred, having himself worried in recent months about the risks Liliana may have taken in her wilder days. "Any other reason?"

"Well, if you go wild, you could easily get hurt psychologically," another female student, whose troubled look reflected problems of her own, volunteered.

"Good point!" Altmann declared. "Men especially get to thinking sometimes, in their wildest fantasies, that it might be great to join in an orgy or, like Don Giovanni, to lay every woman they meet in Italy, Germany, France, or Spain, without much thought of victims, like Donna Elvira, they leave on the trail behind them."

"Donna who?" a male student, whose name still escaped Professor Altmann, queried.

"Donna Elvira," Altmann repeated. "She's the woman who, in Mozart's opera, is lured by Don Giovanni from the cloister where she had been a nun, and then abandoned to her own vengeful hatred and despair after he has exhausted his libidinous use of her. As happens with a lot of women—or men too, for that matter—her impetuous sexual behavior left her psychologically scarred for life. Any other reason why unbridled sex makes no sense?"

"You could lose your reputation," another male student half-shouted from the back of the room.

"And on that account lose your job, or get run out of town or the church you belong to," Altmann added. "So, if you value your good name, your job, or your membership in one or another community, you might want to think twice before going wild, right? Why else . . . Angie?" Getting nothing but a blank stare from the girl whom he had called on precisely because of her tendency to come to class every day attired in the latest fashions of the punk-rock world, he challenged her further by asking: "Are you a wild thing?"

"No-o!" she protested good-naturedly over the laughter of her classmates.

"Of course not," Altmann assured her. "You're a *rational* animal, aren't you, like the rest of us. Were we dogs or pigs, there would be nothing wrong with going wild. But we are not wild things; we are rational by nature, and as even Nietzsche, notwithstanding his defense of the 'blonde beasts,' would admit, it behooves us therefore to keep our wits about us as we engage in sex or anything else. Any other reason? What do *you* think, Joe? Do you think the sex you might find going wild would have any value?"

"Probably not," the Ricky Martin look-a-like admitted with what seemed less than personal conviction.

"You don't seem altogether convinced," Altmann observed. "Well, let's think about it for a moment. What is sex good for? Maria, can you start us off?"

"Reproduction?"

"Yeah. Some people, including non-religious thinkers like Schopenhauer, according to whom the individual libido is a mere instrument of the species' 'will to live,' used to think that sex was good for nothing but reproduction, and we know better than that today, don't we? We shouldn't forget either, however, that sex is still about the only way we have of keeping the species afloat," Altmann remarked, adding with an air of authority that masked his ignorance on the subject, "and fathering or mothering a child can also give one a sense of sharing in Nature's creativity. What other value might sex have? John?"

"It's fun!"

"Right, and we are playful creatures, aren't we; we need to have some fun on occasion; all work and no play makes Jack and Jill dull boys and girls! Sex is not, of course, the only way to have some fun, but it can be one of the better opportunities we have as humans to engage in play. It doesn't always have to be so serious. Just as we sometimes live to eat rather than eat just to keep ourselves alive, so we don't always have to be thinking about contributing to the survival of the human species every time we engage ourselves sexually; sometimes it can just be like a snack, an afternoon delight! What other values might we want to associate with sex?"

"Pleasure!" someone called out anonymously.

"I trust you mean *sensual* pleasure," Altmann observed. "Well, I would agree. Sensual pleasure may not be the end-all of life, but neither is it as bad as some would have us believe; if we don't stop and smell the roses sometime along the way, chances are we'll never find the strength within ourselves to carry on in the pursuit of our long-term goals. And while life has many sensual pleasures to offer, few can match the joy of sex," Altmann theorized, as though he really knew what he was talking about. "What else? Maybe communication? Sex can be a body-language, can't it, and sometimes it may be the only way we have of conveying what we really mean. Or bonding? Traditionally, a couple was not really thought to be married until they had consummated their relationship by an act of sexual intercourse. One shouldn't have to prove one's virility or femininity in bed, but sex can also be a good way for individuals to let each other know who they really are, right? According to Rollo May, it can also expand one's consciousness by lifting one out of the narrow focus of one's everyday affairs and putting one in touch with the cosmos at large. Any other values you can think of?"

Getting no further response, except from one student who flippantly commented that sexual intercourse might also be a good way to lose weight, Altmann proceeded to wrap the discussion up by stating: "So, back to you again, Joe; do you think that the sex one might find by going wild would have any of these values we've identified?"

"It might be reproductive," Joe quipped.

"True, but wouldn't it only be in a negative way, by spawning a lot of unwanted pregnancies?" Altmann demurred. "What about the other values? Do you think, for example, that unbridled sex would really be as playful or pleasurable as *Penthouse*, *Playboy*, or other such rags claim?"

"Probably not," Joe conceded.

"Well, I agree. The main reason for not going wild, therefore, would be to avoid losing all that which makes sex so good, right? And if we use our reason to draw the line on our sexual behavior somewhere, then, it is not because we think of sex as something bad, but rather because we want to preserve its great value. So where *should* we draw the line? Along the line of virtue? Does honesty, patience, or any of the other virtues matter in our sex lives? And what about freedom? Wouldn't we want to conclude that any kind of rape, sexual harassment, or stalking is out of line? But if mutual consent is essential to any good sexual relationship, is that all that is needed to qualify the latter as moral? Don't we also have to consider how old the sexual partners are, or how well they know each other before they have sex? Can we use sex like a handshake just to introduce ourselves to each other, or does it not by its very nature assume prior knowledge, and if so, how much? Does it make any sense to sleep with a stranger or with someone with whom one has nothing to talk about, or for whom one has no real respect or love? Well, these are just a few of the questions we'll have to address the next time," Altmann concluded, as he looked at his watch and noticed that the class hour was about to run out. No sooner did he mention 'next time,' than half the students were out of their seats and heading for the door, leaving their professor once again with the impression of having only the most tenuous of holds on their restless minds.

As he left the classroom and walked down the corridor toward his office, he noticed that not a few of them were already arm in arm with mates and headed, no doubt, for another round of 'afternoon delights'. Entering his office, and closing its door behind him, he dropped his lanky body into the office armchair, threw his legs across the edge of the desk, and reflected in the dark for a moment on how the class had gone. No worse, he mused, than in previous semesters. But the thought gave him little satisfaction, for however smooth his dialogical lecture may have flowed, deep down he knew that like Andre Gide's 'Immoralist,' who had come to despise all the knowledge that had once been his pride and to detest any man of principle, he would probably have jumped into bed with Liliana the first night he had met her had the opportunity presented itself, and if given the chance would this very afternoon follow the example of his more sex-crazed students, forgetting all he and they had talked about in the classroom, and surrendering witlessly to the natural impulses of the erotic moment. Suppressing a tinge of guilt over the hypocrisy of his moral predicament, he promptly lifted himself from the chair, fled the office, and headed for home.

21

Later that afternoon, after lunching on his usual ham and cheese sandwich with a glass of Bud Light, taking a ten-minute nap, and spending an hour or so reading several chapters from Emile Zola's *Doctor Pascal,* Professor Altmann trudged to his upstairs study to check for any email he might have received during the day. In addition to the usual 'junk' from a variety of e-hawkers, there was, much to his delight, another email from Liliana:

<maltmann@netscape.net>; Wed, 12 Nov 1997 10:32 (EDT)

Querido Mauritio,

Que tal? Muy bien, espero! I intended to call you this past weekend, but I got tied down by all kinds of school matters. I am still very busy, and have only a few moments to get this out to you, but I wanted to let you know, first, that Adam and I have decided, after several weeks of intense discussion about how different our basic interests are, that we ought simply to go our own ways, and second, that upon the recommendation of one of my professors here at U of I, Harvard University has accepted me into its doctoral program for Spanish literature, starting already in January. I am so excited, but also a little bit frightened! We'll talk later.

P.S. Any progress on your novel? I hope my earlier critical comments did not discourage you.

Un fuerte abrazo,
Ave sin nido!
Liliana

Shocked as he was to learn that Liliana would be leaving the area altogether and settling down out East a thousand miles away, Altmann suspended for the moment any further consideration of its implications, and reached for his Spanish dictionary to check out the meaning of her closing phrases. In the first of them, he was pleased to discover that he had been right in suspecting that he was being offered a 'heartfelt embrace.' Ignoring what others might have considered the perfunctory nature of such a phrase, he closed his eyes, and momentarily basked in the image of himself being hugged heartily by the lovely Liliana. But whatever delight it brought him was quickly dampened by his suspicion, based on six years of studying Latin in the seminary, and confirmed by another quick check of the Spanish dictionary, that *'ave sin nido'* probably meant that she was referring to herself as 'a bird without a nest.' Having always pictured Liliana to be something like a hummingbird, cheerfully darting here or there to suck one or another floral moment of whatever nectar it might have to offer, he had never given much thought to the possibility of her ever nesting down. And perhaps, he mused, her comment was just a playful reflection on that fugacious side of her being. But even a hummingbird, he knew, needs a nest on occasion, if not in which to rest or sleep—which it generally does on any arboreal branch available—at least to lay its eggs and nurture its offspring. And it saddened him to remember from previous conversations that at thirty-two, Liliana was not a little concerned about her biological clock running out and leaving her childless for the rest of her life. Seeing another prospective mate hit the road, and recognizing that any move to Harvard would delay still further the completion of her doctoral work, had no doubt reawakened such a concern in her mind. And Altmann's heart went out to her. Having let his earlier supposed 'love of wisdom' thwart his own paternal instincts to the point of leaving him now, at the age of sixty-one, without any sons or daughters to dote upon, brag about, or rely upon, he knew only too well the pain any fear of a barren future might inflict upon Liliana, whose warm and generous spirit was the very stuff of which the best of mothers were made. However great her literary achievements might become down the road—and he had no doubt that she would make a name for herself—they could never compensate for the loss of a child's love. As he sat there lamenting her plight, the thought crossed his mind that perhaps he could himself father a child with Liliana, thereby relieving them both of their sense of deprivation. Chagall, he recalled, had done it at the age of fifty-seven with a woman half his age, and even at eighty-one, Goethe was still being lusted after by a twenty-four year old Bettina Brentano as the most desirable 'begetter' around. So, why couldn't he? And what a joy it would be, he mused, to

118

see in the flesh what could be created out of the mixture of his and Liliana's genes, and then to spend the rest of his life working to build and decorate the nest where she could raise the child and provide for all its needs even while pursuing the professorial career for which her doctoral degree would qualify her.

To be sure, he would probably die, or be as good as dead in a nursing home, before any son or daughter could ever reach adulthood, and although he knew of many mothers, like Liliana's own, who had made the best of a bad situation by raising their children well without the help of a husband, it was quite another matter to purposely and consciously bring a child into the world and deprive it of the advantage of having a father. Still, chances were good that he could be around for at least the first twenty years of the child's life, and the considerable amount of wealth he could leave the child and its mother should he die soon thereafter could go a long way toward compensating for his absence when the child would be off to college or getting married anyway. Furthermore, he rationalized, it might be a blessing to take his leave after ten or twenty years of connubial bliss, lest in living into his eighties or nineties he would become a burden upon Liliana and deprive her of a chance to find another mate her own age who might take his place and accompany her gracefully into her own evening years as a distinguished scholar. Finally arresting the flight of fancy, he returned his attention to the computer, and began composing his reply to Liliana's email.

<lcolumbra@aol.com>; Wed, 12 Nov 1997 3:53 (EDT)

Mi colibra querida!

Ave atque vale! It seems that I have hardly had time to say hello before I have to bid you farewell! I am happy for you that you will have a chance to pursue your intellectual interests at so great a school as Harvard. The beauty of the place, as well as its outstanding library and faculty, will surely fire your spirit. And you, no doubt, will add your own spark to its long and noble tradition of scholarly debate. But needless to say, I will miss you terribly. Urbana will not be the same when you are gone. The best of Mozart, Verdi, or Pucini, will not be enough to replace the joy I felt at the opera when you were next to me, and no *crème brûlée* will ever taste so delicious without you being there to share it with me! So, here's hoping that the thousand miles separating us after you head out East will not end our friendship! I'm sorry about Adam. I can imagine how painful the experience has been for you. But if, as you said, your interests were going in different directions, perhaps it's better that you have decided now, rather than waiting till later, to go your own ways. In any event, dear 'little bird,' you know that I have come to care about you very much, and although I may be too old to be building nests, I will gladly help you in any way I can. See you soon!

P.S. Sad to say, no progress to report on the novel, but am collecting a lot of good information about Alaska!

Con carino!
Mauritio

22

Professor Altmann picked up the box left on the front porch of his house by the UPS delivery man, and upon noticing that it had come from Liliana, immediately felt a surge of excitement coursing through his veins. It had been a full two months since he had last seen or heard from her. On the day before her departure for Boston back in December, he had driven to Urbana through a blinding snowstorm to have dinner with her, and they had promised each other to keep in touch. But she had not called or written at all since then. Perhaps it was only because of her preoccupation with finding an apartment and registering for her new program of studies at Harvard. But, with or without good reason, he had begun worrying that despite all her promises to the contrary, she had no real interest in keeping whatever their relationship was alive.

Tearing the brown wrapping away, he found inside the box two smaller packages. The one he opened first contained an exquisitely designed tie of umber and olive hues from the New York firm of Andrew Fezza. The other, a Penquin edition of Ovid's *Erotic Poems* and a copy of Gabriel Marquez' novel, *Of Love and Other Demons*. At the top of the first page of the latter thin book, Liliana had written a birthday greeting, saying how much she appreciated their friendship, and comparing him to one of the songbirds which every morning lighted on the feeder hanging outside her apartment window and dispelled by its joyful chirping some of the melancholy usually clouding her heart at that early hour of the day. It wasn't exactly a profession of anything exclusive or unique about their relationship, asserting as it did that he was only 'one' of her 'birds' and that his singing was only 'some' of the music that added a joyous note to her rising. Still, it was as charming a message as he had ever heard from her before, and he found it rather touching. Beneath the birthday greeting, she had penned one of Shakespeare's sonnets, in which the English bard had tried to capture the atemporal nature of an older man's affection for his beautiful, young lover by highlighting the exchange of hearts between them. As mysterious as was the poem's ironic message, even more puzzling to Altmann was the sentiment that might have prompted Liliana to append it to her birthday greeting.

Not daring to think that she just might be hinting at the possibility of some feeling of love for him, he returned to the other book and began reading one or another of Ovid's poems. As he savored the carnal metaphors conjured up by the Roman poet, he could not resist thinking that Liliana might conceivably be trying to stir his sexual interests. It had been so long since he had been involved in any romantic exchange, that he had all but forgotten what little he had ever learned about the mating game, and he was anything but sure that his interpretation of her intentions had any foundation in fact. Inside the book of poems, however, he also found a postcard inserted by Liliana which on the front side showed a young woman attired in a black bikini posing sensuously on a sandy-white beach against a blue sky and the turquoise waters of Cape Cod, and on the back side, in bold black print, the caption: *'Voulez vous nager avec moi?'* Beneath it, in Liliana's own smooth hand, was inscribed another birthday greeting: *'Feliz Compleanos!'* Had he been no older than she, he would not have hesitated for a moment to interpret the card and its message as a playful come-on. But he knew only too well that he had just turned sixty-two, not thirty-two. Was she, then, merely tweaking him for his own less than subtle vulpine pretensions? Kind soul that she was, he doubted that she would ever want to hurt his feelings by purposely mocking the increasingly fragile character of his aged libido, but he had experienced her mischievous sense of humor before, and suspected that this might be just another instance of her wanting to evoke a little laughter. So, 'Lighten up, Mauritio!,' he muttered to himself, while laying the gifts aside for the moment and going to fetch a cup of coffee. For the rest of the afternoon, however, while doing a quick read of the Marquez novel and some of Ovid's poems, he worried about possibly missing what to others might seem an obvious invitation to love. And finally, after watching the evening news and finishing off what was left of a peppercorn steak from the night before, he decided to chance making a yet greater fool of himself by responding to Liliana's message with at least a hint of his own receptivity toward whatever sexual interest she might have in him.

Dear Liliana,

The beautiful tie and two books you sent me for my birthday (not to mention the bathing beauty!) reawakened the tender feelings I felt toward you from the moment we met. I intend to wear the tie to class tomorrow, and expect to win the oohs and ahs of all the sartorial critics among my students. The Marquez novel is beautiful too. The eroticism it describes is so 'spiritual.' It is paradoxical, but probably very close to the truth, that the most profound spirituality can only be found through the body. Reading the novel along with some of Ovid's poems made me want to start all over again . . . mindful all the while of Ariosto's words that although 'the malady' may already have 'gone too deep to quit the dance and seek tranquility,' he 'who in old age the dupe of love remains, deserving is of fetters and of chains.'

I look forward to seeing you again. In two weeks, we'll be starting our week-long mid-term Spring break, an exciting 'space' which would be nice to fill with a 'flight' (I'm one of your 'birds,' remember!) to Boston! What thinkest thou? There's a lot we need to talk about if we are still planning on a trip to Alaska this summer.

P.S. I am enclosing a photograph of myself when I was your age. Thought you might get a chuckle out of the long hair and sideburns that were thought to be so 'sexy' back then!

Affectionately,

Mauritio

"Your hair is white, but yet you will love!" Altmann murmured to himself as he drove downtown to post the letter to Liliana, gleefully echoing the words uttered by a sixty-five year old Goethe contemplating the consummation of his recently aroused passion for a buxomly, vivacious *Fraulein* of thirty named Marianne von Willemer.

23

"Yeah, but you have to remember that Marianne was only one of the thirteen women for whom Goethe had professed eternal and exclusive love," Dr. Niebling protested, tapping the store of biographical trivia he had culled from six years of graduate study in the field of modern literature.

Although Altmann considered the dean his friend, he had not yet dared confess to him the passion he was feeling for Liliana, and while lunching with him less than a week after having written to Liliana, had initiated the discussion about Goethe's love for a woman half his own age only to test Niebling's sentiments on the delicate matter.

"You don't think he meant it when he told her he'd love her forevermore, and her alone?" Altmann responded with the hint of a smirk that cast some doubt on his own conviction.

"Are you kidding?!" Niebling replied, after washing down a French-fry or two with a gulp from his glass of Heiniken. "The old Teutonic fox was no less a womanizer than Picasso has been in our own time."

"You really think so?"

"I do. Within eight years of his infatuation with Marianne, Goethe, by then seventy-three, was trying to lay a seventeen-year old beauty named Ulrike von Levetzow, evoking from a friend the cynical comment: 'Old as you are, always and ever girls!' Seems to me he was a real Don Juan. Except for one of them, his 'fat better half,' as townspeople liked to call the chubby Christiane Vulpius, whom Goethe actually married and fathered his only child by, he treated the women in his life like mere objects of pleasure."

"I don't know," Altmann demurred. "I think you're wrong on that. My impression is that Goethe's women were mostly 'muses' of one sort or another whom he needed to quicken his poetic vein. Seems to me that he really loved every one of them, but only in a Platonic way that envisioned the sexuality of each as a variation on the theme of eternal femininity."

"So, why, if that were the case, was he attracted only to women much younger than himself? Do women lose the eternal dimension of their being after thirty?"

"Well, according to Plato, you'll recall, it is the woman's physical beauty that attracts a man to her in the first place. As embodied by the individual woman, however, such outward form is, he says, so ephemeral that a man will naturally move from one beautiful person to another, and in the process come to see that physical beauty is not limited to any one individual. He will come to love *all* physical beauty, and by doing so, free himself from any humiliating and trivial passion for one particular person."

"Even of handsome young boys?" Niebling queried, swiping sarcastically at the notoriously pederastic taste of the ancient Greek intellectual community.

"There is no evidence that Socrates' love for Alcibiades ever got physical," Altmann retorted, while taking a bite from his BLT sandwich.

"You may be right," Niebling conceded, "but what about Xanthippe, or for that matter, what about Goethe's wife, Christiane? If Socrates and Goethe were so disinterested in particular persons, why did they ever get married?"

"That's a good question. Socrates' relation to Xanthippe was probably never as bad as Aristophanes made it out to be, and neither Socrates nor Goethe would ever have agreed with the view expressed in Tolstoy's *The Kreutzer Sonata* that marriage inevitably becomes ugly and disgusting. But both certainly did maintain a definite aloofness from their wives and did not consider the ties they had with them to be altogether exclusive of other relationships. Emerson, I might add, came to be of a similar disposition. Notwithstanding his marriage, first to Ellen Tucker, and then, after her death, to Lidian Jackson, he had serious doubts about the permanency of marriage vows, and never let the latter deter his attraction to Caroline Sturgis and a few other lovely ladies, on the assumption, as he wrote in his essay on Love, that 'every soul is a celestial Venus to every other soul,' during the encounter of which 'the world appears as a hymeneal feast.'"

"Sounds like a rationalization for adultery to me!" Niebling—a staunch Roman Catholic who had just celebrated his thirtieth wedding anniversary the month before—protested a bit louder, as the delicatessen where they were lunching began filling with a noisy noonday crowd of local lawyers, businessmen, and other yuppie types.

"You've read Goethe's *Elective Affinities,* haven't you? Was that a defense of adultery? The whole plot revolved around Jesus' admonition that 'He who looks upon a woman with lust has already committed adultery in his heart!,' doesn't it?"

"True, but a novel's characters don't always reflect its author's personal convictions, do they?"

"No . . . or at least not entirely, and certainly not if they are taken out of the context of the author's whole frame of reference. Take Goethe's Faust, for example. It wouldn't make any sense to ascribe to Goethe the lust felt by the old philosopher for the beautiful Gretchen in the first part of the novel. But if one interprets such 'lust' in the context of the whole novel, and sees it as the first inkling of that 'yearning' for spiritual union that climaxes the novel's second part and so many of his other works, like the *Elegy of Marienbad* that was inspired by his passion for Ulrike, then, I think, one would be justified in seeing it as being somewhat representative of Goethe's own view and experience of sexual love."

"Well, I don't know," Niebling mumbled. "You're certainly giving the old boy every benefit of the doubt. But be that as it may, and getting back to your initial question, no, I don't think it makes much sense for older men to be having affairs with younger women."

"History's full of examples, you know," Altmann replied, as the waitress served the coffee and pie they had both ordered. "Not only Goethe, but Rousseau, Novalis, Schopenhauer, Nietzsche, Heidegger . . . and a lot of artists, like Chagall."

"Yeah, I know," Niebling observed with a touch of irritation, "but how long did any of their affairs last? Few for more than a year, and I guess you would say that with Goethe and his like-minded neo-Platonic friends that was precisely what they wanted, lest they lose sight of absolute beauty by becoming too attached to one or another particular woman, but I dare say that that was not the case with Nietzsche, who was crushed by his loss of Lou Salome, or for that matter, with Schopenhauer or Heidegger, and certainly not with Chagall. If I'm not mistaken, the by-then sixty-four year old painter fell into a furious rage when the thirty year old woman he had married seven years earlier walked out on him, claiming that she needed room to 'find herself.'"

"So, what's your point?" Altmann asked rather testily, thinking to himself that he would gladly settle for seven years of connubial bliss with Liliana.

"My point," Niebling replied, "is that even if the men involved in such relationships want them to last beyond a one-night stand or perhaps even 'into eternity,' as one of Marcel's theatrical characters expresses the wish, chances are very slim that their women would stand by them in their evening years. And who could blame them? What young woman, unless she's just a gold-digger, would ever want to be tied down with having to care for a pompous fool like the eighty-one year old Goethe, or—not to mention crazy and cranky septuagenarians like Nietzsche and Schopenhauer—worn-out womanizers like Sartre and Picasso. Incidentally," Niebling added, before Altmann had time to launch a rebuttal, "why this sudden interest of yours in such relationships? You're not having an affair with one of your students, are you?"

"Well, as a matter of fact, there is this lovely blonde who sits in the front row of my summer ethics class and with whom . . ." Altmann feigned, before suspecting that the dean was taking him seriously, and quickly adding, "Just joking, Charlie, just joking!"

"Let's hope so!" the dean replied, trying to cover his embarrassment over having missed his friend's attempt at humor. "You surely haven't forgotten how strict our policy is about professors dating their students."

"Thank you, Herr Niebling, but I'm not senile yet!" Altmann continued to josh. However officious he might be on occasion, the dean, he knew, would be the first to rush to his defense should he ever forget the rules and get into trouble. Altmann took no offense, therefore, to his rather paternalistic solicitude. But neither did he feel comfortable yet in sharing with him whatever story there was to tell of his romantic involvement with Liliana, and instead shifted the conversation to one of Niebling's favorite topics—the stock market. "Not to change the subject," Altmann muttered, "but did you notice yesterday's dramatic drop in the value of Cisco stock?"

"Just a temporary blip!" Niebling asserted.

"So you don't think the bubble is about to burst?"

"No way. It'll be back up tomorrow. Wait and see! I like to think of my relation to the market as being rather analogous to my marriage to Clotilda. While we were dating thirty-five years ago, it was like being on a roller-coaster. Just when our emotions were at their highest peak, some trivial incident would occur to send them on a downward sweep from which we thought we'd never emerge, only to find the next week that the incident had been completely forgotten and we were again flying high. After we wedded there were still ups and downs, but the fluctuations were no longer so dramatic and over the years balanced out to make for what I'd like to believe has been a rather happy marriage."

"And you're still convinced that in the long haul capitalism's flirtation with technology will be a smooth ride?"

"Absolutely!" the dean crowed, while signing his name to the credit-card receipt in payment of both their lunches.

"Well, I hope you're right," Altmann replied, as the two of them headed for the door, "but let's also hope that the 'dating game' is not too rough, as I've never had much of a stomach for roller-coasters."

Upon returning home later that afternoon, and checking his email, Altmann was surprised to discover that Liliana had responded to the letter he had sent her only four days ago.

"It was nice of you to think of visiting me during the midterm break," she wrote toward the end of her rather lengthy email message, "but it will not work out, since I've already made plans for a trip to Cuba that week with a girl friend. Perhaps you could come out sometime in May."

The news that Liliana would be unavailable during the second week of March only mildly disappointed Altmann. Spring weather being as unpredictable as it was, he knew that a two-thousand mile drive to Boston and back in such a short span of time would certainly have been a challenge; waiting till May made more sense. What he found hard to appreciate, however, was the fact that in the remainder of the two page electronic message not one word was said by Liliana about the summer trip to Alaska, the photo of his youthful self, or worse yet, about the 'tender feelings' toward her that he had dared to express in his own letter. She seemed as indifferent to his gentle wooing as was Lolita to Humbert's sexual ecstasy in the Nabokov novel he had recently read again. Like a child ignoring the antics of an adulating adult with irrelevant babble, she seemed to be trying to evade the issue of his feelings toward her by spinning a web of words about the most trivial of events now filling her life at Harvard. But why? To avoid giving him offense, on the assumption that by being ignored, his delicate advances could be less painfully rejected? Or was it that she was too uncertain about her own feelings toward him to want to chance bringing them out into the open before knowing for sure where she wanted to go with them? But why, if the latter, had she herself filled his birthday greeting with such erotic innuendo? Confused, and not a little despondent, he toyed for a moment, while still online, with the thought of checking out the latest 'consolation' being offered by 'Carmenita.' But resisting the temptation, he instead printed out Liliana's email for future reference, shut down the computer, and descended to his living room, where he took to reading another chapter from Zola's novel about the sixty year old, scientistic Doctor Pascal's love for his thirty year old pietistic niece.

24

More than a month passed before Altmann heard again from Liliana. On April Fools' Day there finally arrived a postcard from Cuba that she had sent out to him several weeks earlier. Two days later he received a package from her Boston address containing an enlarged and framed color-photograph of a street scene she had taken in Havana, along with a letter explaining how the photograph seemed to illustrate so well the mixture of joy and sadness she had experienced on the Marxist-dominated island. For all that he could tell from reading her card, her letter and a number of email messages that followed, nothing much had changed in their relationship. She still had given no indication of having taken any notice of his earlier hints of romantic interest, but neither had she reneged on the invitation to come visit her. And as May arrived, his excitement at the prospect of driving out to see her again crescendoed to the point where it was all he could do to concentrate on evaluating his students' exams and turning in their final grades. To convince himself that she would actually welcome his visit, he gave Liliana a last minute telephone call under the pretext of asking her to reserve a room for him at a local motel, hoping that she would instead invite him to stay in her own apartment, as, in fact, she did, causing his heart to flutter all the more as he finally loaded up his car on the second Thursday of May and headed East.

His plan was to make it halfway across Pennsylvania by nightfall, and have a relaxed meal before bedding down at the Holiday Inn in Dubois. But a massive traffic jam caused by a truck accident north of Columbus tied him up for an extra three hours. When finally he did arrive in Dubois at half past twelve, too late to dine, and his nerves on edge from driving at breakneck speeds on roads along whose grassy shoulders he had periodically spotted clusters of grazing deer, he retired immediately after checking in and showering, still in hope of getting a good night's rest. But sleep was slow in coming, and upon being awakened at six o'clock the next morning by the banging of a car door in the parking lot outside his room, he reckoned that he had slept little more than two hours, one of them agitated by a nightmarish dream of the mythological dragon guarding the labyrinthian entrance to the golden fleece. A stack of blueberry, Belgian waffles at the motel's restaurant restored enough of his energy to get him back on the road for the eight hour trek to Boston, but by the time he pulled up in front of the Brattle Street house on whose second floor Liliana had her apartment, he was exhausted and afraid that, because of his weariness, he would look to her even older than he was. It was not a very good start on what he had long been hoping would turn into a romantic weekend.

No sooner did he get inside, however, than his fantasies took a yet harsher blow. For unbeknownst to him, Liliana had agreed to take into her apartment for the rest of the summer a non-English-speaking, female Mexican student who, as she explained it, had been unable to find or afford any other place near the Harvard campus. With the student having pitched her sleeping bag on the dining room floor and arranged her meager belongings around it, any chance of sharing an evening with Liliana in the privacy of her home was obviously out the window. That she had not forewarned him of the foreign student's presence bothered him, but even more troubling was the seemingly casual manner in which she treated the intrusion, as though the loss of their privacy mattered little to her. The thought crossed his mind that she might actually have arranged to have this happen for the sake of avoiding the romantic encounter Altmann had been hoping for. But doubting that her kind spirit would ever allow her to be so devious, he concluded instead that it was perhaps just another instance of Liliana's innate generosity and probably a further indication, sad to say, of her own lack of interest in adding a romantic dimension to their friendly relationship. Trying to make the best of the situation, Altmann feigned an expression of gratitude at being informed by Liliana that, since she would be sleeping on the living room davon, the bedroom she was showing him would be his for the weekend. Depositing his luggage on the floor next to the bed, over which hung one of her own paintings—entitled, she told him with a bit of a chuckle, The Impenetrable Vagina—he quickly took advantage of the moment of semi-privacy to give her a heartfelt hug, and expressed again how grateful he was for having been invited to spend a few days with her. She accepted the affectionate gesture graciously, but also, he noticed, with a touch of passivity.

Later that evening, as they were dining on a meal of Spanish cuisine at one of Boston's finer restaurants, he learned the reason for her apparent reserve. In Cuba, she gently informed him halfway through the meal, she had met a young man with whom she had struck up an instant rapport. Sergio is his name, she announced, and promptly produced from her purse a photograph of a man as darkly handsome and young as herself. Complimenting her good taste, Altmann asked about where and how they had met, and was told that after meeting the young man at a bar, the two of them had gone for a stroll through one of Havana's public parks, and into the wee hours of the morning had carried on a vigorous conversation about the state of the arts in Communist Cuba. "And then?" Altmann queried, not so much to discover whether she had gone to bed with the man that night, as to find out what became of the encounter after her return to the states. "I saw him every evening thereafter until I came back, and since then we have talked at least several times a week on the phone," she confessed. "He thinks he will be coming to New York later this summer in some connection with the Cuban delegation to the United Nations, and wants me to meet him there . . ."

"So, no trip to Alaska this summer, huh?" Altmann mumbled without any attempt to disguise his disappointment.

"Me puede traer un vaso de aqua, por favor?" Liliana requested of the waiter before addressing the question put by Altmann. Reaching across the table and taking Altmann's right hand into her own, she at first said nothing, and tried conveying her feeling for the aging professor instead with a compassionate smile and a slow, gentle stroking of his fingers. "I'm sorry, Mauritio," she finally said, "but I didn't anticipate this happening."

"No need to apologize," Altmann replied sincerely. At thirty-two, Liliana's chances of finding a mate fit to fill her nest, and young and bright enough to keep her company for years to come, were becoming increasingly slim, he knew, and he did not at all begrudge her trying to take advantage of the opportunity Fate had recently afforded her. "I'm happy for you, Liliana!" he added, while squeezing her hand and trying to assure her of his understanding with a courageous smile.

"Perhaps we could take a short trip out to Mt. Evans some weekend in June?" Liliana volunteered. "I'm sure that Sergio would not object, if I explained to him our relationship and the plans we had made previous to my encounter with him."

Reluctant to probe whether such an explanation would say, as he suspected it might, that her relationship to him involved no feeling of love or sexual interest, and on that account represented no competition for Sergio to worry about, Altmann dismissed Liliana's suggestion as being unwise, and tried relieving her of the tinge of guilt she was obviously feeling by joking about how at her age, according to the latest statistical reports, she had about as much a chance of finding a suitable husband as being struck by lightning, and ought not, therefore, miss any chance afforded her. She took the joshing good-naturedly, and the two of them continued their meal with a steady stream of friendly banter, capping it off by sharing, at Liliana's suggestion, a dish of *el flan*. But their 'dance of spoons' was no longer the same. Try as he might to keep a stiff upper lip, and to shift his feelings toward Liliana back onto the plain of friendship alone, he could not escape the sense of having his guts being eaten out.

Later that night, as he lay alone in Liliana's own bed, he was reminded of the frustration Rousseau had once experienced when offered the chance to sleep in the bed usually occupied by the woman with whom he was currently infatuated, but had never found the will or the way to consummate his love for her. It was torture to look around, and by the dim light of the street lamp coming through the room's one window, to see Liliana's presence reflected in the clothes and shoes she had left hanging or lying around, and not to be able to reach out and hold her in his arms. His heart crushed at the thought of possibly losing her forever to Sergio, he thought of going to the living room to invite her to come back to bed with him, but he resisted the temptation, and tried compensating for her absence by wrapping his arms around the second of the two oversized pillows she had left on the bed. They could remain friends, he knew, but the chances of his ever becoming her lover were now, it seemed, next to nil. And although he felt little inclination to blame Liliana for his loss, every fiber of his body screamed out against the cruel Fate that had dangled so lovely a creature before his senescent eyes, only to withdraw her the minute he had reached out to take her into his arms.

25

Driving along Interstate 80 through middle Pennsylvania, Professor Altmann was struck by how different the landscape seemed from just the day before, when filled with excitement in anticipation of seeing Liliana again, he had traversed the same Appalachian foothills and, notwithstanding his early morning stupor, marveled at their rugged beauty. But now, after leaving Liliana to her new-found lover and heading back home with all hope of ever luring her into his own embrace dashed, he saw the jagged outcroppings of limestone for what they really were, little more than the calcareous remains of once living organisms.

Highlighted by the mid-afternoon sun amidst the ragged underbrush and isolated stands of gnarled oak trees, they looked like the vandalized tombstones of an abandoned cemetery, prompting Altmann to suspect for a moment that like Berlioz' Faust, he was on a *Ride to Hell*. A road sign indicating the turnoff to College Station reminded him of the rough and ready football teams that had come out of these Pennsylvania hills and, under the shrewd direction of their craggy-faced coach, captured one national title after another. Although a longtime fan of the Fighting Irish, Altmann had always admired the spunk of the Penn State teams. But recollection of their gridiron mastery now only exacerbated his own sense of defeat as he recalled once again how he had gambled his soul and lost. Hoping to distract himself from the despair he was feeling, he turned on the radio to check out Texaco's Saturday afternoon broadcast from the Met. The opera was already in progress, and he did not immediately recognize from the German libretto exactly which of the musical dramas he was hearing. His ear was good enough for him to tell that the music—lacking as it did any semblance of tonal harmony and full of *bruitistic* sounds and barbaric rhythms—was neither Classical nor Romantic in style, but to which of the German-speaking, 'new-musicians' it belonged—Strauss, Berg, or Hindemith—he was not sure, until listening closely and hearing the high soprano at one point singing: *"Ich heisse nicht Nelly. Ich heisse Lulu!,"* he finally recognized it as a work of Berg by the same name. Given their taste for what was popular, neither U of I's School of Music nor any of the city opera companies in the Midwest had ever presented Berg's *Lulu,* so Altmann had never had the opportunity to attend a live performance of the piece. But after reading Thomas Mann's bitingly satirical depiction of the inventor of the twelve-tone scale as a Faustian figure who goes insane upon losing the only human being he ever truly loved and contracting syphilis from his one and only sexual experience (with a prostitute named Esmeralda), he had become intrigued by the opera and done enough study of its libretto and Berg's sketches of the unfinished third act to be familiar with the horrendous story-line of Lulu's promiscuous and violent behavior. As he listened to the story unfolding on the radio, and heard Lulu singing that she had never pretended to be anything other than she was *("... Ich habe nie in der Welt etwas anderes scheinen wollen, als wofür man mich genommen hat"),* or that she, no less than the older man she had always loved, finally married, and was about to kill in self-defense, had given up her own youth in exchange for the sacrifice of his evening years *("... Wenn Du mir Deinen Lebensabend zum Opfer bringst, so hast Du meine ganze Jugend dafür gehabt."),* he could not help but think of his own relation with Liliana.

There was a major difference, he realized, in that while it was Lulu who had lusted after the older man, it was he himself who had gone in hot pursuit of young Liliana. Still, one way or the other, it was the difference in age that lay at the heart of both relationships. And as the strident sounds of the discordant music filled his car, Altmann shuddered at the thought of Lulu's comic-tragedy having already become the story of his own affair with Liliana. Images of Gounod's damnable Faust down on his knees, watching the soul of his beloved Marguerite being escorted into heaven, crossed his mind, and he uttered a prayer of sorts that good Liliana would find at least some connubial bliss with her Sergio, even though it be in the books, *à la* Marlowe, that he himself "must be damned perpetually," and his soul "plagu'd in hell" forevermore. By the time the soprano had sung the strident notes of Lulu's final scream of pain upon being murdered by Jack the Ripper, however, and he pulled into the parking lot of Youngstown's Super Eight Motel, any touch of consolation he had earlier felt upon comparing his plight to 'The Tragical History of Dr. Faustus' had already escaped him, and as he lay on his bed later that night, staring vacantly at the crazy patterns of the room's ceiling plaster, all he could think of was how right Schopenhauer had been in diagnosing the absurdity of the human situation. Less than a tragedy, whose meaning might be gleaned from some eternal design of things, his own life had become a pathetic joke, no less laughable than the History of Don Quixote.

26

"Damn, Joe, would you look at this!" Tom Czenkowski exclaimed, while absent-mindedly opening one of the files Professor Altmann had asked BCC technicians to transfer onto a larger disk.

A photo of the nude body of a mulatto woman filled the screen of the professor's home computer. Obviously intended to arouse as much prurient interest as possible, it showed a kneeling, half-prostrated woman looking back over her shoulder with a lustful grin on her face, while the intimate details of her genitalia were being displayed from behind with as stark naked singularity as the crevices of an Alpine mountainside on a day of the *Foehn*.

"Doesn't he teach ethics?" Joe Stone asked, as he stopped tinkering with some wires at the rear of the computer and came around the front of it to see what his partner was referring to.

"What's ethics?" Czenkowski mumbled distractedly, while clicking the mouse and bringing one pornographic photo after another onto the screen.

"It's a branch of philosophy that studies morality," Stone explained, "And it seems strange to me that someone teaching others about what is right or wrong would be wallowing in such filth." A practicing Presbyterian, he had devoted a lot of his time in the past year advising a group of interested parents in his parish how they could best protect their children from exposure to all the porn sites and dirty chatrooms now so readily accessible on the Internet.

"I guess he's free to watch whatever he wants in his own home, isn't he?" Czenkowski replied rather defensively, having himself gotten into the habit of tasting the Internet's smorgasbord of hard-core morsels anytime his middle-aged wife rejected the advances of his still raging libido.

"Not necessarily," Stone retorted, upon returning to his work on the machine's backside. "His computer is on a university modem, and so, even though it's in his own home, it's use is still subject to BCC policy, which, if I am not mistaken, clearly prohibits the introduction of material that is obscene."

"Well, I'm not paid to be a cyber-policeman," Czenkowski barked, after clicking the back button to take a second look at an especially lurid shot that had earlier caught his eye. "And I couldn't care less whether he's viewing Carmenita or Mother Angelica."

"Who's 'Carmenita'?"

"Oh, just some Latin American broad I came across a moment ago on one of Altmann's porn sites." Actually, it was her image that Czenkowski had just pulled back onto the screen and whose full frontal nudity was now claiming his undivided attention. "Carmenita Consolata!" he added with a lecherous drawl.

"Now why do you think a man like Altmann would need consolation from some porn star?" Stone asked with a sneer. While pursuing a Bachelor's degree in computer science, he had been required to take a course in philosophy and had fallen so in love with the subject that, except for the need to provide for the two children he had already fathered, he would gladly have switched majors and spent the rest of his life in hot pursuit of wisdom. "You would think," he added, not without a tinge of resentment, "that having the leisure to study philosophy day and night would be consolation enough." He thought of citing a line that he had remembered from his reading of Boethius long ago, but after looking up and seeing his partner's fixation on the dirty picture, knew that he would be wasting his breath, and instead admonished the man to get on with his work and finish the job they were assigned.

Czenkowski reluctantly closed out the files and after another half hour of transferral manipulations succeeded, with the help of Stone, in running all the material on Altmann's old hard-drive disk through BCC's mainframe computer and back onto a new, million-byte disk installed in the professor's machine. "That ought to do the trick," Czenkowski crowed, as Altmann himself ascended the stairs to his study and asked the two technicians how the work was going just as they were finishing up.

"You'll have room to store all the wisdom in the world now," Stone added with a snicker, before handing the professor the form he was expected to sign in attestation of the work done for him.

27

"So, what do you think?" Altmann asked the students in his ethics class. "We've seen what it means to strike a balance between autonomy and heteronomy in regard to parents, religious leaders, and government officials, but what about the boss? Should the boss have any say over what an employee does on his or her own time?"

"What about that nurse down in South Carolina?" a student, whose name still escaped Professor Altmann, queried from the back of the room.

"Which nurse is that?" Altmann asked, relieved at getting some help in keeping the discussion going. He had been up half the night downloading a few more porn sites onto the new hard drive of his home computer, and at one o'clock in the afternoon he was finding it hard to concentrate.

"The one who's become a porn star by stripping down every night on the Internet." As other students in the class began laughing, their mate quickly added—lest they might think, as he suspected they did, that he had himself been cruising the porn sites—that there was a story about the nurse in the *Star* during the previous week.

"So, what about her?" Having recently canceled his subscription to the *Star,* Altmann's only source of news any longer was the Fuss Channel, and if the network had made any reference to the story, he had missed it.

"Did they have a right to fire her?"

"What do you think?"

"Yeah, I think they did."

"On what grounds?"

"Well-l," the student began mumbling, "she wasn't exactly upholding the hospital's reputation."

"Speak up!" Altmann interjected. "Jane up here in the front row can't hear a word you're saying." Actually it was he himself who, at sixty-two, was finding it increasingly difficult to pick up on the generally muffled utterances of his students.

"I said," the student repeated in a louder voice, "that the nurse deserved to be fired because she was not upholding the image of the hospital."

"Just by becoming a porn star?"

"Of course," the student proclaimed emphatically, as though to imply that it would be ridiculous to suggest otherwise.

"And you think that was part of her job, to protect the hospital's good name?"

"Yeah!" the student insisted.

"What do the rest of you think?" Altmann asked. "Jane, what's your view?"

"About what-t?" the blonde beauty in the front row muttered, as she pulled her body up from the slouched position it had taken since the start of class, much to her professor's distraction as he periodically caught a glimpse of the young woman's well-tanned inner thighs under the mini-skirt she was wearing.

"Try to stay with us!" Altmann chided. "Tom, back there" he added after checking the seating chart to find the student's name, "is suggesting that an employee has to uphold the good name of the company for which he or she is working; that implies that the boss, who runs the company, has a right to draw the line on the behavior of the company's employees, even when they're not on the job. Do you agree?"

"Sort of."

"Sort of *what?*"

"Well, I sort of agree that the boss can tell an employee how to behave, but only to a certain extent."

"To what extent?" Altmann prompted, having earlier discovered that 'Jane' was not nearly as dumb as she sometimes seemed.

"Well, only to the extent, I would think, that what the employee is doing on his own time impacts on his job performance," Jane replied, seemingly oblivious to the concerns of her feminist sisters about phallocentric language.

"Good point!" Altmann declared. "But do you think that what the nurse does in the evening has any impact on her job performance during the day?"

"What nurse?" Jane asked with a genuinely befuddled look.

Professor Altmann gave the young woman a bemused stare. With any other of his students, he might have exploded in exasperation over so blatant a lack of attention. But Jane's periodic bouts of moody insouciance rather intrigued him, and wondering to himself what wild sexual fantasies might have been distracting her from the earlier discussion, he took her in a different direction. "Well, let's forget about the nurse," he stated, "and talk about me. Say, for example, that after a week of teaching a heavy load of classes and grading umpteen, mostly unintelligible, student essays,"—he waited for a laugh that didn't come—"I go down to the local bar on Friday night and drink myself into a stupor. Is that any business of our college president, my boss? Would he be justified in firing me on that account?"

"Not if you make it back to class on Monday morning and deliver a good lecture without falling off the podium!" Jane asserted.

"So, as long as I am able to do my job, it doesn't matter what I do at other times, right?"

"Right!" Jane agreed.

"What if your students see you inebriated," another female student named Jessica objected from her seat in the second row, "won't that undermine your ability to teach?"

"How so?" Altmann asked, knowing full well what she would probably say, but still trying to play the good Socratic midwife.

"They would lose their respect for you, wouldn't they?"

"Perhaps they would," Altmann conceded, "but should they? Why should what I do off the job affect the respect my students do or do not have for me as a teacher? Do they have a right to judge my job performance on the basis of my private behavior?"

"Yes!" Jessica insisted. "In my view, it's part of your job to set a moral example."

"You mean I've actually got to practice what I teach?" Altmann exclaimed.

"I think so," Jessica asserted with slightly less confidence, suspecting that her professor might be setting her up for one of his logical assaults.

"So, if I come in here every day spouting Aristotle's theory of virtue, you, as a student, have a right to expect me to be honest, temperate, patient, and so forth in all that I do, whether I'm at school or at home?"

"In my opinion, yes," Jessica stated.

"And if I'm not?"

"Well, then, I would say that the president would have a right to fire you, assuming of course that we're talking about a serious matter."

"I disagree!" Jane interjected without waiting to be called upon. "Teachers aren't preachers! You're not in here to advocate any kind of behavior. All you're supposed to be doing, as far as I'm concerned, is to help us understand the reasons given by Aristotle and other philosophers for acting one way or another; it doesn't mean you agree with them, or that your own behavior has to conform to their way of thinking."

"Good point, Jane," Altmann professed wearily. "You may be right, too, Jessica, in suggesting that setting a good moral example is part and parcel of *some* jobs. Parishioners may have a right, for example, to expect their pastors to practice what they preach from the pulpit each Sunday. And perhaps our political leaders ought to be held similarly accountable. I remember Eric Severaid once saying that, in the final analysis, setting a good moral example is about all the power the president of the United States really has. But the teaching profession is different, isn't it? You think that it is part of my job to inspire you by my personal example, and Tom—it is Tom, isn't it?—Tom would probably add that it is also part of my responsibility to preserve the good name of the college, right? Well, I'm not so sure. I think Jane hit on the key factor, which is the extent to which one's private behavior does or does not impact upon one's job performance. If it does impact, then I would agree that the boss has a right to draw the line even on what one does off the job; if it does not, I would say that what one does on one's own time is none of the boss' business. Whether it does or does not impact on job performance will depend, of course, on how one defines the job. I personally don't think that being a nurse or professor requires that one's private behavior has to always uphold the reputation of the hospital or school, or set a good moral example for one's patients or students. But, you're entitled to your own opinions, so think about it. Next time . . ." Before he could finish the sentence, half the students in the class had already stashed their texts and notebooks into their backpacks and were headed for the door. Altmann made no effort to hold them back, and instead feasted his eyes on the voluptuous lines of Jane's body, the upper proportions of which had come into full view as she leaned down to retrieve several of her books from off the floor next to her chair. As she raised up and noticed her professor still ogling her breasts, she blushed slightly, gave him a nervous smile, and made a quick exit from the room without any word of farewell.

A bit shamed at having an edge of his voyeuristic proclivity detected by one of his favorite students, Altmann trudged back to his office feeling rather depressed. Try as he might, however, to erase the image of the young woman's curvaceous body from his mind by attending to several voice mail messages and a number of other trivial tasks, it would not go away, and instead triggered his recollection of the hundred and one erotic images he had gazed upon for four to five hours the night before. Checking his calendar, he was reminded that in addition to the opening of a colleague's art exhibition later in the afternoon, a student performance of Shakespeare's *Midsummer Night's Dream* was being presented that evening in BCC's Carson Theater. A year ago he would not have thought of missing either of the two events, and even now his past appreciation for anything aesthetic—not to mention a natural penchant for supporting the artistic endeavors of colleagues and students alike—inclined him to arrange the rest of his day to accommodate his attendance at both. But his libido had kicked in, pumping waves of sexual energy from the pit of his body to all its extremities, and pricking his need for sensation to the point where he seemed to himself to have no choice but to go with its flow. Cursing his apparent inability to control any longer the course of his own life, Altmann dejectedly, but with intense excitement, hurried from his office, ignoring several moves on the part of his fellow professors he encountered in the hallways leading out to the parking lot to strike up conversations, and headed for home.

Turning his car off College Avenue onto Pine Boulevard, and driving a mile or so East in the direction of his suburban home, Altmann passed the Bourgeois Inn, whose swank bar and Victorian-styled rooms were known by all who had any interest in such things, to be the best place in town for procuring a prostitute with the least chance of being noticed by the public. Several times of late he had toyed with the thought of frequenting the place in hopes of finding sexual satisfaction more real than he was currently experiencing in the virtual realm of cybersmut. But knowing full well that no matter what precautions might be taken, there was still the chance of being recognized by one of his students or colleagues, he had always steered clear of the place, opting instead for the privacy and secrecy afforded him by the Internet. And once again fear of having his lustful ways exposed prevailed. Careful to stay within the city's strictly enforced speed limits, he cruised on by the Inn toward his home a mile ahead on Elm Street. Just as he turned off Pine Boulevard, however, one of the countless trains traversing the city every day, its diesel engine growling like some prehistoric monster, slowly pulled across the street ten blocks up from where he lived, blocking his path with its string of several hundred cars for at least fifteen minutes. By the time the road had cleared, his irritability had reached a fever pitch, and when another driver, an elderly gentleman to all appearances, cut onto his lane in front of him, he laid on his horn for a full ten seconds and tailgated the man's automobile—a vintage Cadillac from the 1970s—so closely for several blocks that any sudden stop on its part would inevitably have resulted in a rear-end collision.

"Goddamn idiot!" Altmann mumbled, as the Cadillac turned left at the next intersection. Upon getting the lane to himself, however, the stupidity of his having raged over so trivial a matter as the addition of only a minute or two of travel time dawned on the professor, and he promised himself to try keeping his temper under better control in the future, although, given his record of late, he knew the odds would be against his doing so. Whatever little patience he had ever had, had disappeared altogether in recent months, and only the slightest irritation was needed to provoke an angry outburst. Inevitably, on such occasions, he would go away feeling disgusted with himself, and, as now, resolved to not let it happen again, but not at all confident that he was any longer the conductor of his own behavior. Pulling into the driveway of his house, and seeing how bleak the place was looking on its front side, he made a mental note of the need to visit the local lawn and garden shop sometime soon to purchase the mums he was accustomed to planting every fall in the five-foot-long flower boxes that hung under his home's living and dining room windows. A year ago, this late in September, the boxes would already have been aglow with autumnal hues. But like the many other household chores left undone by his recently acquired habit of procrastination, this one too had been delayed until now when, even if he could find the will to act immediately, he would probably be lucky to see any blooms at all before an early freeze would nip the plants in their buds. Distracted by the empty boxes, he drove the car into the narrow garage attached to his house without paying sufficient attention to how close he was to the garage-door's frame on his right side, and for the second time in the last three months heard his side-view mirror being whacked from its fiber-glass base. "Ah-h-h shi-it!" he exclaimed, "there goes another three hundred bucks!" Finally getting the car inside the garage, he walked around it to survey the damage, and upon seeing the mirror dangling by its wires, cursed again upon remembering from past experience how, in addition to the outrageous cost, getting it fixed would consume so much of his time and energy.

Inside, Altmann proceeded to prepare himself a soup and sandwich lunch. His slow, methodical movements belied the tension he was feeling. Anticipation of the euphoria he had come to experience upon losing himself in the world of porn had already sent a surge of excitement through his body, while the scruples generated by years of having protested on rational grounds against everything he had become tugged at his conscience from the opposite direction. But it was a battle, he knew, that he had already lost. However long he might delay succumbing to the temptation facing him by taking his time to open the can of French onion soup or to spread the mayonnaise on the bread sandwiching the lettuce and roast beef he wanted to eat, in the end he would be no more able to resist the attraction of the Internet porn than could a piece of cosmic dust escape the big black hole on doomsday. It was just a game he was playing to kid himself into thinking that he still had some choice, when in fact, as he knew only too well, the porn had so intoxicated his mind as to become altogether irresistible. Still the philosopher at heart, he would frequently wonder how such material could ever have taken so strong a hold on his consciousness. What made it so attractive, so fascinating? The same dreadfulness, perhaps, that still hooked so many people on Hitler and the mind-boggling dirty deeds of his Nazi henchmen? Could there possibly be an element of the sublime, what Kant had identified as the raw force of nature, revealing itself in the ugliness of genital organs being exposed so graphically as the instruments of nature's awful creativity? Or was it not perhaps that the erotic imagery was actually beautiful?

Often in the past Altmann had taken consolation in the fact that he had little, if any, taste for the hardcore stuff, soothing his conscience with the thought that it was only the beauty of the female body upon which he had become so fixated, and reasoning that the pornographic imagery was not all that different from the work of other artists, whose depictions of the nude, contrary to Kant's theory of aesthetic disinterest, invariably left the spectator with some vestige of erotic feeling. But Altmann had never been entirely convinced by his own rationalizing. Plato, he knew, had conceived of beauty in terms of idealized perfection, and more modern thinkers like Stendhal and Santyana, or even Freud, had described such an aesthetic appreciation as a process of chrystalization or idealization whereby the imaginary object of one's desire is over-evaluated or aggrandized to the point of bringing into focus its eternal possibilities. But the soft-porn imagery, he often suspected, did just the opposite. Far from overestimating the beauty of its object, the pornographer's camera, like Rousseau's woman-devouring imagination, seemed to invade the privacy of the individual being depicted to the extent of stripping it of all the soulful dimensions that might relate it to the rest of reality and reducing it to an isolated piece of flesh or body-part, or, as Buber and Marcel might put it, an 'it' or 'thing' that could be exploited to whatever end the gawker might have in mind. But if such pornographic material was not truly beautiful, was his fixation then nothing more than the result of his own distorted vision? Could the porn have appealed only to an eye that was already myopic, to a mind that was already sick? Spoon by spoon, bite by bite, between periodic sips from a bottle of Bud Lite, Altmann consumed the soup and sandwich as he watched Fuss News reporting on President Clinton's latest sexual peccadilloes. All the while, his mind was running ahead of itself, already nibbling at the dessert of erotic imagery to which, willy-nilly, he would soon be treating himself.

Ascending eventually to his second-floor study, Altmann turned on his computer and waited for the machine to hook him up to the cyberworld. With a few more clicks of his mouse, he was into his favorite porn site, and the screen filled with the names of hundreds of 'stars' ready and willing to bare their bodies for his perusal free of charge. He started with the Cs, where from previous experience he knew he would find the sensuous Latin American Carmenita Consolata, checked out a few Asian chicks like Yuri and Sophie Chan in the same category, then moved on to the Ds and Es for a half hour or so of pleasurable viewing of East European babes (as they advertized themselves), before perusing the alphabetical listings under F, and becoming fixated for another hour on the multiple images of Sara Ferrari.

Like all her co-stars on this particular site, Ms. Ferrari displayed her body with full-frontal nudity, but with no less reserve than Professor Altmann was accustomed to seeing in the paintings of nudes by, say, a Giorgione or a Correggio. After sating his erotic desire on such delicate morsels, however, and trying to exit the site, he found himself trapped in a world of much harder porn. Every time he would close a window of one site, another would open—his Back and Home buttons having apparently been rigged again by some clever programer to block his escape from the pornographic loop they had created. In their competitive zeal to lure him and others into their respective corners, the various sites exploited every electronic trick to simulate the sexual thrills they promised to exhibit. As Altmann gawked passively at the chaotic parade of obscene images, he was reminded of paintings by the likes of Titian, Rubens, or Watteau that depicted the bacchanalian pleasures of the 'Garden' or 'Island of Love' with such magical artistry as to disguise altogether any distinction between myth and reality. But such pagan celebrations of *eros* were soon replaced in his mind by a recollection of Hieronymous Bosch's 'Garden of Delights.' With its phantasmagorial display of countless, doomed men and women, enmeshed among their animal and vegetative cousins, hopelessly seeking to satisfy their carnal desire by every conceivable variety of bizarre sensual activity, Bosch's piece left little doubt that far from being the paradise that the current purveyors of cybersmut wanted the public to believe of the electronic garden they were producing, it was really a demonic place, renewing Altmann's impression that if he were not already there, he was, as a victim of his own appetites, certainly on the road to hell.

Finally escaping the trap he was in by simply shutting his computer off, he trudged back downstairs and settled into the lounge-chair facing his TV. It was only five o'clock, but the sun had already begun to set, and with the window's Venetian blinds closed, so little of what gloaming light there was penetrated the living room that its sparse furnishings were barely visible, and of the hundreds of books on the shelves lining the walls only those with the most garish of covers could be seen. Several days of Indian summer had necessitated the running again of the house's air-conditioner, and as its basement fan kicked on, blowing a draft of cool air in his direction, Altmann's sweated body felt clammy, exacerbating the sense of shame that he was already feeling at having failed once again to live up to his oft-repeated resolution not to succumb to his dirty habit. It dawned on him anew that he would probably never be able to stop, and the framed Chagall print of a prayerful Job that he had hung on his living room wall years ago when the embers of his own religious faith had not yet burnt out, and whose greenish hues were now catching a touch of dusky light, only served to mock his feeling of hopeless isolation.

During the previous weekend he had traveled to Chicago at the invitation of a former colleague whose current husband despised opera, to attend a performance of Weber's *Der Freischütz,* and as he recalled the horror and despair of Max, its hero, at the sight of the Black Huntsman emerging from the forest in dark green and flame-colored garb *("Hat mich jetzt der Himmel verlassen?"),* he shuddered at the thought of how much the powers of evil had intruded upon his own life. Would that in the end he could, like Max, win the hand of his beloved, but there was nothing in his recent experience to sustain such hope. He had heard nothing from Liliana all summer long, and could only assume that she was upset over his abrupt departure back in May, or, more likely, had simply become totally preoccupied with trying to develop her relation with Sergio. If he felt inclined to identify with any of the opera's characters, therefore, it was not with Max, but with the devil's own henchman, the wily Caspar into whose tree the 'white dove' had flown, and who, on that account, caught the 'magic bullet' that would doom his soul forever. A shot to the head, he mused, might in fact bring some welcome relief from the gloom he was feeling. Turning on his television with a flick of his remote control, however, he began cruising the forty-nine stations provided by his cable connection, and soon became preoccupied—after passing up late-afternoon reruns of several soap operas—with an especially explicit exhibition of two lesbians making love on HBX.

28

"What's wrong, Joe?" Marilyn Stone asked her husband across the dinner table, after their children had already finished eating and gone off to the family room to watch television or play a computer game. "You haven't been eating half the food I've served for the past week."

Her husband sipped at his cup of coffee, debating within himself whether to reveal to his wife the problem he had been wrestling with ever since he and his fellow technician had discovered all the porn material on Professor Altmann's home computer. He knew what his wife's response would be, and wanted to be sure he would be willing to follow it before soliciting her advice. A Baptist, with a Ku Klux Klan father, by birth, who had joined the Presbyterian church only after marrying her husband, she was even more adamant than he in opposing the spread of pornography. While he had always had a distaste for the obscene material, it had been at her instigation that he had become so involved in their parish's effort to help parents protect their children from cybersmut. He had no doubt that she would push him relentlessly to turn Altmann in, were she to learn of his aberrant behavior. But up to now he had not been able to decide for himself whether he had a responsibility, or even a right, to do that.

"Has something happened at school? You're not in danger of losing your job, are you?" Given a recent drop in enrollment, and the loss in revenues resulting therefrom, rumors were rampant on campus that come January, not a few faculty and staff might be let go. Although her husband enjoyed seniority over most of his fellow workers, one could never be sure whose head would be the first to roll, since in lieu of any formal RIF policy, decisions about hiring and firing at BCC had always been left to the VP of Finance, who was known to have as little respect for worker seniority as for professorial tenure.

"No, no, I'm not at all worried about my position," Joe asserted.

"What is it, then, honey? I know there's something bothering you."

Stone stared back at his wife, eager to unburden himself of the anxiety he was feeling, but still doubting whether the woman he had married ten years ago any longer had the capacity to lend him a sympathetic ear. With every passing year she had grown more cocksure of her own opinions, and seemed to have lost the ability, or at least the will, to engage in genuine dialogue. Whatever the matter he might raise, and however uninformed she might be on the subject, he had come to expect that his every question would evoke a definitive response, leaving little if any room for discussion. Still, with no one else in whom to confide, he finally confessed to her that he was faced with making a difficult decision.

"Last Friday," he began, "Tom Czenkowski and I were asked to transfer the files on Professor Altmann's old hard drive onto a new one that would have a larger capacity. While doing so, Tom happened to click on one of the files and discovered that it was a porn site . . ."

"Professor Altmann, you said!? Isn't he the ethics prof?" Mrs. Stone asked incredulously before her husband could finish half his sentence.

"Yeah, and he also chairs the philosophy department."

"Was this at his home, or at school?"

"At his home, but on a computer hooked up to a BCC modem."

"So it was BCC property, right?"

"Right."

"And you told me before, didn't you, that the college has a strict policy against use of its computers to procure obscene material?"

"That's right, but let me finish what I had started saying. It wasn't just one porn site that Tom found. Upon investigating further, he discovered that the professor's hard drive was chock full of such sites, literally hundreds of them . . ."

"You've got to be kidding!"

"I wish I were," Joe replied, with a touch of sadness in his voice.

"That is outrageous!" his wife exclaimed, adding, just as he had expected she would, that he would have to do something about it.

"What do you suggest I do?"

"Tell the president, of course!"

"I'm not so sure I have a right to do that."

"Why not, if what the professor's doing is against BCC policy?"

"Well, for one thing there is a law of privacy. Had the professor left the pornographic material on his screen, there would be no problem in regard to privacy, and could even have left him open to a charge of sexual harassment."

"How so?"

"As BCC employees we have a right not to be exposed to such material in the workplace; so, if the professor had in fact left one of his porn sites open at a time when he knew that we would be working on his computer, he could conceivably be accused of having harassed us."

"Isn't that what happened?"

"No, as I said, Tom himself clicked on one, and then many more, of the sites."

"Well, after seeing the first one, didn't he have a right to check out the others, to see whether he was participating in the distribution of material he didn't approve of?"

Stone made no move to inform his wife of how his co-worker had become like a pig guzzling swill the minute he had stumbled across the porn sites, and concentrated instead on the questionable legality of what Czenkowski had done.

"The problem is not with the subsequent sites, but with the first one. Did Tom have a right to open that first file, or might not his having done so be considered an invasion of the professor's privacy?"

"So, if you report on the professor, you might be getting Tom into legal trouble, you think?"

"Right, but whatever the legal implications, I'm also concerned about not violating the professor's rights."

"Huh!," Mrs. Stone huffed. "I wouldn't worry about the professor. In my view, one's right to privacy ends when what one is concealing is illegal . . ."

"To my knowledge, Tom found no child pornography, and the rest of the stuff, I think, is still legal."

"But it shouldn't be!" Mrs. Stone retorted. "If its immoral, it should be illegal, and surely you don't doubt that the storing and use of such trash is immoral."

"Not at all!"

"Then, why not turn him in?"

"Well, there's still the problem with Tom."

"I think you're exaggerating the risk. Seems to me that most people would assume that after being asked to transfer the files, the two of you would naturally check to see if the files were actually transferring, and to do that you would have to open one or another of them, wouldn't you?"

"I guess so," her husband conceded.

"What does Tom think? Doesn't he want to report on what he's found?"

"Frankly, I don't think he cares all that much what the professor does in private."

"Well, I do, and I think you should too. Imagine our daughter in a year or two going to BCC and being made to take an ethics course from such a sleazy character! Why he'd probably be ogling her the whole class through, and god only knows what he might try to lure her into, or at least pump into her head. I think you have a responsibility to protect your daughter and all of BCC's students against such a threat."

"You may be right. I'll talk to Tom about it again tomorrow and see if he'll back me up, should I decide to take the matter to the president."

29

The ringing of his phone jarred Altmann from the state of stunned disbelief he had fallen into upon checking out the latest TIAA-CREF report on the Internet and discovering that his growth stocks had taken yet another dramatic dip in value, plunging ten more bucks per unit to settle for the day at more than twenty dollars off the price he had originally paid for them, and more than fifty from the value to which they had soared in the previous year.

"Altmann!," he barked into the phone, unloading onto the party at the other end some of the disgust he was feeling with himself for not having dumped the stock months ago when, notwithstanding Dean Niebling's friendly opinion to the contrary, he was sure the tech-stock bubble was about to burst. Already his delay in acting had cost him tens of thousands of dollars, and God only knew how much lower the market would sink as the bears continued their feeding frenzy.

"Altmann!!," he repeated impatiently, as no response to his initial identification was forthcoming, and the silence had led him to suspect that he was being set up for another of the incessant telemarketing calls that would usually come in the late afternoon from the Democratic Party, the Native American Indians, Disabled Veterans, March of Dimes, the Heart and Lung Association, Parkinson's and Alzheimer's Foundations, or some other charitable organization to which he had begun to donate during the previous years when the growth of his stock investment had left him with the impression of wallowing in wealth.

"Dr. Altmann?" the husky feminine voice inquired hesitantly.

"Yes, it is!" Altmann affirmed.

"Jane Steele, the president's secretary. I wasn't sure it was really you."

"It's me alright; what can I do for you?" Altmann replied rather brusquely, still smarting from the arrogant disrespect the secretary had shown him a couple of months ago when he had tried procuring from the president's office the minutes of the Board of Trustees latest meeting.

"The president would like to have a talk with you."

"Now? Over the phone?"

"No. He'd like to meet with you?"

"Well, sure. When?"

"First thing tomorrow morning. Could you be here by eight?"

"I guess so. Any idea what it's all about?"

"Not really," Ms. Steele claimed.

"Huh!," Altmann grunted, suspecting as did everyone else on campus that next to nothing ever happened in the presidential office without the long-time secretary being privy to it. "Okay then, I'll be there," he finally mumbled.

"Good. I'll inform the president."

No sooner had he hung up than the phone rang again. It was Niebling. "Just saw the TIAA-CREF report," the dean started out, "and thought I'd check to see if you'd jumped from your upstairs window yet!"

"Laugh, you fool!" Altmann retorted only half-jokingly. "If I hadn't listened to you I'd still be a wealthy man! Didn't I tell you a month ago that the bubble was about to burst?"

"Yes, I recall that you did. But you'd said the same thing a year ago, right before the stocks soared to new highs. Anyway, your loss is only on paper, and chances are you'll recover it all before you retire."

"If I don't get fired first!" Altmann interjected.

"Whad'ye mean, get fired? You haven't been challenging Schmidt again, have you?"

"No, but for some reason he wants to see me. Got a summons to meet with him first thing tomorrow morning. Any idea of what it might be about?"

"Not really, unless it'd be that business again with the international student you failed." Midway through the final exam of the previous semester, a student from Ghana whose father was a high official in that country's UN delegation, had approached Altmann's desk at the front of the classroom, claiming through muffled sobs that the recent death of his sister had so upset him that he had not been able to study for the test and pleading for a chance to retake it at another time. Upon letting him do so, however, Altmann had caught the student cheating, and in keeping with his usual policy, had failed him on the spot. The father claimed that the punishment was too harsh, on grounds that his son had a C average going into the final exam, and that the F would keep him from graduating with the degree in business he needed to accept the job he had been offered back home. In a terse, midsummer telephone conversation with Altmann, President Schmidt had suggested to the professor that he might want to reconsider and possibly change the grade to at least a D. But Altmann had refused to budge.

"I thought we'd settled that matter once for all."

"The dad called me again last month and was still pretty irate."

"Well, he can scream all he wants, but he doesn't have a leg to stand on, and if the president thinks I'm going to cave in just because the guy's a diplomat, he's got another thought coming!"

"I suspect the president knows that. But what else could it be? I trust you really were kidding last spring about dating that 'lovely blonde' in your ethics class, weren't you, because if Schmidt ever got wind of anything like that, he'd want your head on a platter in no time flat?"

"Probably would, the hypocritical bastard!" Altmann mumbled, before adding that yes, he had only been pulling Niebling's leg in hinting earlier at a romance with one of his students.

"Well, perhaps he just wants to tell you what a great professor you've been, and offer you some extra merit pay!"

"Yeah, sure! Or maybe even a year's sabbatical so I'll have more time to write critical articles for *Academe* about the ineptitude of most college administrators!"

Niebling laughed at the recollection of how perturbed Schmidt was reported to have been over Altmann's piece in the August issue of AAUP's monthly journal. "He surely didn't take it personally, did he?"

"No more than I took the opinion he voiced about the bankruptcy of modern philosophy in that ridiculous commencement address he gave last May!"

"That *was* rather insulting, wasn't it. Perhaps he's just looking for a chance to apologize."

"Ha! That will be the day!"

"So what do *you* think it is?"

"I don't have a clue," Altmann answered honestly.

"Well, good luck. I doubt that it's any more serious than what's happening in the market, so don't throw in the towel yet!"

"That's reassuring! But thanks, anyway. I'll keep you posted."

30

Altmann arrived at the president's office the next morning in a despondent mood. After having cruised the Internet for an hour or two before retiring the night before, he had tossed and turned the whole night through, intermittently fantasizing about Liliana's beautiful body and rehashing in his mind for the thousandth time during the past year what he might have done differently not to have lost her loving embrace. As the realization had once again dawned on him that his hope of ever winning her affection had been crazy from the start—if for no other reason than their having been born so far apart in time—he had felt his will to live weakening, and when finally during the wee hours of the morning he had fallen into a deeper sleep, he had dreamed, not of some Wagnerian *Liebestod* whereby he and Liliana, locked arm in arm, might have transcended time's cruel walls by throwing themselves together off some romantic alpine cliff, but instead, to the accompaniment of Schopenhauerian howls of laughter, of a lonely plunge all by himself into an apocalyptic black hole out of which no being could ever hope to crawl in one piece.

"Good morning, Professor Altmann," Ms. Steele uttered with all the pathos of a nurse welcoming a patient whom she knows is about to be informed by his physician of a terminal illness, reinforcing Altmann's suspicion that notwithstanding earlier disclaimers, she was well aware of everything happening in the president's office. "Did you get a good night's sleep?" she added in a tone that Altmann interpreted to be less than sincere or even a bit sarcastic.

"As a matter of fact, I didn't," Altmann muttered without any attempt to explain himself. "Is the president in yet?"

"No, he just called and said that he is running a few minutes late, but would be here shortly. So you might as well take a seat."

Altmann looked around the waiting room at its collection of furniture, most of which, except for two solid oak armchairs, appeared to have been placed there for no other reason than to highlight BCC's hundred years of academic life— a 19th century, leather-covered, walnut-rimmed writing table, two Victorian-styled, high-backed dining-chairs from the 1930s with their original floral patterns barely visible, an empty, redwood bookcase with glass doors covering every shelf, and most impressively, a Chippendale love-seat which, according to the small plaque attached to its back, had once belonged to BCC's first president and his beloved spouse, but across which a silken cord had now been hung to keep any romantically inclined students or other visitors from actually sitting upon it. Selecting one of the oaken armchairs, Altmann seated himself and stared vacantly at the piece of antique furniture, oblivious to whatever passions its curvaceous lines might once have enveloped. He had almost dozed off when President Schmidt finally appeared on the scene, ten minutes after the appointed hour, and like his secretary before him, greeted Altmann with exaggerated solicitude.

"Ah, Professor Altmann!" the president exclaimed, upon entering the waiting room, shaking Altmann's hand, and ushering him through a door toward a chair in the presidential office. "Would you care for a cup of coffee?" he asked, and then, upon getting an affirmative answer, instructed Ms. Steele to fetch him one.

Altmann began sipping pensively at the coffee handed him, not a little suspicious of the dramatic shift from what he had expected would be the president's disposition.

"So, Maurice, how is your research work going?" Schmidt inquired.

"Slow," Altmann responded rather guardedly, in view of the fact that the president had never before shown an interest in any of his publications other than the *Academe* piece, and was known around campus to be of the opinion that for a community college such as their own, scholarly research was of little value.

"Hard to find enough time, I guess, huh?"

"Having to teach fifteen hours doesn't help," Altmann mumbled.

The reduction of teaching loads had long been a bone of contention between Schmidt and BCC's faculty, but the president had no intention of debating the issue, and inquired instead about the professor's health.

"I'm doing alright," Altmann replied hesitantly, "a few aches and pains now and then, but nothing serious." Even if he had been dying of cancer, Altmann would never have told the president, in whose excessively solicitous tone of voice he had detected a sinister note.

"Getting enough sleep?"

"I have a bad night occasionally, but generally get five, six hours."

"That's not much, is it?"

"It's enough for me."

"You live alone, don't you, Maurice?"

"Yeah, I do. Why do you ask?

"Oh, I was just thinking, that you must get very lonely on occasion, especially doing all that research work. Ever think about getting married?"

"At my age?," Altmann replied with a self-effacing smirk, still suspicious about where all the president's paternalistic blather was leading.

"What are you, sixty-one, sixty-two?"

"Sixty-two," Altmann acknowledged reluctantly.

"That's not so old; lots of folks have discovered connubial bliss later than that. BCC's first president, you know, was already sixty-five when he first got married, and to a woman only half his age at that."

"That was in the 1890s," Altmann scoffed, fearing that Schmidt had somehow gotten wind of his own earlier involvement with Liliana, and not wanting to be lured into confessing anything more about the relationship.

"A different time, to be sure, but still the same human nature," Schmidt opined.

"Having been married for thirty years, I'm not an expert on the subject, but I would guess that living alone is no less stressful now than it was back then, and the latest studies would indicate, I think, that all that stress can greatly reduce one's life expectancy."

"You may be right," Altmann replied impatiently, "but may I ask what all this has to do with me? Surely you didn't summon me here for marriage counseling, did you?"

"Well, it's probably none of my business," Schmidt drawled, "but since getting this report yesterday, I've been thinking that had you been married, perhaps you wouldn't have been so vulnerable to this kind of stuff."

"What report is that?" Altmann asked with increased agitation. "Stuff? What stuff?"

"All that *porn* our technicians found on your computer last week," the president replied emphatically. "One of them informed me yesterday that while transferring your files onto a larger disk as you had requested, he and his assistant discovered all kind of obscene material."

"Like what?" Altmann mumbled defensively; "They didn't find any child pornography or even any of the hardcore adult stuff, did they? Just some photos of naked women."

"*Some* photos?" Schmidt exclaimed. "More like thousands of them, wasn't it?"

"Maybe so . . . but there's no law against that, is there?"

"No law, but certainly our college policy. Have you ever read our policy on computer use, Professor Altmann!?"

The presidential shift from the personal to a more formal address did not escape Altmann's notice, and he suspected anew that the paternalistic solicitude the president had earlier shown had been nothing but a guise for setting his rebellious professor up for deeper embarrassment when finally confronted with the evidence against him. "I perused it once or twice," Altmann asserted.

"And do you remember reading that the introduction of any obscene material on any school computer is strictly prohibited?"

"I can't say that I do."

"Well, perhaps you should have, for I can assure you that's what it states, and everyone I've talked to about this matter, including our college attorney, is of the view that you are in clear violation of the policy," the president declared, having dropped any pretense of concern about the lonely life that might have prompted Professor Altmann to indulge his voyeuristic tastes, and relapsing into his usual stentorian tones.

"It was on my own computer, wasn't it?" Altmann protested.

"Was it really? The computer was in your home, but according to my information, it was BCC property, and operating off a BCC modem. Isn't that correct?"

"I guess so, but did that give the technicians the right to snoop into my files and tell you what they'd seen?"

"They weren't snooping, Altmann! They were simply doing their job, and our attorney tells me there was nothing whatever improper or invasive about their actions."

"What about my right to *privacy?* Doesn't the policy also say that reading another user's files is the same as 'breaking and entering'?"

"It does, but that refers only to unauthorized intrusions, and is certainly no license for improper use; our attorney also tells me that Illinois and federal law clearly mitigate the right to privacy by allowing administrators to monitor their computer systems for any abuse by employees."

"Okay then, so you've caught me perusing a little soft porn. It never dawned on me that the college might actually try to dictate what a sixty-two year old man can or cannot watch in his home. But if it's that big of a deal to all of you, I guess I'll have to switch over from the college modem to a line of my own!"

"Well, it won't be quite that simple," the president responded, obviously relishing Altmann's unease, and intent upon not letting him slip so easily out of the mess he had gotten himself into.

"What do you mean?" Altmann asked, suspecting full well what Schmidt had in mind. Publishing the *Academe* piece had been a gutsy thing to do, and he had known all along that the president would be looking for any opportunity to strike back. The frustration of his desire for Liliana, however, had left him in a reckless state of mind, and far from deterring him from publishing exactly what he was thinking, the threat of retaliation had only fanned the flames of his masochistic mood. Even if he had remembered what the school's policy on computer use was, the danger of getting caught and possibly having his career wrecked right on the eve of retirement, would probably have only made his attraction to the world of cybersmut all the more irresistible. It was as though his passion for Liliana had been seeking its own destruction.

"What I mean," the president began expounding, "is that it's too late to be thinking simply of stopping your improper use of our system. That is to be taken for granted, since our policy states that anyone abusing computing privileges will immediately have them revoked. But the policy also calls for abusers to be disciplined. And after conferring with my VPs and the attorney, I have decided that it will be in the best interest of the school that you resign your chairmanship of the philosophy department." The president paused to watch his chief antagonist among the BCC faculty registering the shock of being stripped of half his professional identity. When none seemed to be forthcoming, he continued: "Frankly, Altmann, it amazes me that after all this school has done for you, you have shown so little concern for its public image, or for that matter, your own reputation. What do you think people in town are going to be saying if they find out that the chairman of its philosophy department has been using taxpayers' dollars to wallow in pornography?"

"Who, apart from you and your staff, knows about it?" Altmann queried defiantly.

"Probably no one at this point, and on that account I am willing to let you announce that you are resigning for reasons of poor health. But let me warn you. It is nigh impossible to keep anything like this from leaking out, and if it does, as I fully expect it will, I will have no choice but to explain to the public that your behavior is altogether out of line with what this college is all about. There is no way that we can stand by and let you sully the good reputation we have all worked so long to build up in the eyes of our fellow citizens. Furthermore, one of the technicians tells me that his wife is already complaining about the possibility of her daughter having to take an ethics course from you next semester, and when this story hits the headlines—as it no doubt will sooner or later—I suspect there will be others expressing similar concerns. And I must say that it escapes my comprehension how you ever thought that you were fit to teach our students about virtue when you yourself were acting so shamelessly."

"It was never my impression that I had been hired to *preach*," Altmann protested. "Isn't that the chaplain's job?"

"Nobody's saying you were supposed to be preaching, Altmann, but surely it was part of your job to encourage students to put into practice what you were teaching them, and wouldn't the setting of a good example be essential to such a task? In any event, before I allow you to continue in the classroom I'm going to require that you get some psychological counseling. From what the technicians have told me, there must have been tons of that trash in your files, which leads me to believe that you must have become addicted to the stuff, and won't be able to break the habit on your own. So, if you're willing to seek the help you need, I'll grant you an immediate leave of absence from your teaching duties and give you till next Fall to straighten up."

Looking at the disgruntled professor before him, and not detecting any sign of gratitude for what he had thought was a rather merciful gesture on his part, Schmidt added icily, "But if you can't bring yourself to do at least that much for yourself and the students you are supposed to be serving, you may as well consider yourself fired! So, which will it be? It's your choice."

"I'll need some time to think about it?"

"What's there to think about?" Schmidt asked incredulously."I'm offering you a second chance; you spurn it, and your career and reputation are down the drain; is that what you want?"

"Give me a day," Altmann insisted.

"Well, okay then, but come tomorrow morning you'd better have made up your mind, for if by then you are not ready to announce to your colleagues in the philosophy department your leave of absence as a professor and your resignation as their chair, I will be telling them every gory detail about our decision to have you fired. *Verstehen Sie?!*"

Schmidt was notorious around the BCC campus for relapsing into his native tongue anytime his pride had been piqued. Long used to it, Altmann let the president's tough talk blow past him like a waft of bad breath. Muffling a gut reaction to laugh in the president's face, he nodded his head in acknowledgment of the conditions laid down, picked himself up from his chair, and exited the office without another word.

31

"My doctor tells me that I need to get out of here for a while," Professor Altmann announced to his surprised colleagues from the philosophy department. For better than half of the previous night he had lain awake wrestling with the options offered him by the college president. Around two in the morning he thought he had finally reached a decision to stand up to Schmidt and take his chances at being fired, reckoning that, notwithstanding the virtual collapse of Nasdaq and the loss of no small part of his investment funds, he didn't really need the job anyway. So, why bother to go on, making believe that he still had a meaningful role to play in the family of man? Better to put an end to the charade and let the devil have his due! He had wagered on Liliana keeping his soul alive, but with her now gone, it was as good as dead, and he might just as well abandon himself to the world of porn and let it go to hell on a binge of euphoric lust. But later that night, toward the dawn of day, he had been visited in a dream by none other than the lovely Liliana. Attired as he had often seen her before in the white tee-shirt, blue jeans, and leather sandals that always made her look even younger than she actually was, she had caught up with him as he was walking dejectedly toward the exit gate of some imaginary university campus his subconscious mind had conjured up.

"Mauritio, wait up! It's me, Liliana! Why the long face?," she had crooned in that warm and spirited way that had always melted his heart in earlier times, and all the more so when, as now again, she would flash her angelic smile.

"I can't live without you and am on my way to hell!" he had muttered in his sleep.

"Oh Mauritio, Mauritio," she had gently chided him, "you are so *melodramatic!* Does my friendship mean so little to you?"

At that moment a garbage truck making a pickup at the junior high a block from Altmann's house had banged a metal container against its bed, waking up half the neighborhood, and ending before it had hardly gotten started the dream of the conversation he had been having with Liliana. But he had heard enough to make him think twice about the decision he had reached earlier in the night. And within an hour he had been on the phone to Schmidt, informing the president that after conferring with his doctor he would be at the ten o'clock philosophy department meeting to announce his resignation and leave of absence.

"I've tried to cover it up," Altmann continued, "but as some of you may have detected anyway, I have been suffering depression for several months and, quite frankly, have not been coping with it very well of late. I have therefore decided to follow my doctor's advice both to resign as department chair and to take a temporary leave of absence from my teaching position." In a release to the school's student newspaper, Altmann stated only that "after much thought I have decided for personal and professional reasons to relinquish some of my responsibilities."

Coming as it did in the middle of Fall semester mid-term exams, Professor Altmann's resignation immediately raised suspicions across the BCC campus. Some faculty claimed to have noticed that Altmann had not been himself in recent weeks, and seemed disposed toward accepting his public explanation. But most were not. Students also were skeptical that the popular, long-time professor would ever have stepped down of his own free will midway through the semester. Rumors were rampant among both faculty and students about what had actually happened to force his sudden departure.

Within days, the Brookfield *Tribune* treated them and all its readers to the real story: "ALTMANN'S OUSTER LINKED TO PORN," the banner headline of its October 13, 1998, edition read. There followed a detailed account of what had gotten the professor into the trouble he was in, how the president had handled the matter, and what Altmann's colleagues and students thought of what he had done and how he had been treated. "Had Altmann been chair of the physics department," one faculty member was quoted as saying, "it might not have mattered all that much; but philosophy? That's a different story; they're supposed to be teaching 'values,' for god's sake!" But most of the comments reported were more sympathetic to the beleaguered professor, challenging the right of the college officials to intrude upon Altmann's privacy or to act as though they owned his whole life. Having long ago canceled his subscription to the local paper, Altmann himself tried ignoring what others were saying about his past behavior, and devoted his time instead plotting the moves he would need to make next to break out of what Liliana had labeled the 'melodrama' of his self-destructive, masochistic attempt to cope with the frustration of erotic desire.

32

"Paul! This is Maurice . . . say, I was wondering if you might have some time to join me for lunch. I've got something I'd like to talk to you about."

"Sure. Where would you like to meet?" Professor Mason replied. As BCC's psychology professor for the past twenty years, he had developed a good working relation with his colleague in the philosophy department, and after hearing of the latter's recent troubles welcomed the chance to have a word with him.

"How about Donario's?" Although its cusine was nothing special, and its decor at least thirty years behind the latest trends, Donario's had long been the favorite meeting place of the two professors, mainly because its booths were isolated enough to allow for vigorous conversation without the risk of being overheard by anyone.

"Fine. What time?"

"Eleven o'clock?"

"See you there."

Upon arriving at the restaurant, Altmann found his colleague already seated at a booth. "Thanks for coming, Paul," he stated rather humbly. Still reeling from the shock of having had his private life exposed in the local newspapers the week before, he was grateful that his fellow professor was not too embarrassed to meet him in public.

"No problem," Mason replied. "I was rather hoping you would call."

"I guess you read the reports in the paper?"

"Yeah, I did, and I think it's a damn shame the way the information was released."

"Needless to say, I wasn't very happy about it either!" Altmann replied, while pointing to his colleague's mug of beer and motioning for the waitress to bring him one also. "But I guess there's no one to blame but myself for the mess I'm in, and I regret any embarrassment I've caused you and other of my friends."

"No need to worry about that," Mason responded. "I talked to a few of them since the story broke, and their only concern seemed to be how they could help you get through this in one piece. Incidentally, how's Liliana taking the news?" Mason had been the only colleague with whom Altmann had confided about his infatuation with the younger woman, but had told him nothing about the disappointment he had experienced earlier in the summer.

"I doubt if she knows about it," Altmann mumbled.

"You haven't told her?"

"No . . . in fact I haven't talked to her for close to five months. I think she's either mad at me, or . . ."

"Why would she be mad at you?"

"Well, I never told you about this, but last May I went out to Boston to visit her, thinking that because of the birthday presents she had sent me back in February, our relationship just might have some chance of becoming a bit more. . . well, you know . . . a little more romantic."

"Must have been some birthday present!" Mason joked.

"Oh, it was just some rather erotic poems and a card that were probably meant by Liliana only to tease me, but . . . well, anyway, I guess I was indulging in a bit of wishful thinking, but I thought that she might be trying to tell me something. So, like a fool I suppose, I wrote back to her, hinting at my own affection for her, and including a photo of myself at the age of twenty-four along with a piece of erotic prose that I had been working on. Although she ignored all of this in her reply, she did invite me to come out to Boston for a visit after she would return from a trip to Cuba with a girlfriend. I drove out there in May, and had planned to stay the whole weekend in hopes of finding a little . . . well, I know this sounds ridiculous . . . but, well, I was feeling especially lonely, and hoped that maybe Liliana and I could get a little closer than we had earlier been by just being friends." Altmann paused to take a sip of his Bud Lite.

"So, how did it go?" Mason prompted.

"Not very well!" Altmann murmured. "She had invited me to stay at her one-bedroom apartment. But when I got there, I discovered that she also had a foreign student living with her, thereby reducing next to nil any chance of me and her enjoying any privacy together. Then during the meal that evening, she informed me that while on her trip to Cuba she had become enamored of a young man named Sergio, who would soon be coming to the States on UN business, and with whom she would want to be spending as much time as possible. Well, needless to say, I was rather disappointed. Deep down, I knew I had no reason to be upset or even surprised, and I tried being as understanding as possible. But after tossing and turning the whole night through in the bed she offered me, while she herself slept on the living-room davon and her foreign guest in a sleeping bag on the dining-room floor, I got up the next morning and promptly announced rather gruffly that I would be leaving shortly. I did not volunteer, and she did not ask for an explanation. But from the sad look on her face, I suspected that she knew very well what I was thinking, and if it did not anger her, it probably did disappoint her."

"Why would *she* be angry or disappointed? Weren't you the one getting hurt?"

"Because I think it was the first time she ever doubted our friendship. I suspect that my surly attitude that morning made her think that perhaps I had been out to use her from the very start."

"Had you?"

"Not really. I know that from the first minute I set eyes on her, I was intoxicated by her physical beauty," Altmann observed, after pausing to take another sip of his beer. "And I can't deny fantasizing," he added, "about someday making love to her. But I was attracted as much by her intelligence and warm personality as by anything else. We had a lot of common interests, and found it easy to talk to each other. Just being with her was always so exciting. Not infrequently, after a round of conversation, going for a walk, or riding for hours on end with her in the car, I would feel so happy I could hardly resist taking her in my arms. And now that I think about it, perhaps that's all I was really looking for in the first place. Maybe I'm just the last of the troubadours!"

"A troubadour?!" Mason queried skeptically.

"Yeah, the *aged* troubadour!" Altmann replied with a bit of a chuckle.

"Well, I get the 'aged' part," Mason joshed, "but why the 'troubadour'? I've never known you to write any songs."

"Had you come to my reading last summer," Altmann chided, "you might have noticed that I *have* made a little music of late. But anyway, I wasn't really thinking of the troubadours' songwriting so much as their notion of pure love."

"Pure love?"

"Right!"

"Never heard of it!," Mason confessed.

"Well, I hadn't either until some years ago when, while doing a study of early medieval literature, I came across a couple of lyrical pieces by the first troubadours. They were all waxing poetic about how in love that is 'pure,' the lover longs to see his beloved's naked body, to kiss, touch, and embrace it, but without any intention of ever engaging in sexual intercourse."

"Sort of like Tantrism, huh?"

"There is some superficial similarity. But the troubadours had no interest in the kind of mystical illumination of *sunyata* that might result from using passion to exhaust passion. They weren't trying to purge themselves of desire; theirs was an attempt to idealize it."

"Sounds rather Platonic."

"It does, and in fact, is based to some extent upon the example of Socrates himself, who, as you may recall from your reading of the *Symposium,* seemed infatuated by the beauty of several fine young men, like Alcibiades, with whom he even slept on one occasion, but, much to the chagrin and amazement of the young man, without ever going beyond a warm embrace to show his affection. The troubadours, of course, had no access to the Platonic dialogues, but they might have read Arab Neoplatonists, like Avicenna and Ibn Hazm, who also championed the notion of pure love. I just happen to be reading Avicenna's *Treatise on Love* again. Want to hear what he has to say?"

"Yeah, sure; lay it on me."

Reaching into a satchel of books he had brought with him, Altmann pulled out a Puffin paperback, and turning to a page he had marked earlier, began reading: 'Upon encountering a beautiful human being, man's animal soul first experiences an urge to embrace that person's form, then secondly to kiss it, and thirdly to have sexual intercourse with it' . . . ."

"Spoken like a true man!" Mason interjected, before Altmann could finish reading the passage.

"No, no! Let me finish. He's not at all trying to justify the typical male's lust for erotic pleasure. Quite the contrary. Genuine love for the beautiful form, he says, will be devoid of any desire for sexual possession. He recognizes that engaging in sexual intercourse can easily destroy a loving relationship. But he considers the 'urge' to embrace and kiss the beautiful form to be in a different category altogether, and is nothing to be ashamed of, but rather the mark of 'a man of nobility and refinement.' Let me read more of what he has to say: 'As for embracing and kissing, the purpose in them is to come near to one another and to become united. The soul of the lover desires to reach the object of his love with his senses of touch and sight, and thus he delights in embracing it. And he longs to have the very essence of his soul-faculty, his heart, mingle with that of the object of his love, and thus he desires to kiss it.' All this occurs, he says in another passage, through the cooperation of man's animal and rational souls, whereby the physical beauty of the beloved reminds the lover of absolute beauty or goodness in itself."

"So, that's what the troubadours were after, the contemplation of absolute beauty?"

"Yes, but not exactly in the same sense as Plato and his followers had in mind. The troubadours had no interest in absolute beauty as some abstract ideal that lay beyond the object of their love. In their view, the beloved is herself the absolute embodiment of beauty. Appreciation of her physical beauty, therefore, was not just a means to, or step toward, some higher form of spiritual love; it was an end in itself, giving rise, as one of them—a poet named Bernart de Ventadorn — described it, to 'an unspeakable joy!'"

"Joy? Out of such frustration?"

"Yeah. In his view, the spiritual energy derived from stopping short of sexual intercourse intensifies the poetic idealization of the beloved and replaces the note of sadness that inevitably accompanies coitus with the ecstacy of basking in the beloved's eternal beauty."

"I don't know," Mason mumbled, "sounds rather unnatural to me. Do you really think you or anybody else could play with fire like that and not get burned?"

"Probably not, if it's just a matter of self-control. But I'm not sure that's what they had in mind. From my reading of their lyrics I didn't get the impression that the troubadours were talking about erotic desire being controlled by the human will. What they meant, I suspect, was that as the senses of the lover become increasingly enraptured through seeing, kissing, touching, and embracing the beloved's beautiful body, his imagination is fired to the point of inhibiting the natural aim of the sexual impulse and re-directing it toward a spiritual goal of writing songs that will further celebrate the beloved's beauty."

"Is that any different from what Freud meant by sublimation?"

"Seems to me it is. Both have in mind the re-channeling of sexual energy into poetic creativity, but with the troubadours the contemplation of physical beauty of the beloved remains much more closely connected with the creative act, both as its subject and object, than in the case of Freudian sublimation."

"So you think that's the kind of love you had for Liliana?"

"Certainly not all of the time, for I'm sure there were moments when I was feeling nothing but raw lust. I don't know. But I think I can honestly say that there were also times when my desire to look at her and hold her in my arms was rather pure."

"And you really think the joy you found thereby exceeded any you might have experienced by having sexual intercourse with her?"

"The troubadours would have thought so!"

"And is the 'last of the troubadours' still of the same opinion?"

"Well, I haven't really thought about it all that much until rather recently, but yeah, I think I am."

"How can you know if you've never had sexual intercourse with her, or for that matter . . . ?"

"With anyone else?" Altmann proffered, completing the sentence his friend had thought better of finishing. "Well, that's a good point, and I'll probably go to my grave never knowing for sure. But I do know I've had some moments of sheer delight being with Liliana. Blinded by my occasional lust, I probably didn't realize at the time how happy I was. But now as I look back on such moments, it's hard to imagine how I could have been any happier."

"And you're thinking that maybe you can recapture some of those moments in the future?" Mason asked.

"The thought has crossed my mind," Altmann confessed, "assuming, of course, that she might ever be free again, and want to revive our friendship."

"I don't see why that should be so impossible."

"Well, I hope you're right, but any chance of that happening will certainly require getting myself out of the mess I'm presently in."

"Anything I can do to help?" Mason asked, after pausing a moment to let the waitress take their order of the luncheon special of salad and lasagna.

"Well, as you probably read in the paper, President Schmidt has conditioned my return to the classroom on getting some professional counseling. At my age, I could, of course, just retire and tell them to get lost, but I'd hate to go out on such a sour note. Furthermore, as I said before, I need to get myself back in shape if I'm ever going to have any chance with Liliana. So, I guess I'll try to do what he says. That's why I wanted to talk to you. Know any good psychiatrists?"

"Are you sure that's what you need? If your only problem is that you now and then view a little porn, I doubt that you need a psychiatrist."

"It's more than 'a little'; I'm afraid I may have become hooked on the stuff."

"Well, in that case, you might want to consider Sex Addicts Anonymous; I think they have a chapter up in Springfield," Mason replied rather prosaically, while trying to ignore the bewilderment he was feeling about how a fixation on porn could ever have coexisted with a love that is pure.

"Is that anything like Alchoholics Anonymous?"

"Yeah, they've adapted the AA Twelve Step approach to curing sexual addiction."

"Humm-m, I don't know if I'm ready for that. It involves a lot of religion, doesn't it?"

"Right. The steps are all based upon the assumption that one is powerless to help oneself and that the only solution is to turn one's life and will over to God. You're Roman Catholic, aren't you?"

"I was, until I started reading a lot of Nietzsche several years ago. Nietzsche, as you know, wanted to replace the god whom he declared dead with a passionate humanity in control of its own impulses."

"But isn't the problem with sexual addiction precisely the loss of control over one's passions?"

"Here's your lasagna, boys!" the middle-aged, red-headed waitress interjected.

"Thanks, Loretta," they both replied, pushing their salad bowls immediately aside to make room for the steaming hot dishes, and digging right in.

"Right," Altmann conceded to his colleague upon returning to the discussion at hand, "and Nietzsche himself would no doubt have despised my current weakness, but would still have insisted upon my regaining control through the strength of my own will, rather than waiting for some *Deus ex machina* to pick me up."

"And I would agree with him were the God of Christianity nothing more than the divine troubleshooter Nietzsche made him out to be, and not without some reason, given the way a lot of Christians in the past were inclined to lean on God to solve all their problems. But you ought to read Dietrich Bonhoeffer someday."

"I have."

"The Letters and Papers from Prison?"

"Yeah."

"Well, you'll remember then how Bonhoeffer describes the Christian God as a *Deus Otiosus,* or in other words, a God who, in order to get mankind to stand on its own two feet, reveals himself in the crucified Christ as useless, and one, therefore, whom humans can only enjoy, but never use."

"Yes, I do remember that line of thought, and was really excited about it when I first read it ten years ago. Nietzsche himself would probably have been open to it. But it certainly wasn't what he was hearing from the nineteenth century Christianity he was rebelling against, and I can't say that I've ever found many Roman Catholics thinking along such lines—certainly not the present pope and his episcopal legions. Nor, I suspect, would the AA crowd have a clue of what Bonhoeffer was talking about."

"In theory, perhaps not; but in practice, I daresay they probably come rather close to what he had in mind."

"How so?"

"Well, by inviting its practitioners to surrender their wills to God, AA doesn't have in mind to excuse them from making every effort to help themselves; in fact, it is precisely their faith in God that seems to goad them toward whatever other steps they need to take to recover, including psychological counseling. In any event, there's no reason why you couldn't interpret the AA program of surrender to the divine will along Bonhoefferian lines, and let your faith strengthen your resolve to turn your life around by seeking whatever psychotherapy you think you might need."

"Well, that could be. But in my present mood, I think I'd rather keep the two more separate. Any alternatives?"

Reluctant to dismiss so readily the importance of religion in the therapeutic process or to recommend any psychiatrist relying solely on strictly Freudian psychoanalysis, Mason tried recalling the name of the elderly man he had met in St. Louis the previous summer at the annual APA meeting. During a break in one of the sessions, the two of them had struck up a conversation, and Mason had learned that fifty years earlier the man had studied at the University of Chicago under the renowned Adolf Meyer, and ever since had been trying to inculcate into his own psychiatric practice the principles of psychobiology advocated by his Swiss mentor. Upon returning from the APA meeting, Mason had done some research to refresh his memory of Meyer's theory, and had been pleased to learn anew of the latter's insistence that the patient be studied as a *whole,* and that to do so, *all* of the patient's past life had to be scrutinized, and not merely, as Freud had thought, unresolved conflicts of early childhood. Upon further reflection it had dawned on him that it was probably Meyer, more than anyone else, who had given American psychotherapy its eclectic orientation, and encouraged the likes of Albert Ellis, Carl Rogers, Abraham Maslow, B.F. Skinner, or even Erik Erikson and other neo-Freudians, to pursue more person-centered therapeutic work from a variety of behavioral, humanistic, cognitive, and existential perspectives. "There's this psychiatrist out in St. Louis," Mason mumbled pensively, "who might be just the man you are looking for. I met him last summer at the APA convention, and was really impressed. He's about seventy-five, but is as lucid as an owl, and is still very active. I've got his name written down somewhere back home, and will give you a call when I find it."

"I would appreciate that, Paul. It might be especially helpful to have someone older than myself, and there aren't many such fellows around anymore!" Leaning back in his chair, Altmann motioned for the waitress, and when she finally found time to get back to their table, he asked her to put both dinners on his own check.

"You needn't to have done that," Mason stated as he rose from his chair and offered his friend a parting handshake, "but thanks. I'll be calling you soon. So, hang in there. We're all pulling for you."

"I'll try," Altmann promised.

33

"Welcome to St. Louis, Professor! Have you ever been to this metropolis before?" Dr. Stein inquired as Altmann hesitantly entered the spacious office, and took the seat offered him across from the huge walnut-wood desk behind which the elderly psychiatrist himself was seated.

"Not recently," Altmann replied. "But back in my youth I was an avid fan of the Cardinals and would occasionally make the trip out here to see them play. In fact, until I turned about sixteen and discovered that I was too tall to any longer catch a grounder, I had always dreamed of one day playing shortstop for them."

"*C'est la Vie!* I guess at some point we have all had to accept the hand that fate has dealt us! So, what brings you here this time? I recall from our telephone conversation that you were recommended to me by a friend I made at last summer's APA convention, but unless my senility is playing tricks on me again, I don't think you mentioned exactly what your problem is."

"You're right, I didn't; and let me thank you first for being willing to see me on such short notice and with so little information on which to make a judgment."

"*Nichts zu danken!*" Dr. Stein replied, lapsing jovially into his mentor's native tongue, which he himself had had to learn upon entering the field originally dominated by the likes of Breuer, Freud, Adler, Jung, and other German-speaking scientists. "I was only too happy to reciprocate for the kindness shown me at last summer's convention by Dr. Mason. You would think that a gathering of psychologists would be about the last place in the world to encounter any prejudice against an older man. But until Dr. Mason came along at one of our meetings and

175

struck up a conversation with me, I was beginning to feel like a *persona non grata*. Most of the younger crowd didn't seem to think or care that I was still alive . . . but anyway, back to your problem; what is it that's bothering you?"

"Well, I seem to be addicted to porn," Altmann confessed, while diverting his eyes to avoid the psychiatrist's warm, but penetrating stare, and surveying instead the shelves of books lining the office walls except where here and there a landscape painting or two had been hung. "About a year and a half ago, at a time in my life when I was about to throw in the towel, I happened to meet a lovely woman about half my age who expressed some interest in having a relationship. Probably all she had had in mind was a friendship based upon our mutual interest in philosophy and literature. But attracted by her exceptional beauty, I began entertaining the hope of something more romantic. My erotic desire had been stirred as never before by the encounter with her, and excited still more by an accidental trek into the world of cyberporn, I found myself fantasizing ever more about the possibility of making love to her. When that never happened, and she informed me back in May that she had fallen in love with another man, I surrendered to the lure of Internet pornography to the point where I now think that I am addicted to the stuff. It has already gotten me fired from my administrative position, and will cost me my teaching job also unless I can change my behavior."

"I see," said the doctor in a gentle, non-judgmental voice. "I'm not so sure that what you are experiencing should be called an addiction in the strict sense of that word, but it certainly is problematic, and probably symptomatic of a deeper neurosis. Whatever we call it, it will require a lot of work on both our parts to find a cure. As you may know, my therapeutic method is known as psychobiology, because in its concern about the whole person, it has as one prerequisite thorough and detailed physical and mental examinations of the patient. So, you will first have to go through a lot of testing. Are you willing to do that?"

"Yes, sure, if it's the only way you can get the information you need."

"Well, it's not the only way, but it is an essential component of my approach. After all the testing is done, we will then have to do a lot of talking. There is much disagreement among the various schools of psychiatry about what therapists and their patients should be talking about, or about how the talk should be conducted, but few would challenge the importance attached early on by Freud to the curative value of the patient's talking. And I am certainly not one of them. At some point, with my help, you will be expected to tell me the story of your whole life, and especially more of the details about the encounter with the younger woman you mentioned earlier. Some of my patients have found it difficult to be so open and talkative. But I guess with your philosophical background, and love of dialogue, that won't be any problem, right? Or did you buy into Walter Benjamin's depiction of Socrates as exploiting the erotic dimension of the *dialektike* only to hound his youthful disciples for answers he already knew?"

Surprised at the doctor's familiarity with Benjamin's esoteric critique of the Socratic method, Altmann explained that Benjamin had written his essay on the ancient Greek while he was still a very young man and had probably based it on a misinterpretation of comments by Nietzsche. "But to answer your first question," he added, "no, I won't have any problem talking. It's a good way to get to know oneself, I guess, and that's our motto, isn't it: *Gnothi seauton!*"

"Good," Dr. Stein responded, acknowledging his familiarity with the motto of ancient Greek philosophy with a warm smile. "My Freudian friends like to have these talking sessions every day until a cure is found, but I've always thought that once a week suffices. So, after you've had all the aforementioned tests, we'll get started talking."

"Where's your couch?" Altmann asked, after looking around the office and seeing nothing approximating the proverbial analytical-bed.

"Oh, that was just Freud's way of covering his own shyness, and helped keep the therapist in a passive role. I prefer to be more active. Our talks will be *tête-à-tête.*"

34

"You seem to have an exceptionally low tolerance for pain," Dr. Stein stated. After several months of preliminary probing of Altmann's motives for consultation, his medical and family history, and a long series of somatic and neurological examinations—during which it was discovered that his PSA had jumped to an ominous 4.6, requiring a biopsy that showed no signs of prostate cancer yet—the psychotherapist was finally getting around to discussing with his patient what he thought was at the heart of the professor's problem and how best it could be cured.

"It's an occupational hazard," Altmann muttered. "Shakespeare, you know, once wrote that he had never met a philosopher yet who could tolerate a toothache!"

"Well, combined with what would also seem to be your insatiable appetite for pleasure, that makes you very vulnerable to addictive behavior," Dr. Stein replied, after dutifully chuckling at his patient's self-effacing humor.

"So, you think I am in fact addicted to that porn stuff?"

"Not so much to the porn itself, as to the pleasurable euphoria you derive therefrom. Your voyeuristic recourse to the pornographic material may be just one of the several paths you have been taking in recent years while trying to achieve pleasurable results."

"Like chasing after Liliana, you mean?"

"Perhaps; it depends on how you conceived of your relationship to her. In both Goethe's and Guonod's *Faust,* which I recall you saying you have read and seen, Faust is initially enamored of Margaret by nothing more than a vision of the young girl's beautiful body. Can you imagine a man falling in love with a woman on the basis of nothing more than her picture?"

"Not really," Altmann conceded.

"Neither can I. And I suspect that the relation of Faust to Margaret was initially little more than a desperate pursuit of pleasure, and that goes for Marlowe's Faust too, since he seemed in the end to be satisfied by nothing more than a kiss from the imaginary Helen of Troy. So, what about your own relation to Liliana? Was it any different from that of Faust to the Helena-look-alike, Margaret? Were you really in love with her, or merely intoxicated by the beauty of her body? Would you have settled for a mere *nuit de plaisirs?*"

Altmann winced, knowing full well that although it had been Liliana's lively spirit and brilliance as much as her physical beauty that had initially captivated him, there was some truth in what the psychoanalyst was implying.

"Well, if in fact that is all you were after," Dr. Stein continued without waiting for a response from his patient, "then, I would have to say, that your relation with Liliana was actually little more than a variation on your addictive behavior. Instead of seeking a real relationship that might actually have eliminated the cause of your pain, you were probably trying simply to drown the latter out with the passing sensation of euphoria provided by the pleasure you got from fantasizing about having sexual intercourse with her, right?"

"Well, yeah. I know I lusted after Liliana, but I'm not sure that's all there was to it." Altmann replied, still entertaining the thought of being, perhaps, the 'last of the troubadours.'

"And I'm not saying that it was," Dr. Stein responded gently. "You may very well have had some other feelings for her too, or at least developed them along the way, but I think that if you are honest about it, you would have to admit that your initial attraction to Liliana involved a good deal of lust, and to that extent was just another pleasurable way you had of trying to escape the pain you were feeling. And much the same could probably be said about your frenzied research work over the past five years."

"So I'm also a workaholic?"

"Based on what you've told me, that's the impression I've gotten. Your primary motivation for writing all those books and articles seems to have been merely the immediate gratification you derived therefrom? It doesn't mean that other factors were not operative in your life, but it does imply that what was driving you to work so feverishly was the satisfaction you got from being able to rack up yet another publication every two years or so. My suspicion is that the quantity of your achievements mattered far more than their quality, and that is almost always a sign of an addictive personality."

"So, how exactly would you describe the pain that I was supposedly trying to avoid by working so hard or by being in such hot pursuit of Liliana?"

"Well, from what you've told me about your sleepless nights, constant fatigue, despondency, and especially your occasional thoughts of suicide, I can only conclude that you are suffering major depression."

"Hum-m," Altmann mumbled pensively. "And why am I so depressed?," he added, fully suspecting what the answer would be.

"Well, your loss of Liliana may have been a contributing factor. Any man would feel disappointed and hurt over such rejection. And my Freudian friends would no doubt be inclined to say that the feelings of guilt and self-loathing you are now experiencing in your depressed mood are simply the product of the anger you are turning against yourself instead of against the potential lover you have lost. They would say that it all goes back to the loss of, or rejection by, a parent in your childhood years. But I don't recall you telling me of any such loss or rejection, did you?"

"No, I actually felt rather loved by my parents, both of whom lived well into their nineties."

"Furthermore, you were feeling depressed long before you encountered Liliana, weren't you? In fact, as I implied earlier, your attraction to Liliana in the first place may have been precipitated by an attempt to medicate yourself against the pain you were feeling."

"Probably so. I know I was tempted to do myself in while driving to Urbana on the very day I first met her."

"And why was that? Why were you feeling so suicidal at that time?"

"Well . . . I hesitate to identify myself with Goethe's great hero, but like his Faust, I had fallen into a terribly agnostic mood. Remember the lines of his opening monologue, in which he bemoans the fact that after studying philosophy and theology for nigh on ten years, and 'pulling his students by their noses to and fro, up and down, across and about,' and being left with the impression that there was nothing that he or they could ever really know? Well, that was my own feeling back then and still now; I guess you could say that I am a burnt-out case."

"That could be," Dr. Stein replied. "Burnout generally strikes people like you who have worked hard but feel their efforts have borne little fruit. And it can certainly contribute to a feeling of depression. But tell me, why would the realization that reality is ultimately mysterious depress you? I can understand Goethe's Faust, or the many modern philosophers who share his initial assumption that all of nature's mysteries can be reduced to mere problems to be solved by the magic of scientific empirical observation, becoming frustrated and depressed by their inability to come up with a theory of everything. But wasn't it at the heart of the Romantic and Idealistic philosophies you were studying that neither philosophy nor science could ever exhaust the mystery of reality?"

"That's correct."

"Why then, if you shared their views, as I gather you did, would the lack of knowledge you claim to have experienced not have given rise to a sense of wonder rather than that of a bitter agnosticism? Wasn't it Socrates who said that the wonder which is the beginning and end of philosophy arises out of the experience of human ignorance?"

"Right. Humans can and do wonder, he said, precisely because unlike the gods and brute animals, who are incapable of wondering because they either know everything already or have no knowledge of what they do not know, they know that there is much about reality that is perplexing."

"So, if in fact all your study had left you deeper in the dark, it should only have enhanced your sense of wonder, right?"

"Assuming that it wasn't just an exercise in obscurantism . . . Yeah, it would seem so," Altmann conceded.

"And if it didn't? What would that tell you?"

"Well, probably that I had succumbed to the attitude of the very demystifiers opposed by the philosophers I was studying."

"Yes, I think that in a roundabout way that is probably what happened. I don't think that you consciously or purposely embraced their belief that through reason and empirical observation you could exhaust the mystery of reality, but from what you've told me, I do suspect that you were operating subconsciously under some such assumption. And in the process of trying to conceptualize the mystery of reality and to reduce it to an intelligible object, you lost your sense of wonder. Outside such a wondrous frame of reference, the lack of knowledge you experienced upon not being able to completely define reality naturally became a source of frustration. But even then, I suspect that it was not so much the agnostic mood, as it was the alienation brought on by your attempt to conceptualize everything, that caused you so much pain. The mysterious dimension of reality became for you a mere abstraction; it was no longer a reality to which you could relate in a personal way, or in which you could participate and find yourself as a part in the whole. As a result, you felt cut off from the reality you were studying. What you said and wrote became mere verbiage. For a while it had enough force to sustain your intellectual assent, but it no longer really moved you. There was no love involved, no real interest. You were living, but 'only partly,' as T. S. Eliot would put it. Needless to say, this did not do much to enhance your self-esteem, right?"

"Right," Altmann confessed. "While everyone was telling me that I had achieved so much, and I was getting praise and awards from every direction, I actually felt like I was falling apart. I remember reading once about how in his later years, the author of *The Great Gatsby*, Scott Fitzgerald, one day looked in a mirror and got the impression of seeing not only his face, but the whole of his life, all fragmented like a porcelain vase. Well, that's what I felt like. I couldn't any longer see how all the different pieces of my life fit together. I felt like I was losing my identity."

"And you no doubt found that very painful."

"Oh, terribly so. I recall a nightmare I once had of dying, and as Democritus had predicted, seeing all the atoms of my body disintegrating and being sucked into a big black hole. Although the thought of dying itself did not especially frighten me, the thought of falling apart before I was actually dead certainly did. But that is exactly what seemed to be happening to me during my waking hours, and I've never since been able to get the nightmare completely out of my mind."

"So, the question then, I guess, is how do we put Humpty Dumpty back together again?" Dr. Stein observed with a solicitous smile.

"And a sixty-three year old Humpty Dumpty at that!" Altmann joked. "You don't think it's too late to try?"

"It's never too late! You can't ever really die if you're not in one piece."

"So, what do you recommend?"

"Well, since you've shown no sign of any repressed childhood conflicts, catharsis-conducive analytical insight will not be of much help."

"*That's* a relief!" Altmann muttered half-jokingly, without a clue of what the psychiatrist was talking about.

"But I don't think that merely trying to modify your bad behavior through one or another aversive or punitive tactic will do the trick either," Dr. Stein continued, undisturbed by his client's rather cynical interjection. "Certainly, one of our goals will be to break the pattern of your addictive behavior and get you into behavior of a sort that will allow you to express your feelings in healthier, less self-destructive ways. To do that, however, we are going to have to work on changing the way you think. In most general terms that will mean trying to recapture the sense of wonder which your frenetic pursuit of philosophical speculation over the past ten years seems to have killed. More specifically, it will mean trying to change the image you have of yourself. From the story you've told me of your life, my impression is that you had a very idealized image of yourself in your earlier years when your sense of wonder had not yet been suffocated by excessive rationalization. By inclining you to see yourself again as a soulful creature, or, in other words, as a part of some larger, unfathomable whole, recapturing your sense of wonder will certainly take some of the wind out of the inflated image you have been cultivating in recent years. It will no doubt humble you. But, paradoxically, it will also remind you of the potential you have of becoming far more than a mere ego by enticing you to lose yourself in the infinite ocean of being around you. That will take a lot of the bite out of the frustration you are currently experiencing as a result of having tried so hard to actualize yourself along merely egoistical lines."

"And how do I resurrect a sense of wonder? One can't just get up one morning and decide to wonder, can one?"

"No. In the final analysis it can only be acquired and sustained through experience of that which is wonderful. You no doubt remember the story of how Percy Byssche Shelley broke out of his earlier rationalistic mind-set only after fleeing the scientific laboratory and losing himself amidst the majestic power and beauty of nature during a trip into the Alp mountains back in 1816. Prior to that excursion he had been convinced that nothing could be considered true unless it was verifiable by the senses or logically deducible therefrom."

"You're right."

"So, one way to recover your lost sense of wonder might be by trying to reconnect with nature. It worked for Shelley, and I dare say that if you just get out of your ivory tower for awhile and spend more time out in the woods or in the mountains, you will be far less inclined to idolize reason and far more likely to begin wondering again at yourself and the world around you. Such a back-to-nature move on your part, however, will also have to be complemented by a renewed effort to engage yourself more personally with other people. Persons, after all, are the most mysterious dimension of reality, and you'll never regain your sense of wonder without encountering the people around you as being more than mere objects of your pleasure."

"Including Liliana?"

"I wouldn't rule her out altogether."

"You don't think it's crazy for a man as old as I to fall in love with a woman half his age?"

"It's happened repeatedly throughout history. And I see no reason why love is any less able to transcend the limits of age than those of race, nationality, or religion. Had you approached Liliana along more personal lines from the start, as a real 'thou,' in other words, and not a mere 'it' about which you could fantasize, I dare say your relationship with her could have gone a long way toward relieving you of your loneliness and depression, even if it had never been consummated by sexual intercourse."

"Like the troubadours, you mean?" Altmann interjected with a boyish grin.

"The troubadours?" Dr. Stein inquired, obviously failing to see the connection.

"Yeah-h," Altmann replied rather hesitantly. "They had this idea of pure love, where lovers bind themselves to each other by modest looks, kisses and embraces without ever having sexual intercourse."

"That's not exactly what I had in mind," Dr. Stein asserted with a smile, "and I'd be rather skeptical about something like that ever working. It'd certainly take a couple of very special people."

"Like poets, perhaps?" Altmann suggested, not without a hint of hope that he and Liliana might qualify along such lines.

"Did Ovid or Goethe refrain from having sexual intercourse with the object of their love?"

"Probably not," Altmann admitted, "but unless they were consummate liars, troubadours like Bernart de Ventadorn or Guillaume of Aquitaine certainly seem from their writings to have done so."

"Perhaps they did, and far be from me to cast aspersions on them. Freud, I'm sure, would have dismissed their behavior as being neurotic, and ascetical-minded religious folks would probably label it hypocrisy, preferring even outright fornication or adultery. But I don't know . . . the Greeks of old had Calliope and other muses to inspire their poetry, and maybe the troubadours were on to something similar."

"They certainly thought they were," Altmann asserted. "By stopping short of sexual intercourse, they apparently had in mind to fire their poetic imaginations all the more."

"And you no doubt are thinking that some such relationship with Liliana might help to inspire your own creative imagination?"

"Well, it was certainly my fascination with her beauty that inspired me to write that first chapter of the novel I told you about."

"Then maybe you ought to do more of that," Dr. Stein suggested.

"I would except that I've been at a loss about where to take the story next, given the fact that I based it on our own relationship and am now so confused about where it can ever go."

"Perhaps you'd be better off trying your hand at painting again, since that would require less development, and give you a chance to focus more on capturing one or another moment in the life of the subject . . . you did say that you now and then painted in the past, didn't you?"

"Yeah, I did," Altmann acknowledged.

"Well, in any event, my dear professor, it's not just your relation with Liliana that you need to work on—which after all may not even be open to you in the future; you also need to re-engage others in general . . . and perhaps even *der ganz Andere!* Studies indicate that religious people suffer far less depression, and I've always been of the view myself that religion has great therapeutic value for those who can find the will to believe. I gather from what you've told me that you are not exactly disposed to believe in the existence of God at this point in your life, right?"

"It's not that I'm convinced there is no God, but that I can't bring myself either any longer to the conviction that there is."

"And it's certainly not my intention to try proving to you that there is one; even if I could convince you intellectually, I doubt it would solve your problem. I know the Greeks of old were of the view that recognition of an eternal divine plan could afford the victim of tragedy a catharsis of sorts, but I suspect that so long as your faith would consist of nothing more than intellectual assent, it would only provide your anger with another target. Unless you can experience God as a real Other, or, in other words, as a loving Person, the mere acknowledgment of his or her existence will give you little relief. But until you can rediscover the mystery of nature and human love, I doubt that you will ever again sense the presence of God either."

"That's interesting. Maybe it will all come together for me in the end if and when Liliana and I can ever head out for the mountains. I remember a friend of mine telling me a few years ago that he had his first real religious experience while climbing the tallest mountain in the world."

"Everest?"

"No, Alaska's Mt. McKinley. Everest, of course, is higher, but its peaks start on the Tibetan Plateau, at eight thousand feet, while Denali has a vertical rise of eighteen thousand feet. A short guy standing on a chair may be taller than Shak ONeal, but . . ."

"Sounds like you have done a lot of research on Alaska."

"I have. As I think I told you earlier, Liliana and I had planned on traveling to Alaska last summer, but that was before she hitched up with Sergio."

"You had planned on climbing Mt. McKinley?"

"Oh, no!" Altmann replied with a laugh. "That would be foolhardy even for someone as young as Liliana. I *had* planned, however, that on our way to Alaska we would at least drive up Colorado's breathtakingly beautiful, fourteen thousand two hundred sixty-four foot-high Mt. Evans."

"Well, perhaps you can look forward to doing that in your evening years."

"Like Florentino with his Fermina, huh?"

"Like who?"

"Oh, just a couple of fictional old folks who sailed up the river of time on a surge of octogenarian sexual bliss," Altmann replied with a touch of sadness. Recalling how young Liliana would still be when he was already in his eighties, he knew his analogy to the Marquez couple limped considerably.

"You'd better get yourself back in shape, then!" Dr. Stein joked, before rising from his chair to shake his patient's hand and bid him farewell until their next session.

35

An hour before midnight on New Year's Eve Professor Altmann sat alone in his living room, listening to the haunting sounds of Mozart's Piano Concerto Number 21in C Major, and poring over a collection of photographs he had taken of Liliana since first meeting her a year and a half ago. Several friends had called him earlier in the evening to invite him to join them in their usual end-of-the-year pagan ritual of throwing themselves, half-inebriated, to the wind, but he had turned them down, first with the excuse that his inguinal hernia could not take another round of their foot-stomping polka-dancing, and then, when they had insisted that he come anyway and at least sit and drink with them until the new year could be ushered in, with the claim that a degenerative spinal disc would make it impossible for him to sit that long on the hard chairs of the Elk Lounge where they were all planning to congregate. The fact was that he was feeling quite depressed, and notwithstanding the advice of his psychotherapist to seek the company of his friends at precisely such times, much preferred staying at home, and even had his groin and back not been giving him trouble, would have fabricated some story to have kept himself there.

After dining on a Caesar's salad, Fettucini Alfredo, and an extra large slice of Coconut Cream pie, that he had ordered for home delivery from the newest restaurant in town, he had settled down in his living room recliner to read a chapter or two from Philip Roth's latest novel, *American Pastoral*. Its graphic description of Swede Levov's erotic play with the former Miss New Jersey, however, had ignited his own libido, firing his imagination with the tantalizing recollection of the naked Carminita Consolata he had so often devoured before while cruising the Internet's world of porn. Sensing the danger of relapsing into his old, dirty habit, he had quickly put the book aside, and in hopes of distracting himself, decided to do some work on several photographic albums he had begun assembling in previous weeks.

Among the hundreds of prints he had periodically tossed into a shoebox during the past two years, he was pleasantly surprised to discover that no less than fifty of them were of Liliana. One of them, shot within the first month of their encounter, showed her, clad in black Levis, a lime-green, tight-knit blouse and Puritan-style, black sandals, leaning casually against an old revolutionary-war canon that had been mounted on a limestone platform in Urbana's Peace Park. A fire-engine-red, Jeep Cherokee could be seen parked in the background, accenting the gun's phallic aspect, but with Liliana standing next to it the way she was, with a smart, confident grin across her face and one leg projected slightly in front of the other to make her look taller than her actual height, it was hard to imagine the old weapon ever having had any real fire power. It reminded him of one of her own paintings he had seen hanging on her bedroom wall when last he had visited her out in Boston. He recalled her entitling it 'The Impenetrable Vagina,' and he marveled now at how close the witty label came to capturing the picture of gentle toughness radiating from the photo he had in hand. No macho-man, he recognized anew, would ever lord it over this woman! And however much her mild rebuffs of his own subtly sexual advances had hurt his masculine pride, he had nothing but admiration for the strength of her character. Laying the print aside to include in an album he had in mind to eventually devote to pictures of her alone, he turned to another set of photos he had taken of Liliana on the July evening prior to their attendance at a performance of Tschaikovsky's *Onegin*. She had already donned the ruby-red dress she would wear to the opera, and at his invitation, had gone barefoot out into the grassy backyard of her house to let him get some shots of her in what was left of the day's sunlight. In contrast to the feline toughness exuding from the earlier 'Peace Park' photo he had been viewing, in these, except for one, she was all playfulness. For one of his shots, she had posed, like Copenhagen's coquettish little mermaid, on a boulder next to the fish pond, gazing dreamily off into the distance, as though waiting to be picked up by some passing, bonny sailor desperately in search of love. In another, she had seated herself on a bench for two that stood at the edge of the yard against a small wooded area, and was captured by the camera just as her sinuous body was doubling up in laughter—probably, he recalled, because of some cynical comment he had made at the time about the pinnated stalks of poison sumac growing up through the bench's wooden slats in the empty space alongside her, symbolizing her self-imposed impenetrability. A third print had her again on the pond-side boulder, this time standing in a relaxed posture, as though she were taking a shower, with one arm dangling at her side and the other raised effortlessly to pull her hair away from her face and to the back of her outstretched neck. From the hint of a smile on her lips it was obvious that Liliana had been aware of the humorous nature of her pose, and was only doing it for the sake of entertaining her friend's creative fantasies. But with what one of his colleagues had labeled his cosmic view of reality, that always inclined him to take things more seriously than they were actually meant to be, the photo at first reminded Altmann of Arthur Lee's famous sculpture of *Dawn,* until, observing more closely its relaxed lines, he concluded that it could better symbolize the dusk, the gloaming, in other words, when the work of the sun had been consummated, and as Hegel had put it, the Owl of Minerva could begin spreading her wings. Still other photos in the set had caught Liliana playfully mimicking the look of an Amazon superwoman, clinging in an overly seductive manner to the bare trunk of a blue gum, eucalyptus tree, or strutting out of the forest's undergrowth growling like some jungle cat intent upon devouring the first thing that moves. The one exception to these humorous shots was a closeup he had taken of her face as she seated herself in a patio swing, behind which hung a pot of petunias in full bloom. Against the background of the multiple, sun-splashed, green-leafed sprays of scarlet flowers, her countenance, lightly shadowed by long strands of her still undried, disheveled hair, had taken on a special warmth, revealing through the soft lines of its deep-set, brown eyes, fine nose, and full lips, the thoughtful, compassionate person he had early on discovered Liliana to be. Sighing sadly over his apparent loss of so delightful a creature, he placed the set of photos aside, and was about to take up another, when his cell phone rang.

"Altmann!" he mumbled into the receiver, fully expecting, even at so late an hour, to hear another of the telemarketers who had been badgering him recently to switch telephone companies.

"*Hola, Mauritio!*" the hesitant voice at the other end saluted him.

"Liliana?!" Altmann exclaimed in disbelief.

"*Si, Si! Como estas?*"

"I'm okay," Altmann responded softly, "but you are not going to believe this; I was just looking at some photographs of you that I had taken over the past several years."

"Really?" Liliana murmured, in a voice as melancholic as an autumnal breeze. "So you haven't forgotten what I looked like after all these months?"

189

"Oh, Liliana! A thousand years," Altmann started waxing poetically, before catching himself and shifting to another, less effusive, assertion of how no period of separation, however long, could ever erase from his memory the beauty of her being.

"You're hopeless, Mauritio!" Liliana responded with a laugh. "My elderly, Italian friend, Maria, tells me in her inimitably honest manner that my looks are of an *average* sort at best, and none of the men I've dated lately seem overly enamored of what you call my beauty, or at least not enough to keep them from abandoning me and going off in hot pursuit of some other, younger and apparently more attractive woman, and yet to hear you tell it, you'd think I was the *very incarnation* of Helen of Troy!"

"It takes a philosopher to see *real* beauty!" Altmann retorted. "From what you've told me before, Maria has become something like a second mother to you, and we all know how mothers like to deflate their daughters' self-image! And as for all those men . . . Are you talking about Sergio? He hasn't dropped you already, has he?"

"Apparently, he has," Liliana stated. "We had what I thought were several great weekends together in New York City, and before going back to Cuba, he had promised to keep in touch. But notwithstanding the number of emails I sent him in subsequent months, I've gotten absolutely nothing back from him."

"The blind bum!," Altmann protested angrily, genuinely upset that any man would treat so cavalierly a woman for whose embrace he would himself—were he not so *damn* old—swim across any sea.

"Well, life is full of adventures, and Sergio was only one; I'm sure there will be more down the road," Liliana said, "But enough about me, what's going on with you? Why aren't you out celebrating the new year?"

"That's probably what my psychotherapist will be asking also," Altmann mumbled, a bit hesitant about admitting to the fact of being in the care of a mental health professional, but wanting at the same time to give Liliana a true picture of where he was at.

"Your *psychotherapist?!*" Liliana queried.

"Yeah," Altmann responded, "not long after I last saw you back in May I became addicted to Internet porn to the point where, after BCC found out I was using one of their computers to store the stuff, I ended up losing my chairmanship and being suspended from my teaching position until such time as I could get some counseling on how to cope with the problem."

"Oh, Mauritio, that's terrible! I wish I had called you earlier!"

"It wasn't your fault," Altmann protested.

"Maybe not," Liliana replied, "but I could at least have provided you some friendly support."

"I never doubted your friendship," Altmann replied, "but it's good to hear you reaffirm it."

"So, how's it going now? Are you better?"

"Dr. Stein seems to think so." Altmann answered. "The key to breaking the addiction, he says, is to revive somehow the sense of wonder that I apparently let die during years of rationalistic speculation, and he claims to see some improvement already in that regard. But he also thinks that if I'm ever to recover fully, I'm going to have to get back to nature, and work on my personal relationships."

"Sounds like its time we head for Alaska, my friend!"

"Are you serious?!"

"Yeah, why not?!"

"In July, perhaps? It will take a whole month, you know, to make such a trip?"

"That would be great; I could save some money by subletting my apartment for the whole month."

"So . . . should I start making reservations? From all I read last year, it's never too early to start."

"Yeah, let's go ahead with it."

"There *is* one problem, though . . . well, not necessarily a *problem*, but . . . well-l, what should I do about our sleeping accommodations? There may be times when only one bed will be available, especially if we stay at any of the bed and breakfast places, which I think you told me before you much prefer to motels."

Before Altmann could ask whether it would bother her to sleep in the same bed with him, Liliana dismissed the matter with a laugh. "No problem," she replied jovially, "I generally curl up in one corner of the bed anyway, and you'll have all the room you need."

That wasn't exactly the answer he was looking for, but the prospect of actually having Liliana share a bed with him was almost more than Altmann's confused psyche could absorb at this point in his life, and he pressed the matter no further than to mumble, "Well, then, I'll see what I can arrange."

"Keep me posted!" she chirped gleefully.

"I will," he assured her, and bade her good-bye. Looking at his watch, he noticed that it was already half past twelve and that the two of them had been altogether oblivious to the birth of another year being celebrated by his friends. "So much the better," he mused to himself, before boxing up the photos again, and heading off to bed. Time, he knew from his reading of Kant, was nothing more than a mental construct, and probably did more harm than good by differentiating so cruelly one year from another, or between, say, the young and the old, like himself and Liliana. Better, perhaps, he continued musing while waiting to fall asleep, to forget time altogether, and try finding already here and now a bit of the atemporal Nirvana promised by the Enlightened One. It was comforting to realize that, willy-nilly, he and Liliana had launched the new year on such an ancient note of wisdom. But how long would it last before reality would again set in and leave the two of them categorized in worlds apart? Finally succeeding at turning his brain off, Altmann rolled over onto his side and surrendered his body to the law of gravity's soporific, if not yet fatal, force.

36

"*For I see that the flower of her age is blossoming, while mine is fading; and the eyes of men love to cull the bloom of youth, but they turn aside from the old. This, then, is my fear—lest Heracles, in name my spouse, should be the younger's mate . . .*"

Altmann paused to let Deianeira's pathetic lamentation register on Liliana's distracted mind, while at the same time catching a nervous glimpse of the speedometer. After escaping the congested traffic on the west side of St. Louis, where they had bedded down for their first night on the road, he had turned the wheel of his brand new Monte Carlo over to Liliana, and to help break the monotony of the Missouri-leg of the twelve thousand miles they would be traveling to and from Alaska, he had been reading aloud to her the poetic lines of Sophocles' *Trachiniae.*

"The sexy beast!," Liliana smirked, playing off the title of the English flick they had gone to see the previous evening after dining at the city's famous Cheshire Inn.

"Have a heart!," Altmann retorted only half-facetiously. For six months he had been spending his every spare minute preparing for this trip, always with the thought at the back of his mind that by agreeing to travel with him for such a long time Liliana just might still be open to the possibility of letting their relationship become a bit more affectionate. Trying to be as delicate as possible, he had booked a room with two queen size beds for their first night together, and had let her claim one of them for herself without his having made any move, apart from a perfunctory good-night hug, to lure her into his own. With at least another thirty days and nights ahead of them, he had reckoned that there would be ample opportunity for whatever feeling of affection there was between them to surface. It was to probe her real thoughts in that regard, however, that he had brought along the works of Sophocles and other writers who had dealt with the subject of human love between older men and younger women. Liliana's instantly cynical appraisal of the aged Heracles' sexual appetite for Iole had given Altmann little encouragement, and he quickly tried to rebut her comment, by adding: "I know that Sophocles shared the view of Hesiod and other Greek thinkers of old that Eros is a 'wild and beastly force,' and to that extent might have agreed with you that by succumbing to his sexual desires Heracles had become a 'sexy beast'. But you also heard Sophocles saying, didn't you, that Heracles' soul had been smitten and *'utterly vanquished'* by the *'overmastering love'* and *'passion'* inspired by the younger woman's beauty?"

"So Iole's to blame for Heracles' wildness?!"

"Well, I don't think he's trying to *blame* Iole for anything; he states explicitly that she is innocent. But he does seem to be saying also that Heracles couldn't help himself. I remember reading somewhere that when Sophocles himself got too old to any longer have any sexual desire, he celebrated his loss of it as though he had 'escaped bondage to a raging madman,' and I suspect he would have thought of Heracles as having been similarly 'enslaved' by his male libido."

"A victim of love, huh?" Liliana snickered, while accelerating the Monte Carlo up to eighty-five and speeding past some slower moving cars.

Altmann made no immediate response, holding his breath instead until Liliana had safely executed the maneuver. "Well, yeah," he said hesitantly, "if you believe, as Sophocles apparently did, that the sexual drive is so strong in men that it is beyond their control. And I might add that according to Euripides, it's no different with women. In his play *Hippolytus*, which incidentally I thought we might want to read next, we are told that although Phaedra was already up in years, *'her heart was seized with wild desire'* for her husband's young and handsome, bastard-son?"

"Yeah, but that's a rare case, a piece of fiction that's hardly true to life. It's usually only the older *men,* and not the women, who claim to be victimized by their sexual desires."

"Why? Because the feminine libido is weaker?"

"No, not really! I think it's due rather to the keener interest women have in childbearing and family life; this inclines them early on to develop a more mature attitude toward sex, and to be more interested in long-term relationships."

"Whereas most men never grow up sexually, you're saying?"

"Many don't. Like teenage boys, they seem to think that sex is all about immediate gratification; if they think about long-term relationships at all, it's only on the assumption that their sexual partners will remain forever young and physically attractive. As Sophocles said, their *'eyes love to cull the bloom of youth, but turn aside from the old.'*"

"Why? Because men are just wired differently?"

"Could be. It no doubt has something to do with our animal past, but I'm sure there are cultural factors involved also. Your beloved Plato can probably be blamed for much of the problem."

"I assume you're referring to his taste for idealization?"

"Exactly. By claiming that the idea of womanhood was more real than any particular woman, he encouraged men to idealize the objects of their sexual desires, and although he himself may not have identified the ideal woman with mere physical beauty, much of the literature influenced by his philosophy, especially the Romantic stuff, would later do so."

"Wasn't it the beauty of Gretchen's *soul* rather than her physical attractiveness that in the end captivated Goethe's Faust?"

"You may be right, but how consistent the concluding scene of Goethe's drama was with Faust's initial fascination with Margaret or his later fixation on the imaginary Helen of Troy is certainly debatable."

"I'm not so sure. Plato, you know, recognized that the pursuit of absolute beauty always starts with discovery of the physical attractiveness of young men and women and that it is this experience of physical beauty that awakens one to, or reminds one of, the idea of absolute beauty. So, perhaps Goethe was trying to imagine the striving of Faust maturing along similar lines."

"Maybe so, but judging from Goethe's own womanizing proclivities, my suspicion is that the old boy conceived of the eternal feminine more in terms of young, physically attractive women than in any sort of *'seelenshoenheit.'* And I dare say that that is the way men in most cultures, and especially my own Latin American one, have been brought up to think, namely, that the ideal woman is always young and physically beautiful. That's why so many of them feel the need to have mistresses, or like Heracles, to dump their older wives and shack up with younger women, some of whom, sad to say, are often their own relatives, or even their own daughters. As Garcia Marquez seems to be saying in his novel *A Hundred Years of Solitude,* the whole phenomenon reeks of incest, and has contributed significantly to the havoc prevailing today in many Latin American countries."

"I can see how that might happen," Altmann conceded, "if the Platonic idealization causes men to measure particular individuals over against some perfect model, especially if the latter is conceived of in terms of physical beauty alone. But does it have to be that way? As I said before, Plato himself would never have identified the perfect woman in terms of her physical beauty alone. Furthermore, isn't it conceivable that instead of coming up with some abstract ideal of feminine beauty, and then measuring individual women over against such a model of perfection, as Plato admittedly seemed to encourage, isn't it possible that one could idealize the beauty of the particular woman whom one encounters, sort of like Rousseau imagining Julie—his nouvelle Héloïse—as the perfect embodiment of feminine beauty?"

"Would that be any different than Don Quixote's idealization of Dulcinea, and nothing more, therefore, than an exercise in egoistic delusion?"

"Well, there certainly is a touch of that in Rousseau, especially in his dramatization of *Pygmalion,* in which Galatea is represented as a work of the imagination alone, or even in *La Nouvelle Héloïse,* since at least in its first two parts, Julie is clearly Rousseau's invention of an ideal woman to compensate for the sexual frustration he was experiencing in real life. In the rest of the novel, however, which he finished only after meeting and falling in love with the young Countess d'Houtetot, the idealization of Julie is far more concrete. He himself says that he endowed Madame d'Houdetot with all the perfections he had attributed to Julie, but it could also be argued that it was in fact the particular attributes of Madame d'Houdetot that he ascribed to his idealized, fictional character. Julie, in other words, may be seen as the realization of Madame d'Houdetot's beauty, rather than the other way around. And to that extent, it seems to me that Rousseau can be dubbed a 'troubadour' of sorts."

"A troubadour?" Liliana asked skeptically, drumming her fingers impatiently against the steering wheel as a line of cars to her left cut off her path around the semi in front of her.

"Yeah, you know, the twelfth century, singing poets like Bernart de Ventadorn."

"I know who they are, but how are they like Rousseau?"

"Well, as I was saying, Rousseau—at least in the latter half of his novel— idealizes the beauty of a particular woman, and it seems to me that that is exactly what the troubadours were inclined to do; they didn't first come up with an abstract idea of feminine beauty and then apply it to particular women; rather, they used their poetic skill to sing the praises of the particular features of the women they met; their poetic songs, in other words, treat the particular woman herself as the supreme instance of beauty; it is in her unique features that they see the ideal of feminine beauty."

"So, what happened to Rousseau and Sophie?" Liliana asked on a more practical level. "Did they ever get married?"

"No, they didn't. Just as Julie, in the novel, ends up marrying someone other than Saint-Preux, so in real life, Sophie married her first lover, a man named Saint-Lambert. Unlike Saint-Preux, however, Rousseau never even had sexual intercourse with his beloved, and had to settle for a *ménage à trois*, deriving whatever pleasure he could from viewing Sophie from a distance, and savoring the idealized beauty of her that his mind never ceased imagining. But that just makes him all the more like the earlier troubadours, who also purposely stopped short of consummating their sexual desires so as to fire their erotic imaginations still more."

"Rousseau's abstinence wasn't on purpose, though, was it?"

"Apparently not. He would gladly have consummated his relation with Sophie had he been given the chance, and to that extent he did not exactly live up to the troubadour notion of a *fin'amor*. Still, once he saw the futility of trying to have sexual intercourse with her, he did at least accept reality and tried elevating his love for her onto a purer level."

Liliana made no reply, but from the inquisitive look on her face, Altmann sensed that she was intrigued by what he was saying, or at least less cynical than she had earlier been about Heracles lusting after Iole. Satisfied at having had the chance to plant the thought of a possibly different scenario to their own relationship, he went back to reading from the Sophoclean text, and over the next hundred miles gave her the pleasure of hearing again how—thanks to what the poet describes as the 'great cruelty of the gods'—Deianeira inadvertently causes her husband's death with the very gift by which she had had in mind to charm his soul and win back his love.

"*Consummatum est!*" Liliana joked wickedly.

"How about some breakfast?" Altmann asked, ignoring Liliana's irreverent, pithy commentary on the ignominious end of Heracles' sex life, and pointing to a sign at the exit ahead advertizing an International House of Pancakes. Anxious to get out of St. Louis before the traffic had gotten any worse than it actually was, they had foregone the complimentary breakfast promised them by the hotel, and had been on the road since sunrise. Apparently no less hungry than he, Liliana promptly followed his suggestion and pulled the car off the Interstate and into the

IHOP parking lot. As they entered the eating establishment, a 1930s diner that had seen its better days, Altmann noticed that not a few in the crowd of people already seated in the place were turning around to look them over. Liliana had put on an especially short and sassy summer dress that morning, and Altmann could only imagine what the folks staring at them might be thinking upon seeing her coming into the restaurant at midmorning in the company of an older man. He couldn't have cared less what they were thinking about himself, but it bothered him greatly to suspect that they might be dismissing Liliana as nothing more than a highway tramp he had picked up at one or another truck stop along the way. How anyone seeing the elegant and dignified way in which she carried herself could conclude that she might ever have put her body up for sale, was beyond his conception. But he had himself earlier experienced the capacity of the public to imagine the worst of anyone, and he would not at all put it past the clientele of this place now to be thinking that way. Realizing that that might actually be their impression, he felt guilty at having subjected Liliana to their judgmental gawking. But ushering her to the only open seat at the rear of the diner, he observed that the stares of the crowd had hardly registered on her consciousness. If she felt any embarrassment at being seen in his company, she gave no sign of it, and instead returned the crowd's cold stares with her usual warm and friendly, confident smile, and throughout the breakfast carried on with the male waitress as though it were as natural for her to be with Altmann as it was to be eating bacon with her eggs. Her unapologetic attitude pleased Altmann so much that upon finishing the meal and exiting the restaurant, it was all he could do to keep from taking her up into his arms and, in full view of the gawking crowd, carrying her across the parking lot to the sexy Monte Carlo waiting for their return beyond.

As they climbed into the car, however, and set out again, with Liliana still at the wheel, down the interstate toward Kansas City, Altmann mused to himself for the longest while how it was that she could rise so cooly above what she must herself have suspected were the thoughts of others—even of her own friends or those of Altmann, not a few of whom, upon learning of his plans, had jokingly accused him of erotic intentions—about her making such a long trip with a man so much older than herself. It was not, he hoped, altogether out of question that during the past six months since the renewal of their relationship, their many exchanges of emails and telephone conversations had warmed her heart enough to stir some affection for him, and that it might, therefore, be something like a wall of love that was protecting her against whatever suspicions friends and foes alike might be harboring. But that, he feared, was probably just wishful thinking on his part. Suppressing it, he toyed instead for the moment with the thought that perhaps she was able to suffer the public scrutiny of their relationship so well only because she had come to think of him as something of a father-figure. Given the variation between their respective heights, complexions, and other physical features, it was not very likely that anyone would ever mistake him for her biological father. But with adoption, any mix might play with the public, and since she had in fact lost her own father so early on in her life, she just might be looking for a surrogate to take his place. Catching a glimpse of her profile as she smartly negotiated the Monte Carlo in and out of a line of heavy traffic, he thought to himself what a joy it would be, childless as he had always been, were she ever actually wanting him to play such a role, to have so lovely a creature for a daughter. But it would also mean, he knew, canceling out or rendering incestuous the kind of amorous feelings he had been cultivating toward her all along. And he was not at all sure that he could yet bring himself, or even want to try, to make such an emotional shift. In any event, Liliana herself had never given him any indication of wanting to convert their relationship into such a paternalistic affair of filial love, and upon further reflection, Altmann concluded that in all likelihood she saw him at best as a good traveling companion, for whose friendship she, being a woman of thirty-three with a mind and will of her own, owed an explanation to no one. Slightly depressed at the realization of where, in reality, he probably stood with Liliana, and seeing the city's skyscrapers up ahead, Altmann tried distracting himself by mouthing the words from 'Oklahoma' about 'everything being up to date in Kansas City'. His off-key attempt brought a bemused smile to Liliana's lips. "You don't like my singing?" Altmann murmured with a feigned look of hurt on his face.

"You sing *beauti*fully!" Liliana lied.

"So what would you rather hear? Mozart? Smetana? Beethoven? I brought half my collection of classical music along, so take your pick!"

"How about Patsy Cline?" Liliana suggested, while reaching behind the driver's seat, and blindly fetching the leather-encased file of her own favorite CDs.

"Never heard of her, but it's fine by me," Altmann replied, taking the case from Liliana and flipping through its multiple pages to find one of Patsy's pieces.

"You've never heard of Patsy Cline?" Liliana asked incredulously. "She's one of the great country stars from the fifties and sixties."

"I spent my youth in the seminary, remember? They didn't allow us to listen to the radio in those days."

"Shame they didn't," Liliana joshed. "Listening to her now and then, chances are you would have been singing a different tune the rest of your life, arm in arm with some sweet thing from southern Illinois!"

"Here's one!" Altmann exclaimed, as he came across a CD entitled *'I Fall To Pieces'*, pulled it out, and inserted it into the car's stereophonic player. "I see what you mean," he moaned as he sat back and let the lyrics of Ms. Cline's sad song tear at his heart: " . . . *You want me to forget; Pretend we never met; And I try and I try; But I haven't yet; You walk by and I fall to pieces!*" Glancing to his left, he caught a glimpse of Liliana staring dreamily ahead of her, and swaying her body gently to the rhythm of the country music. It seemed obvious to him that she was absorbed in reminiscence of some past lover, and was altogether oblivious to the pathos the song had stirred in his own heart.

37

Late in the evening, several days into their trip, Professor Altmann sat with Liliana in a swing on the porch of the Grand Lake cabin he had reserved for their stay in Rocky Mountain National Park. Upon arising that morning at the crack of dawn and seeing the cloudless, azure sky all around, he had decided it would be a perfect day for ascending Mt. Evans. Despite her usual early-morning stupor, Liliana had welcomed the plan with enthusiasm, quickly jumping from bed and, after showering, donning the hiking clothes (blue jeans, white sweat-shirt, and boots) she had brought along for such occasions. After a hearty breakfast in the lodge restaurant to ward off the possibility of altitude sickness, and a quick stop at the local gas station, they had driven south along Granby Lake, over the Berthoud Pass, and through Idaho Springs, where they picked up the back-country road that would take them to their destination. Within two hours they were already half-way up the mountain, far ahead of any other tourists who might have been contemplating a similar trek. The sun had just risen above the distant, jagged horizon, bathing the forest of gently swaying lodgepole pine and Engelmann spruce through which they were driving with a wash of blue-green light, and sporadically accenting some of the trees' normally grayish trunks with brilliant streaks of amber hues. At a point called the Mt. Goliath Research Natural Area, Altmann had stopped the car, and the two of them had climbed out to get a closer look at a virgin stand of the bristlecone pine that according to the brochure given them by the park ranger were at least sixteen hundred years old. "Just imagine," Altmann muttered, "some of these very trees had already sprouted before the fall of the Roman Empire!"

"Or the rise of Machu Picchu!," Liliana added from a less Eurocentric perspective. "They must be very tough! Whole cultures—Inca, Aztec, and Mayan—have come and gone in the meantime!"

"Yeah, that's amazing," Altmann observed, as he put his arm around Liliana's shoulder and led her forward to the edge of a precipice from which they could see far into the distant valley, eleven thousand feet below them. Child of the Andes that she was, the panoramic vistas were nothing new to Liliana, but she had thrilled to the sights all the same, or perhaps all the more, to the extent of being reminded, after years of American big-city life, of how blessed had been the youthful years she had spent growing up in a mountain village of her native Colombia. For some ten minutes they stood there, saying nothing to break the silence that, except for occasional squawks of competing ravens or the whistle of winds gently buffeting their bodies, was nearly total, bringing to both their countenances a smile as blissful as that of a Buddhist monk contemplating the ultimate *sunyata*. Returning finally to their car, they drove on, across a precipitous, four mile long, windswept escarpment, and past Summit Lake, where the winding road took a sudden, sharp turn upward. The higher they drove, the more childlike Liliana seemed to have become, asking Altmann one question after another about the identity of the pika, the marmots, the ptarmigan, and other wildlife that could be seen scampering about the rocky outcroppings along the way. At about fourteen thousand feet she spotted a female goat nursing a kid some fifty yards off to the side of the road, and almost before Altmann could obey her command to stop the car, she leapt from it, and with camera in hand, began stepping delicately from rock to rock across the Alpine tundra, until no farther than ten feet away from the animal pair, she prostrated herself on a rocky patch of ground and waited for the perfect shot. The goats seemed to sense a kindred spirit and tolerated her presence with nary a second glance.

Pulling the car off to the side of the narrow road, Altmann got out and with his binoculars brought the scene of Liliana and the goats into closer view. As impressive as was the picture of the female goat, with its dagger-like horns and newly acquired, snow-white coat, nursing the seemingly defenseless kid, even more wonderful to Altmann was the sight of Liliana abandoning herself, as usual, to the experience of the moment. It was this spontaneous, total absorption in whatever she was doing that, more than anything else about her, had always fascinated him. And once again, seeing her stretched out on the ground amidst thousands of tiny Violets, Alpine Sandwort, Bitterroot and other brightly colored mountain flora, oblivious to all but her interaction with the goats, he could only wonder at what divine scheme of things had dropped her into his life, and what on earth he was supposed to do with so marvelous a gift—if indeed that's what she was, and not a curse sent by a wrathful god to torture him in his old age for the sins of his youth. He watched in awe as she put the camera aside for the moment and began stroking with the little finger of her right hand the petals of a cluster of purple violets blooming alongside her outstretched arm. Seemingly satisfied with merely feasting her eye on their *splendor formae*, the thought of plucking one of the flowers or uprooting it from its natural environment apparently never entered her mind. And it crossed Altmann's own mind that perhaps there was a lesson to be found therein for his relation with Liliana, that ranunculaceous flower of Colombia that he had suddenly discovered in the backyard of his life.

"Look at her! Admire her! And maybe even embrace her! But don't try to possess her!" he felt himself being warned, as he watched her crawling about on her belly to get ever closer to the goats, and then creeping along behind them as they began moving up higher to join other female members of the herd—all the billy goats having been driven off by the protective mothers—reclining on a huge boulder overlooking the mountainside. Recalling how, at the age of thirty-three, Liliana had already created a bed of her own in which to sleep, it dawned on him anew how unnatural it would be to try luring her now into his own, as unnatural, he mused, as for a troubadour of old to have thought that the noble, virtuous, and possibly even married lady to whom he was singing his song of love could ever be wooed across the feudal boundaries separating them! "So." the voice kept telling him. "Feast your eyes on the beautiful sight, the graceful body, the bright face, the sweet glance, and fine manners, but respect the distance—the seemingly infinite abyss of time between her youth and your own old age! It will make a better man of you, doubling your will to live!"

"Sure it will!" Altmann scoffed to himself, only too mindful of how his encounter with Liliana had fired his passion and triggered his earlier sexual addiction that almost led to his suicide.

"Nobody to blame but yourself," his conscience shot back. "Purge yourself of lust, and nature will take a different course!"

"I'm trying!," Altmann mumbled, as he got back into the car and drove it up the last leg of the steep and serpentine road to the parking lot above.

Liliana was still climbing among the monumental boulders at the southern edge of the lot in pursuit of one or another of the more elusive goats that had taken refuge there from the hot sun. So totally absorbed had she become in what she was doing that it was not until she had exhausted the new roll of film he had put into her camera earlier that morning, that she finally became aware again of the fact that she was not alone, leaving Altmann with a melancholic suspicion that he was little more in her life than a vassal, or worse, a serf, to whom she would turn only when needing a ride or service of some other sort. Never once, during her rendezvous with the wild, had she ever thought of waving back to him, or tried in any other way to engage him in the excitement she was herself experiencing. "I, alas, whom love forgets!," he moaned in a surge of self-pity worthy of any medieval knight. But no sooner did she return to the car, and with that inimitable, wide-eyed look and sweet voice of hers, asked him to load up the camera again, than his heart recovered its rhythm of love and filled him with gratitude for the chance to do her the favor.

"Going up?," Liliana asked, beside herself with the joy of having merged so intimately with Nature, but like a Resphigi *crescendo,* pregnant with anticipation of a yet higher synthesis.

"I'd better not," Altmann replied. The mountain's peak was only another hundred and thirty-four feet higher than the parking lot, but the steep, zig-zag path leading up to it was much longer, and given the scarcity of oxygen at such a height, he was wary of overtaxing a heart that a doctor had long ago told him had a congenital defect of sorts—a minor leakage that had never given him any real problem, but which he had taken seriously enough in subsequent years to finally get off the daily pack of cigarettes he had started smoking in his college days in hopes of enhancing the image he had had of himself as a budding philosopher. "But you go ahead," he added, "I'll document your ascent."

Taking a pocket-size, Kodak disposable camera from the glove compartment, he got out of the car and accompanied Liliana the first fifty feet or so until the trail turned sharply upward. A black, ominous cloud had suddenly appeared from out of nowhere on the western horizon, and seeing it moving toward them, he warned Liliana against the danger of being struck by lightning. But she had paid him no heed, and continued merrily on her way, pausing periodically only long enough to wave back and let him snap another photo, before pushing on to the next level. Upon reaching the peak, she mounted a boulder, stretched her arms out to the sky above, and just as a bolt of lightning streaked out of the base of the cloud behind her, shouted something at the top of her voice, which—given his distance from her and the din of thunder rumbling through the mountain valley below—escaped his comprehension. But he had snapped a photo of her at what he reckoned to have been the precise moment of the lightning strike, and for a second or two delighted in the thought of having possibly captured such a dramatic incident on film. Coming back to his senses, however, and remembering what he had read somewhere about the large number of people being struck by lightning each year on the treeless ridge-tops of Colorado's Rockies, he began waving frantically for her to descend immediately. She did as she was bade, but at her own pace, and upon returning to the car, into which Altmann had already rushed for cover, she dismissed his expression of concern with so angelic a smile that he was left feeling guilty at having feared that so divine a creature could ever have incurred the wrath of Zeus.

"So, what was it that you shouted from on high?," he asked finally, while shifting to a lower gear as they approached an especially wicked curve on their way back down.

"What do you think?" Liliana teased.

"Well, let's see," Altmann mused aloud with a pensive smile. Mindful of her rather scornful levity toward the gods, her defiance of death, and passion for life, he ventured the guess that she might have been echoing from the mountain top the ancient cry of Sophocles' Oedipus or Albert Camus' Sisyphus: *"All is well!"*

Altmann's guess led to an intense discussion on how the absurd hero of modern Existentialist literature can find dignity, or even a touch of happiness, through the futile effort of rolling a rock up a hill time and time again, but while confessing to a rebellious streak or two in her own character, Liliana denied in the end having voiced any such absurdist sentiment from Mt. Evans' peak. And after they had stopped for a while to photograph a flock of Big Horn sheep that had approached their car looking for a handout, and were continuing their descent, she challenged him to try again.

Having repeatedly observed her apparent readiness to accept whatever hand she was being dealt in her life of love and other affairs, and given what he knew was her taste for Nietzsche, he guessed that she might have used her Olympian perch to punctuate, in a Latin or French key, some such sentiment of resignation to the inevitable course of human events like *Amo Fatum!* or *Que sera, sera!* "Or did you, perhaps," he queried along another closely related, Nietzschean line—without waiting for her dismissal of his first suggestion—mouth Zarathustra's encomium to all things earthly: *'That is life . . . Very well! Once more!'*"

"Had I thought of it, I might have," Liliana admitted, "but I'm not as tuned in to the philosophical *dialektike* as you might think. My thoughts generally run along more mundane lines."

"Like *'I want a man!'*" Altmann joked, playing off of the crazy scene in the autobiographical, Fellini film, in which the famous Italian director pictured himself as a frustrated, younger man up in a tree at the center of town, screaming at the top of his voice: *"I want a woman!"*

"I'm not that desperate yet . . . And never will be," Liliana retorted with a laugh.

"Well, then . . . how about *'Bring on the good times!'*" Altmann guessed again, mischievously paraphrasing a line he'd recently heard in a song by Shakira, the sexy Colombian Rock star, who in her younger, leaner years at least, could have passed for Liliana's twin.

This time Liliana did not laugh. Recognizing the source of the lyric, she began lecturing Altmann instead on how disgusting she thought it was that so many young Colombian girls were being turned into beauty queens or sex idols as a result of the traditional penchant of Latin American culture to idealize love. "Erendiras, one and all!," she protested, adding for Altmann's elucidation a summary of the Garcia Marquez short story in which a beautiful young girl, who is sold into prostitution by her avaricious grandmother, eventually loses her own soul in her lust for gold and the emancipation she thinks it will buy her.

Embarrassed by his insensitivity to Liliana's deepest convictions—convictions that he knew had grown to some extent out of the tragic events of her own life, at the start of which her father, already a married man, had lured her then young and very attractive mother into sexual intercourse, only to walk out on her upon learning that he had gotten her pregnant—Altmann refrained from any further guessing, and for the rest of the trip down the mountain road hardly a word passed between them. But after stopping in Idaho Springs to check out a local art gallery, and then again in Winter Park to lunch at the Rome on the Range Restaurant, their conversation resumed on a less contentious note, and Liliana, her playful spirit revived, again challenged him to guess what she might have proclaimed from the mountain top. Try as he might, however, Altmann was unable to put his finger on it, and that evening, after having returned to the Lodge and suspended the game for a late afternoon nap and dinner, he was still trying to read her thoughts as the two of them had retired to the front porch of their cabin to have a cup of coffee.

"So what was it?" he finally pleaded, eager to pick up again on another subject—the possibility of a *fin'amor* between themselves—he had hinted at during their drive across Missouri two days earlier.

"You give up?" she teased playfully, while drawing her feet up onto the oscillating swing and wrapping her arms around her elevated knees.

"*Concedo!*" Altmann declared, adding with a grin that he was a fool to have thought in the first place that he could ever have read so great a mind! "So, let's have it! What was it that you said?"

"Nothing terribly profound," Liliana demurred, pausing for a moment to admire the full moon rising over Grand Lake, "just that '*I am woman! I am invincible!*'"

"I should have known!" Altmann exclaimed. Driving down Interstate 70 that morning on their way to Mt. Evans, they had heard the Helen Reddy classic being sung on the radio, and it had struck him then how close a resemblance the lyrics of the song bore to the message of one of Liliana's own paintings. "Speaking of invincible women," he added. "Remember that first installment of the novel I sent you last year?"

"About Professor Klauer and the young woman he meets at the opera?"

"Yeah, Teresa was her name. Well, after writing that first chapter I became rather lost for words, and haven't been able to write another chapter since then, mainly, I think . . ." Pausing to debate within himself whether to confess openly that his writer's block was simply the result of confusion about where his own relation with Liliana was going, and deciding not to, he continued: ". . . mainly, as I was saying, because I couldn't imagine what further direction the relationship between Teresa and the professor might take. Initially, I had planned on letting it develop along the lines of Goethe's Faust . . . you know, the old philosopher becomes infatuated with the beautiful young woman, she falls madly in love with him, they have intercourse during their *nuit d'amour,* she dies shortly thereafter, but not before inspiring him to strive anew toward the ideals of truth, beauty, and goodness, and thereby to snatch his soul back from the devil and win eternal salvation alongside his beloved Marguerite. The more I thought about it, though, the less inclined I was to take the story in that direction."

"So much the better!," Liliana interjected, "As I've told you before, I think the Romantic idealization of love is a dead-end road, not because it leads to some kind of tragic *Liebestod,* as Goethe and his kind liked to think, but in the sense that it inevitably contributes to the incestuous exploitation of women."

"You're probably right," Altmann conceded hesitantly, still reluctant to write off for good the possibility of ever consummating his erotic desires toward Liliana, and suspecting that she was more aware than she was letting on that their current conversation was as much about their own relationship as it was about the fictional characters of Professor Klauer and Teresa. "But that's why, as I said, I was having trouble figuring out where to take the story next, and haven't been able to get beyond the first chapter. You'll recall from our conversation the other day, however, that I've been reading a lot of literature lately again about the medieval troubadours, and have become rather fascinated by their notion of pure love. What do you think? See any possibility of letting the story of Klauer and Teresa unfold along some such line?"

"Well, it still seems to smack of Platonic idealization, but tell me more. Where exactly would it take them?"

"Okay. Let's say Klauer comes to see that because of their age difference and Teresa's invincible determination not to settle for anything less than true love and the kind of family life it alone can deliver, he will never have a chance to realize his erotic dream of a *nuit de plaisir,* falls still deeper into the depression that his latter-day agnosticism had earlier generated, becomes addicted to cyberporn, almost loses his job and life, and begins to pull himself back together only after seeking psychological counseling, during the course of which, while reading Rousseau's autobiographical *Confessions* and some love songs by Bernart de Ventadorn, he gets to thinking that even if his erotic desire for Teresa must go forever unconsummated, he might still find a way to share with her his feelings of love ."

"Why does all this sound so familiar?" Liliana joshed kindly, between sips from her cup of cappucino.

"Can't imagine," Altmann replied with a sheepish grin, before returning to his story line. "So-o, after Teresa, who has just lost another boyfriend, invites him to take a month-long trip to Alaska with her. . ."

"To Alaska, huh?" Liliana interjected, almost spilling the precious caffeine onto the pink sweater she had donned for the cool evening.

Except for a knowing smile, Altmann ignored Liliana's comment, and promptly resumed his unfolding of the story's plot: ". . . knowing full well that on such an extended trip they would generally be sharing a room and maybe even, on occasion, a bed, he got to thinking that this would perhaps be his perfect opportunity to test their chances of ever finding a pure love together. Vowing to himself not to try luring Teresa into any act of sexual intercourse, he determined all the same to use his every poetic trick to woo her occasionally into letting him feast his eyes on her naked body, and then, with the purest of intentions, to kiss and touch it, and finally to take it into his arms for a long and soulful embrace. So, they set out on their trip, and come about the third night, Klauer is ready to make his move."

"And?" Liliana prompted, as Altmann stopped in mid-sentence and stared vacantly out into the moonlit darkness beyond the cabin porch.

"Well, I'm not sure," Altmann finally mumbled. "It takes two to tango, you know, and I'm not altogether clear on how a woman might be expected to react to such amorous overtures. What do *you* think? Would it make any sense to imagine Teresa joining Klauer in such a dance of love?"

"We're talking fiction, right?"

"Yeah, of course," Altmann lied.

"Well, in the fictional realm anything is possible, and I suppose that in the love songs of your beloved troubadours the women to whom they are being sung do sometimes show signs of returning amorous sentiments."

"Not always," Altmann admitted. "In a few of them, the fair lady actually seems uncomfortable in being placed on so high a pedestal, and scorns the effusive praise being heaped upon her. In others, she denies her suitor the affection he is seeking on grounds that while she recognizes his goodness, she has no fondness or affection in her heart for him. 'Grievous, I woo a woman who won't unbend,' Bernart sings in one of them. But there certainly are some also in which the lady reciprocates with an affectionate glance, a tantalizing smile, a kind word, a kiss, or even by allowing him to see and embrace her naked body, 'bidding him,' as Bernart again sings in one of his songs, 'to the room where she unrobes, so that I right by her bed sink to my knees and from her tendered feet draw the shoes,' or, as he sings elsewhere, 'see the white beauty under her clothes,' the 'nude body' in comparison to which the 'snow is brown!'"

"Well, it might have worked in medieval literature, but I'd be skeptical about how well it would play in modern times. Kawabata, I know, touched upon a similar theme in his *House of the Sleeping Beauties*, but although Marquez expressed his admiration for it, and based one of his own short stories on it, a lot of readers found it to be rather weird."

"And understandably so, given the fact that the young, naked virgins with whom the novel's main character—an old man of sixty-four, named Eguchi— is given a chance to sleep, are duped with drugs to the point of being reduced to mere fragments of flesh by the matron of the house. The troubadours would never have dreamed of trying to exploit the objects of their love in that way."

"That may be, and, of course, neither Kawabata nor Marquez themselves had in mind to justify the practice they described. But be that as it may, I still suspect that the reading public today, numbed by decades of exposure to soap operas and romance novels, would find even the troubadour notion of 'pure love' rather silly."

"The majority probably would," Altmann conceded, "but I'm not interested in writing for the masses; all I really care about is how you and a few of my other friends might react to the story. Would you think it stupid of me to imagine Teresa responding favorably to Klauer's knightly wooing?"

"Will you have Teresa involved in any other romantic relationships?"

"Not while they are actually on the trip, but, as I noted earlier, she was just coming off of a romantic experience right prior to their departure, and I wouldn't rule out the possibility of her having more such relationships, or even getting married to another man, after their return."

"I don't know," Liliana demurred, "sounds rather unrealistic, even for the world of fiction!"

"What's so unrealistic about two people who know what they are doing and want to do it, letting their souls mate and 'in single Being both together be' for an eternal moment, as my friend, Bernart, would put it?"

"Nothing, I guess, if they can bring it off without getting burnt in the process, and if both of them really want it."

"And if Teresa agrees to travel with Klauer for thirty days and nights, knowing full well that they will often be sharing the same bed, would it be so unreasonable of him to assume that she might be open to the possibility of affording him a bit more intimacy than a perfunctory good-night hug—especially after they have spent a whole day bonding with each other under the influence of Nature's beauty? How could they not," he asked further, after recalling how irresistibly attractive he had found Liliana that day on the mountaintop, "long to hold each other in their arms and bask in a oneness that must surely transcend the joy of any coital union?"

"You know that for a fact?" Liliana queried.

"No, but the troubadours attested to it, and I find their claim imaginable."

"Well, you have to follow your own instincts. Nobody can tell you what to write. But, frankly, I think it would be a hard sell!"

"Would *you* buy it?"

"Your novel?"

"No, the possibility of *fin'amor!*"

"Between Teresa and Klauer?"

"No, between you and me! Oh, Liliana, I'm down on my knees! Remember that song by Otis Redding you played for me coming across Kansas yesterday?

The one about *'These arms of mine . . . Yearning from wanting you.'* Well, I don't know what thoughts it stirred in you, but it captured perfectly what I so often feel as we drive together for hours on end, engaging in non-stop, lively conversation, laughing sometimes till our sides hurt, or, like this morning, when we were just standing next to each other on that precipice overlooking the valley eleven thousand feet below us, saying nothing, abandoning ourselves to the wind, and letting it strip us of our every egoistic desire. Don't you ever feel it, too?"

His amorous intentions now clearly out in the open, Altmann reached over to put his arm around Liliana's shoulder to draw her nearer to himself. She made no effort to resist, but neither did she seem to put her heart into the embrace she let him have.

"I'm sorry, Mauritio," Liliana finally uttered after a long pause. "You are a wonderful person. I too enjoy our companionship immensely, and am truly honored by your affection for me, but I can't honestly say that I feel the way you do. I hope I did not lead you on to think otherwise. I suspected all along we'd have to have a talk like this sooner or later. I guess I should have cleared the air long before luring you out onto the road like this, but . . ."

"Is it my age?" Altmann inquired, his spirit crushed by the apparent finality of the hard news Liliana had delivered. Withdrawing his arm, he let her move back to the other end of the swing, and muttered something beneath his breath—just loud enough for her to pick it up—about how he'd thought their mutual reading of Marquez' *Love in the Time of Cholera* had inclined them both to imagine the possibility of love transcending the fictional boundaries of time.

"It can," Liliana gently insisted, "and did I feel the way you do, I doubt the difference in our age would matter all that much. But there is something magical about falling in love. Before I can honestly say I love a man, I've got to feel enamored of his whole being."

Bitter thoughts raced through Altmann's mind, and he was tempted to ask whether this magic she was talking about was anything more than the sex appeal of a young, hard body that he could no longer claim for himself. But swallowing his pride and biting his tongue, he inquired of her in only a slightly less cynical way, how, if it was the magic that mattered so much, her conception of love was any different from that of the romantics, whose idealization of love she was constantly knocking, but whose literature always relied also upon some magical means, like the philter drunk by Tristan and Iseult or Leontes' ritualistic kiss for his dead wife, to carry its lovers beyond the empirical laws of nature into the realm of the ideal?

"I was thinking of something more ordinary," Liliana replied, "like a certain spiritual chemistry about the man that immediately enraptures all my senses."

"I'm not sure I know what you're talking about, but I gather that whatever it is, I don't have it."

"That doesn't mean that someone else couldn't fall in love with you. And it certainly doesn't mean that I have no feelings for you. They're just of a different sort. You're the best friend I have, Mauritio, and to have our relationship injected with a dose of eroticism would almost seem incestuous to me."

"I wasn't thinking of *sex!,*" Altmann protested, stunned by Liliana's assertion that there might even be something perverse about his intentions.

"I believe you," she replied, "but I seriously doubt if the kind of love you had in mind was as pure or innocent as the troubadours liked to think."

Waves of resentment rushed through Altmann's veins, as the suspicion grew in him that Liliana had let the theme of her doctoral dissertation color her personal life to the point where, because of his age, he'd never had a chance with her from the very start, and never would. He thought of suggesting that they should probably call their trip off and go back to their separate ways, but another sudden surge of love tied his tongue, and after a long pause, he solemnly announced instead that since it was already eleven o'clock, and they would be wanting to head out for Yellowstone early the next morning, they should probably get to bed. Liliana complied without a comment, and within ten minutes they were retired, she wrapped cocoon-like in a blanket in one corner of the king-size bed, he lying on his back, spread-eagle, and only half naked, in the rest of it.

38

Early one afternoon, a month later, Professor Altmann sat at his computer, reflecting on what he might want to say to Liliana about where the trip they had just completed had left their relationship. Midway through their travels she had been informed that her director, who had been kept in the dark about most of her travel plans, was expecting her back in Boston for a meeting on the third of August regarding a dissertation prospectus she had earlier submitted. This had required her catching a flight out of Denver's International Airport on the day following their attendance at an 8 PM performance of Debussy's *Pelléas et Melisande* in Santa Fe.

The long drive from Santa Fe to Denver had begun on a very chilly note. Notwithstanding her rejection of his amorous advances back on the cabin-porch of Rocky Mountain's Grand Lake Lodge, and her equally unsympathetic dismissal the next day of his melodramatic—as she had labeled it—interpretation of how the loss of her love would eviscerate his creative spirit, he had continued hoping all along that their evening at The Santa Fe Opera might still trigger some affectionate feelings on her part and bring their Alaskan trip to a beautiful climax. And, to be sure, the opera itself, as well as their dinner before it, had lived up to his every expectation. After they had checked into the Hacienda Hermana, where Altmann had reserved a room with a single, king-size bed for the night, Liliana had attired herself in an elegant, rose-colored, satin evening gown, and accompanied him to the Bishop's Lodge Restaurant and the opera house in an as ebullient a spirit as he had ever found her. But the rest of the evening had turned into something of a nightmare. Already during the opera's intermission, his heart had begun to sink a bit upon noticing her using her cell-phone to call an acquaintance who had moved to Santa Fe after graduating from Harvard, and whom she had indicated earlier she might want to contact while visiting the city. And no sooner had the opera ended than she announced that she had made plans to have him meet her yet that night for what she described as "a drink or two." When finally, at about midnight, the friend had arrived to pick Liliana up, Altmann had hinted that he might like to join them for a "drink or two" on the hacienda's covered patio, thinking that he could thereby limit better the time Liliana would be spending with the man. But she was on to his old tricks, and promptly squelched the idea by claiming that she and her friend needed some time together alone to discuss employment opportunities for a mutual acquaintance back in Boston. So, off to one or another Santa Fe bar they had gone, leaving a distraught Altmann behind in the hacienda all by himself. For two hours he had waited for her return, sitting in a huge, oversized armchair that stood next to the foyer's fireplace, staring vacantly at the room's white-washed, stucco walls, and wondering what kind of fool he must have been to have thought that things could have turned out any way other than they had. Finally stripping himself of the tie and other fancy clothes he had worn to the opera, he locked the door to the hacienda, and threw his half-naked body dejectedly onto the king-size bed. But his brain would not turn off, and as he lay there, with another round of thunderclaps shaking the hacienda to its foundations, the thought of Liliana and her friend possibly making love to each other crossed his mind, and despite his every effort to suppress them, left him wallowing for another hour in feelings of resentment and self-pity. Resolving to rouse Liliana as early as possible the next morning to leave Santa Fe without taking even a minute to tour, as they had planned, the city's historic, downtown area, he finally surrendered to sleep, only to be awakened ten minutes later by the sound of Liliana trying to open the hacienda door. He'd assumed she had taken a key with her, and, despite his anger, had never intended to lock her out. But hearing her fumbling at the door's latch, and recalling how shabbily he thought she had treated him, he was tempted for a moment to do so, and although he resisted the temptation, he was as cold as he could be when finally he went to open the door and let her in. She must have sensed how upset he was, but thinking apparently that he had no real reason to feel that way, she offered no word of apology or any other, and after disrobing from her opera attire and donning her usual pajamas, crawled onto a corner of the bed and was fast asleep within five minutes.

Two hours later, at six o'clock, Altmann was up and packing, announcing rather huffily to his drowsy, dreary-eyed bed-companion that they would be leaving in one hour. Liliana had taken it all in stride, rising promptly to shower, clothe herself, and pack her belongings, with still enough time to partake of the breakfast being offered by the hacienda's matronly owner. So cheerful, in fact, was Liliana during the breakfast with other hacienda guests that Altmann could not help but relax his sulking and now and then join in the conversation. And by the time they had loaded the car, he had relented enough to drive downtown after all, under the pretense of wanting to pay a last-minute visit to the city's famed cathedral. Once inside the church, Liliana had raced off to a side chapel dedicated to the Virgin Mary, while Altmann stood admiring the beautifully decorated wooden screen over the main altar. The Franciscan version of the crucified Christ touched him deeply, reminding him of Bonhoeffer's suggestion that the Christian God was good for nothing but revealing the forgiveness that is ours when we too, like Jesus, forgive those who offend us. And before Liliana had returned from her brief pilgrimage to the Virgin's shrine, Altmann had resolved to forgive her whatever wrong, if any, she might have done him the night before, knowing full well that were he not able to bring himself to do so and rise above his feelings of resentment and self-pity, it would only be a matter of time before he would again be wallowing in the swamp of cybersmut. All the same, as they exited the church and headed out of town, there was still a chill in the air between them. And although they carried on a lively conversation all the way to Denver, when they finally parted company at that city's international Airport twelve hours later, much remained to be said about where they stood with each other.

Hoping to clear the air once for all, Altmann began processing again the letter he had been trying to write to Liliana for the past week:

Dear Liliana:

Seldom in all my many years have I ever felt such excitement in the company of another person as I did while traveling with you to Alaska and then, down the coast of Oregon and California, to San Francisco, Las Vegas, and Santa Fe. Almost every day—and not only when we were riding the rapids of the Nenana River, basking in the soothing waters of Radium Hot Springs, or admiring Pacific sunsets—you exuded a joy in living that made being with you nothing less than exhilarating. The spontaneity of your interaction with the dam and her kids atop Mt. Evans, with the black bear and her cubs along the Alcan Highway, Denali's caribou, the seal pups on Prince William Sound's floating icebergs, or the dolphins and whales swimming alongside us through the Inside Passage, was a

215

delight to behold, as was also your instant infatuation with Haines' bald eagles and the Chilkat salmon—not to mention their Tom Cruise-look-alike keeper! Your seemingly fearless plunge into grizzly-infested back-country, like your helicoptor excursion or your periodic ninety-mile-per-hour bursts of speed out on the highway, made me fret occasionally about your safety and what I would tell your mother should you end up getting mauled or mangled, but there was also something very fascinating about your nonchalant defiance of death. Equally impressive was the vigor with which you raced up the last leg of Mt. Evans' majestic pinnacle, or down and up again in record time the iron stairwell to Yellowstone's Lower Falls, the steep trail to Glacier National Park's Hidden Lake, or the Grand Canyon's Bright Angel Path.

Notwithstanding my own periodic reticence, I also really admired the instant rapport you seemed to strike up with all the people you met along the way, like Lake Louise's cliff climbers, Watson Lake's 'Bear Lady,' Fritz and Hilda at *The Raven* in Haines Junction (where we had such wonderful meals), 'Gypsy Rose' and her bohemian husband in their roadside cave of a place on the Alaskan border, the captain of the *Rocinante* off the coast of Seward, the boat people sailing with us through the Inside Passage, or the B & B proprietors, like Stella and Tom (and the neighborhood children) at Lincoln Beach, or the Lord and Lady of Eureka's Victorian mansion, Charles and Lou. It was amazing to watch all these previously unknown people coming alive in response to your friendly smile and probing conversation, and may even have prompted me to open up a bit more—no mean challenge for a man of North German roots!

It was inevitable, of course, that when traveling twelve thousand miles together by car in a single month any two individuals would experience some stress. And I know that on occasion your free spirit was tested rather severely by my Teutonic need for *Ordnung*, just as your periodic pouting or seeming insouciance sometimes challenged my patience. But such moments were, to me at least, mere ripples in the wonderful, month-long pool of time we had together. More serious, however, was the rather sour note on which the trip seemed to end, and I would like to offer an apology for that.

After the verbal shower you gave me on the porch of our cabin in Rocky Mountain National Park, I should probably have given up on ever luring you into my arms for any kind of love, accepted reality, and

216

shifted the gears of my psyche to make the best of the friendship we had. But as the old saying goes, 'Hope burns eternal in the human heart!,' and I found it hard to let go. Perhaps it was just the last gasp of my aged libido, aroused by your youthful sensuality, those seductive perfumes, or the daily display of laundered lingerie in the intimate quarters we had to share on the road. But I refuse to believe it was nothing but lust. Many times, after a lively exchange of ideas or sharing one or another adventure, I just wanted to hold you and tell you how happy I was to be in your presence. Every good experience we had along the way added fuel to the fire burning in my heart, and by the time we got to Santa Fe, I had completely forgotten, or suppressed, I guess Freud would say, the stoical rationale you had earlier provided me for not responding in kind to my amorous advances, and was again fantasizing about a post-operatic *nuit d'amour*—nothing coital, mind you, just a touch of *fin'amor!* When, therefore, you chose to spend the rest of the night drinking with your friend, and left me alone back at the hacienda, I was deeply hurt. And I must say that I still find it hard to understand why you had to do it with such seeming indifference to my own feelings. Was it your version of tough love? The only way you knew of bringing me back to reality? But be that as it may, I had no right to get angry or to pout the way I did for the rest of the night and much of the next day. You owed me nothing— notwithstanding my rationalization to the contrary that because of your having agreed to travel with me on such intimate terms for a whole month long, I had been given some kind of *licentia amoris*—and I should have accepted the fact that you did not share my feelings of affection, and respected your freedom to reject my advances. Nor did I have any reason to begrudge you time with a friend you had not seen for so long, and about whom you had fully alerted me before our arrival in Santa Fe. So, please accept my apology for having acted so foolishly and spoiling what should have been a happy conclusion to our trip.

Still, my dear Liliana, I have to tell you, in the words of my favorite troubadour, 'I am, was, and ever shall be your sworn man.' Your beauty has completely captivated my soul. 'I'm caught! Like a fish leaping to the bait, I've leapt into loving you, and can't break away!' And so, while I shall remain your friend, and cheer you on in your search for a man to love and father your children, 'I will content myself with rarefied love and live elated, forever contemplating your beauty from a distance.'

217

Fare thee well!

Maurice

Printing the letter out and laying it aside to mail at a later time, Altmann shut off his computer, and walked across a hallway to a guest bedroom where he had earlier begun working on a painting. Stepping up close to the easel again, he studied the outline of the figure of a woman's nude body he had already drawn on the canvas. Although he had never seen Liliana disrobed, he had taken many a photograph of her during the last year of her stay in Urbana. In one of them he had captured her in a half-seated position leaning against the railing of her backyard porch. Supported by arms outstretched behind her, her upper torso was slightly twisted backward from its protruding lower half, highlighting in an early-morning ray of sunlight the sensuous curves of her breasts, and gently elevating the left shoulder against which, with her eyes closed, her lips pursed, and her dark brown hair falling down around her long neck onto one side of her chest, she was inclining her cheetah-like head. It was from this photograph that he had been working, and although he had had no difficulty imagining her body nude, arranging its lines and colors into an aesthetic composition that would adequately reveal what he had always perceived to be her deeply spiritual sensuality was another matter. Twice he had tried and failed, each time erasing the lifeless lines he had drawn, and sighing disgustedly over the suspicion that he had lost forever the ease with which he had once—before deciding at the age of thirty to devote all his time and energy to the pursuit of scholarly research and writing—been able to trace onto canvas any image conjured up by his creative mind. But eyeing his third attempt, in which he had cropped Liliana's figure at mid-thigh, causing the rest of her body to flood the canvas like an alluvial fan, he was pleased at what he saw, and nodding pensively, contemplated his next moves to animate the figure still further. Mixing first a palette of beryline greens, grays, and indigo blues, he proceeded to lay down a misty, hazy background, against which Liliana's body, now shown to be leaning against a rocky outcropping at the water's edge, would seem all the more to be a gift from the sea. Then turning to the warmer colors, he began filling the empty spaces outlined by her body with a sensuous combination of yellow, amber, and—for the sake of shadowing—rose hues, while accenting the nipples of her breasts and the lips of her mouth with a final touch of peach. With dense black strokes and impasto brushwork he next traced anew the sinuous contour of her body and strands of dark black hair around her head, one of which he let fall gracefully like a rivelet of sweat over her right shoulder into the fleshy armpit below, and then finally, with a few swift strokes of a much finer brush, touched in the delicate lines of her face, the soft curvature of her breasts and the dance of pubic hairs across the top of her *mons Veneris.*

Dropping his brush into a can of kerosene, he walked to the other side of the guest bedroom and sat down on the edge of the bed, facing the easel. With a quick glance at his wristwatch, he calculated that he had completed the piece in less than two hours of actual painting—much faster than he had ever worked even during the days of his youth when his artistic skills had supposedly been at their best. But for all the speed with which he had executed the painting, he saw nothing sloppy about it, and in fact liked it better than anything he had ever done before. Despite its straightforward portrayal of her naked body, it exuded, he thought to himself, a certain shamelessness that came very close to capturing, as he had hoped it would, the unabashed spirit of Liliana's erotic femininity. As he sat there, basking in the joy of having created something that at least to his own eyes seemed so beautiful, it dawned on him that never once throughout his several hours of work on the piece had he entertained a dirty thought about the woman he was portraying.

EPILOGUE

Several years later, on a cold February morning, after his philosophy students had reported his failure to show up for class, Professor Altmann was found dead in the bed of his own home, an apparent victim of a heart attack. College officials who, alarmed by his absence, had broken into his home to see if he was in need of help, were not only shocked to find him deceased, but were equally stunned to discover that dispersed around every room of the house were hundreds of paintings of the one, same woman. Executed in what one of BCC's art professors later identified as a distinctly Modigliani style, the paintings all depicted the woman in the nude, and from almost every conceivable angle. Who she was, none of them could guess, until a week or so later, after the opening of his Last Will and Testament, it was learned that the childless professor had left the whole of his estate—now, since the recovery of the market, again worth more than half a million dollars—to one Liliana Aquileur, nee Columbra. When asked how to dispose of the paintings, Ms. Aquileur insisted that, except for the one of them that showed her leaning against a boulder at the edge of the sea, and which she wanted to keep for herself, they should all be burned and the ashes of the canvases, along with the professor's own, thrown to the wind off the side of Mt. Evans' highest peak. Several of Altmann's family members objected to such a course of action. But after several months of legal haggling, a judge eventually ruled that in his Last Will, the professor had clearly given Ms. Aquileur final say over how he and the whole of his estate were to be disposed of. And later that summer, while driving alone through Colorado, on her way to attend the American premier of Kaija Saariaho's *L'amour de loin* in Santa Fe, Liliana drove to the top of Mt. Evans and released the ashes of the professor and his paintings from the two separate canisters in which she had borne them reverently across the plains and up the mountain. As she did so, a sudden breeze swirled gently around her, embracing the ashes from both and blending them into a single gray cloud that danced momentarily across the flower-bedecked tundra before being carried out into the wild, blue-green abyss beyond and dropping out of sight.

"Consummatum est," she uttered softly, to the accompaniment of the bewildered bleating of a lone billy goat that had strayed onto the scene.